… at the same time I slipped my hand into her bosom and for the first time took possession of the two most beautiful globes which adorned it. Louie did not draw back. She in no way tried to prevent my caressing her there. I was more than tempted to let my hand stray much lower …

Harper Perennial
Forbidden Classics

Venus in India

or

Love Adventures in Hindustan

'CAPTAIN CHARLES DEVEREAUX'

HARPER PERENNIAL

London, New York, Toronto, Sydney and New Delhi

Harper Perennial
An imprint of HarperCollins*Publishers*
77–85 Fulham Palace Road, Hammersmith
London W6 8JB

www.harperperennial.co.uk
Visit our authors' blog at www.fifthestate.co.uk

This Harper Perennial edition published 2009
1

Previously published by Wordsworth Editions Limited 1996

A catalogue record for this book is available from the British Library

ISBN 978-0-00-730042-6

Set in Minion by Newgen Imaging Systems (P) Ltd, Chennai, India

Printed and bound in Great Britain by Clays Ltd, St Ives plc

Mixed Sources
Product group from well-managed
forests and other controlled sources
www.fsc.org   Cert no. SW-COC-1806
© 1996 Forest Stewardship Council

FSC is a non-profit international organisation established to promote the
responsible management of the world's forests. Products carrying the FSC
label are independently certified to assure consumers that they come
from forests that are managed to meet the social, economic and
ecological needs of present and future generations.

Find out more about HarperCollins and the environment at
www.harpercollins.co.uk/green

Contents

1

A Call to Arms

The war in Afghanistan appeared to be coming to a close when I received sudden orders to proceed, at once, from England to join the first battalion of my regiment, which was then serving there. I had just been promoted captain and had been married about eighteen months. It pained me more than I care to express to part with my wife and baby girl, but it was agreed that it would be better for all of us if their coming to India were deferred until it was certain where my regiment would be quartered on its return to the fertile plains of Hindustan from the stones and rocks of barren Afghanistan. Besides, it was very hot, being the height of the hot weather, when only those who were absolutely forced to do so went to India, and it was a time of year particularly unsuitable for a delicate woman and a babe to travel in so burning a climate. It was also not quite certain whether my wife would join me in India, as I had the promise of a staff appointment at home, but before I could enter upon that I had of necessity to join my own battalion, because it was at the seat of war. But it was annoying to have to go, all the same, as it was clear that the war was over, and that I should be much too late to participate in any of its rewards or glories, though it was quite possible I might come in for much of the hardship and inconvenience of the sojourn, for a wild, and not to say rough and inhospitable country is Afghanistan; besides which it was quite possible that an Afghan knife would put an end to me, or that I might fall a victim to a common murder instead of dying a glorious death on the battlefield.

Altogether my prospects seemed by no means of a rosy colour, but there was nothing for it but to submit and go, which I did with the best grace possible but with a very heavy heart.

I will spare the readers the sad details of parting with my wife. I made no promise of fidelity, the idea seemed never to occur to her or to myself of there being any need for it, for although I had always been of that temperament so dear to Venus, and had enjoyed the pleasure of love with great good fortune before I married, yet I had, as I thought, quite steadied down into a proper married man, whose desires never wandered outside his own bed; for my passionate and loving spouse was ever ready to respond to my ardent caresses with caresses as ardent; and her charms, in their youthful beauty and freshness, had not only not palled upon me, but seemed to grow more and more powerfully attractive the more I revelled in their possession. For my dearest wife, gentle reader, was the life of passion; she was not one of those who coldly submit to their husband's caresses because it is their duty to do so, a duty, however, not to be done with pleasure or joyfully, but more as a species of penance! No! With her it was not, 'Ah! no, let me sleep tonight, dear. I did it twice last night, and I really don't think you can want it again. You should be more chaste, and not try me as if I were your toy and plaything. No! Take your hand away! Do leave my nightdress alone! I declare it is quite indecent the way you are behaving!' and so forth, until, worn out with her husband's persistence, she thinks the shortest way after all will be to let him have his way, and so grudgingly allows her cold cunt to be uncovered, unwillingly opens her ungracious thighs, and lies a passionless log, insensible to her husband's endeavours to strike a spark of pleasure from her icy charms. Ah! no! With my sweet Louie it was far different; caress replied to caress, embrace to embrace. Each sweet sacrifice became sweeter than the one before, because she fully appreciated all the joy and delight of it! It is almost impossible to have too much of such a woman, and Louie seemed to think it quite impossible to have too much of me. It was, 'Once more, my darling! Just one little more! I am sure it will do you good! and I should like it!' and it would be strange if the manly charm which filled her loving hand were not once more raised in response to her caresses, ready once again to carry rapturous delight to the deepest, richest depths of the trembling voluptuous charm for the special benefit of which it was formed, a charm which was indeed the very temple of love.

Having ascertained from the adjutant general, that my destination was Cherat, a small camping ground, as I heard, on top of a range of mountains forming the southern limit of the valley of the Peshawar, and having received railroad warrants, via Allahabad, for the temporary station of Jhelum, and dak warrants from that spot to Cherat itself, I made my preparations for the long journey which still lay before me; amongst the necessaries for mind and body I purchased were some French novels which included that masterpiece of drawing-room erotic literature *Mademoiselle de Maupin* by Théophile Gautier.

The route from Bombay via Allahabad to Peshawar runs almost entirely through a country as flat as a table. Only once on this journey, about which I fear I may become tedious, did the tempter accost me, and then so clumsily as quite to frustrate his well-meant intentions. I had to make a few hours' stay in Allahabad and to pass that away pleasantly I wandered about, examining the tombs of the kings and princes who reigned in past times over the banks of the Ganges and the Jumna, and in seeing such sights as I could find to amuse and interest me. As I was returning to my hotel a native accosted me in very good English.

'Like to have woman, sahib? I got one very pretty little half-caste in my house, if master like to come and see!'

Oh! dear *Mademoiselle de Maupin*!

I felt no desire to see the pretty little half-caste! I put this self-abnegation down to virtue, and actually laughed, in my folly, at the idea that there existed, or could exist, a woman in India who could raise even a ghost of desire in me!

The station beyond Jhelum is reached, I having but one mighty river to pass before I leave the bounds of India proper and tread the outskirts of central Asia, in the valley of the Peshawar. But it took some two or three days and nights of continuous travel in a dak *gharry* [carriage], before I reached Attock. The dak *gharry* is a fairly comfortable mode of conveyance, but one becomes tired of the eternal horizontal position in which it accommodates the weary traveller. Crossing the Indus in a boat rowed over a frightful torrent with the roar of the waters breaking on the rocks below, was a very exciting experience, especially as it happened at night, and the dark gloom added a magnifying effect to the roar of the suspected danger. Another dak *gharry* waited, into which I got, lay down and went to sleep, not to waken until I reached Nowshera.

Ah! *Mademoiselle de Maupin*! What a lovely girl! Who can she be? She must, I fancy, be the daughter of the colonel commanding here, out for her morning walk, and perhaps, judging from the keen expectant glance shot in at me through the half-open sliding door of the *gharry,* expecting somebody, perhaps her fiancé; perhaps that is why she looked so eager and yet so disappointed!

Oh, dear reader! just as I opened my eyes I saw, through the half-open door, this perfect figure of feminine beauty! A girl clothed in a close-fitting grey-coloured dress with a Teria hat archly sloped on her lovely and well-shaped head! That beautiful face! How perfect the oval of it! What glorious, yet rather stern eyes! What a delicately formed nose! Truly she must have aristocratic blood in her veins to be so daintily formed! What a rosebud of a mouth! What cherry lips! God! Jupiter! Venus! What a form! See those exquisite rounded shoulders, those full and beautiful arms, the shape of each so plainly visible so close does her dress fit her; and how pure, how virgin-like is that undulating bosom! See how proudly each swelling breast fills out her modest, but still desire-provoking, bodice! Ah! The little shell-like ears, fitting so close to the head. How I would like to have the privilege of gently pressing those tiny lobes! What a lovely creature she looks! How refined! How pure! How virginal.

And all these impressions flashed through my mind from a glimpse, a very vivid glimpse it is true, and she seemed so absolutely and completely removed from ordinary mankind that I never dreamt I should ever see her cunt; according to plan I was going to change horses at Nowshera and proceed immediately to Cherat.

But on arriving at the post office, which was also the place for changing horses, the postmaster, a civil-spoken Baboo, told me that he could give me horses only as far as Publi, a village about halfway between Nowshera and Peshawar, and that from that place I must make the best of my way to Cherat, for there was no road along which dak *gharries* could be driven, and my good Baboo added that the said interval between Publi and Cherat was dangerous for travellers, there being many lawless robbers about. Moreover, he added, the distance was a good fifteen miles. He advised me to put up at the public bungalow at Nowshera until the brigade major could put me in the way of completing my journey.

This information was a great surprise and a great damper to me! How on earth was I to get up to Cherat with my baggage if there was no road? How could I do fifteen miles under such circumstances? To think I had come so many thousands of miles, since I had left England, to be balked by a miserable little fifteen. However, for the present there seemed nothing to be done but to take the excellent Baboo's advice, put up at the public bungalow and see the brigade major.

The public bungalow stood in its own compound, a little distance from the high road, and to get to it I had to drive back part of the road I had travelled. I dismissed my driver, and called for the *khansama* [house-steward], who informed me that the bungalow was full, and that there was no room for me! Here was a pretty state of affairs! but whilst I was speaking to the *khansama,* a pleasant-looking young officer, lifting the *chick* [bamboo blind] which hung over the entrance to his room, came out on to the verandah, and told me that he had heard what I was saying, that he was only waiting for a *gharry* to proceed on his journey down country, and that my coming was as opportune for him as his going would be for me. He had, he said, sent at once to secure my dak *gharry,* and if he could get it, he would give up his room to me but anyhow, I should, if I did not dislike the idea, share his room which contained two bedsteads. Needless to say I was delighted to accept his kind offer, and I soon had my goods inside the room, and was enjoying that most essential and refreshing thing in India, a nice cool bath. My new friend had taken upon himself to order breakfast for me, and when I had completed my ablutions and toilet, we sat down together. Officers meeting in this manner very quickly become like old friends. My new acquaintance told me all about himself, where he had been, where he was going to, and I reciprocated. Needless to say the war, which was now practically over, formed the great topic of our general conversation. Getting more intimate, we of course fell, as young men do – or old, too, for the matter of that – to discussing love and women, and my young friend told me that the entire British Army was just simply raging for women! That none were to be got in Afghanistan, and that, taking it as a general rule, neither officers nor men had had a woman for at least two years.

'George!' he cried, as he laughed, 'the Peshawar polls are reaping a rich harvest! As fast as a regiment arrives from Afghanistan, the whole boiling lot rush off to the bazaars, and you can see the Tommy Atkinses waiting outside the knocking shops, holding their pricks in their hands and roaring out to those having women to look sharp!'

This was of course an exaggeration, but not to so great an extent as my gentle reader may suppose.

We had just finished our cheroots after breakfast, when the young officer's servant drove up in the same dak *gharry* which had brought me from Attock, and in a few minutes my cheerful host was shaking hands with me.

'There's somebody in there,' said he, pointing to the next room, 'to whom I must say goodbye, and then I'm off.'

He was not long absent, again shook my hand, and in another minute a sea of dust hid him and the *gharry* from my sight.

I felt quite lonely and sad when he was gone, for, although the bungalow was full, I was left in a small portion of it walled off from the rest, so that I didn't see any of its other occupants – though I might occasionally hear them. I had forgotten to ask who my next-door neighbour was, and indeed I did not much care as I was so bothered, wondering how I should get up to Cherat. It was now nearly ten o'clock, the sun was pouring sheets of killing rays of light on the parched plain in which Nowshera is situated, and the hot wind was beginning to blow, parching one up, and making lips and eyes quite sore as well as dry. I did not know what to do with myself. It was much too hot to think of going to the brigade major's, so I got another cheroot, and taking my delightful *Mademoiselle de Maupin* out of my bag, I went and sat behind a pillar on the verandah, to shelter myself from the full force of the blast and try to read; but even this most charming damsel failed to charm, and I sank back in my chair and smoked listlessly whilst my eyes wandered over the range of lofty mountains which I could just distinguish quivering through hot, yellow-looking air. I did not know at the time that I was looking at Cherat and had I had any prescience of what was waiting for me there, I should certainly have gazed upon those hills with far greater interest than I did.

Reader dear, do you know what it is to feel that somebody is looking at you, though you may not be able to see him, to be aware for a fact that somebody is looking at you? I am extremely susceptible to this influence. Whilst sitting thus idly looking at the most distant thing my eyes could find to rest upon, I began to feel that someone was near, and looking intently at me. At first I resisted the temptation to look around to see who it was. I felt so irritable, that I resented, as an insult, the looking at me which I felt certain was going on; but at last this strange sensation added to my unrest and I half turned my head to see whether it was reality or feverish fancy.

My surprise was unbounded when I saw the same lovely face which I had caught a glimpse of that morning peering at me from behind the slightly opened *chick* of the room next to mine. I was so startled that instead of taking a good look at the lady I instantly gazed on the hills again, as if turning my head to look in her direction had been a breach of good manners on my part; but I felt she was still keeping her eyes fixed on me, and it amazed me that anyone in the position which I imagined she held (for I was firmly convinced that I was right as to my surmise that my unknown beauty was a lady, and a colonel's daughter) should be guilty of such bad manners as to stare at a perfect stranger in this manner. I turned my head once more, and this time I looked at this lovely but strange girl a little more fixedly. Her eyes, large, lustrous, most beautiful, seemed to pierce mine, as though trying to read my thoughts. For a moment I fancied she must be a little off her head, but just then, apparently satisfied with her reconnaissance, the fair creature disappeared from sight. From that moment my curiosity was greatly aroused. Who was she? Was she alone? Or was she with the unknown colonel in that room? Why was she staring at me so hard? By Jove! There she was at it again! I could stand it no longer. I jumped up and went into my own room and called the *khansama*.

'Khansama, who is in the room next to mine?' and I pointed to the door which communicated with the room the lady was in, which was closed.

'A memsahib, sahib.'

A memsahib! Now I had been in India before, this was my second tour of service in the country, and I knew that a memsahib meant a married lady. I was surprised, for had anyone asked me, I should have said that this lovely girl had never known a man, had never been had, and never would be had, unless she met the man of men who pleased her. It was extraordinary how this idea had taken root in my mind.

'Is the sahib with her?'

'No, sahib!'

'Where is he?'

'I don't know, sahib.'

'When did the memsahib come here, *khansama*?'

'A week or ten days ago, sahib!'

It was plain I could get no information from this man, only one more question and I was done.

'Is the memsahib quite alone, *khansama*?'

'Yes, sahib: she has no one with her, not even an *ayah* [maid].'

Well! this is wonderful! How often did my young friend who had only gone away this morning, know her? You, gentle reader, with experience, no doubt have your suspicions that all was not right, but for the life of me I could not shake off the firm notion that this woman was not only a lady, but one exceptionally pure and highly connected.

I went back to my seat on the verandah, waiting to be looked at again, and I did not wait long. A slight rustle caught my ear. I looked around and there was my lovely girl showing more of herself. She still looked with the same eager gaze without the sign of a smile on her face. She appeared to be in her petticoats only, and her legs and feet, such lovely, tiny, beautiful feet, and such exquisitely turned ankles, were bare; she had not even a pair of slippers on. A light shawl covered her shoulders and bosom, but did not hide either her full, well-shaped, white arms, her taper waist or her splendid and broad hips. These naked feet and legs inspired me with a sudden flow of desire, in spite of the fact that her lovely face and its wonderful calm yet severe expression had hitherto driven all such thoughts from my mind.

Giacomo Casanova, who certainly is a perfect authority on all that concerns women, declares that curiosity is the foundation on which desire is built, that, but for that, a man would be perfectly contented with one woman, since in the main all women are alike; yet from mere curiosity a man is impelled to approach a woman, and to wish for her possession. Something akin to this certainly influenced me. A devouring curiosity took possession of me. This exquisite girl's face inspired me to know how she could possibly be all alone here at Nowshera, in a public bungalow, and her lovely naked feet and legs made me wonder whether her knees and thighs corresponded with them in perfect beauty, and my imagination painted in my mind a voluptuous motte and delicious cunt, shaded by dark locks corresponding to the colour of the lovely eyebrows, which arched over those expressive orbs. I rose from my chair and moved towards her. She instantly withdrew and as instantly again opened the *chick*. For the first time I saw a smile wreathe her face. What a wonderfully different expression that smile gave it! Two lovely dimples appeared in her rounded cheeks, her rosy lips parted and displayed two rows of small perfectly even teeth, and those eyes which had looked so stern and almost forbidding, now looked all tenderness and softness.

'You must find it very hot out there on the verandah!' said she, in a low, musical voice, but with a rather vulgar, common accent which at first grated on my ear, 'and I know you are all alone! Won't you come into my room and sit down and chat? You will if you are a good fellow!'

'Thank you!' said I, smiling and bowing as I threw away my cheroot and entered whilst she held the *chick* so as to make room for me to pass. I caught the *chick* in my hand but she still kept her arm raised, and extended; her shawl fell a little off her bosom which was almost entirely bare, and I saw not only two most exquisitely round, full and polished globes of ivory, but even the rosy coral marble which adorned the peak of one of them. I could see that she caught the direction of my glance, but she was in no hurry to lower her arm, and I judged, and rightly, that this liberal display of her charms was by no means unintentional.

'I have got two chairs in here,' said she, laughing such a sweet-sounding laugh, 'but we can sit together on my bed, if you don't mind!'

'I shall be delighted,' said I, 'if sitting without a back to support you won't tire you!'

'Oh!' said she, in the most innocent manner, 'you just put your arm round my waist, and then I won't feel tired.'

Had it not been for the extraordinary innocent tone with which she said this, I think I should at once have lain her back and got on top of her, but a new idea struck me: could she be quite sane? And would not such an action be the very height of blackguardism?

However, I sat down, as she bade me do, and I slipped my left arm around her slender waist and gave her a little hug towards me.

'Ah!' she said, 'that's right! Hold me tight! I love being held tight!'

I found that she had no stays on at all. There was nothing between my hand and her smooth skin but a petticoat and a chemise, both of very light muslin. She felt so awfully nice! There's something so thrilling in feeling the warm, palpitating body of a lovely woman in one's arms; it was only natural that not only did my blood run more quickly, but I began to feel what the French call the 'pricking of the flesh'. There she was, this really beautiful creature, half naked and palpitating, her cheeks glowing with health, though paler than one is accustomed to seeing in our more temperate Europe, her lovely shining shoulders and bosom almost perfectly naked, and so exquisite! The nearer I got my eyes to the skin the better did I see how fine was its texture. The bloom of youth was on it. There were no ugly hollows to show where the flesh had receded and the bones projected. Her beautiful breasts were round, plump and firm looking. I longed to take possession of those lovely bubbies! To press them in my hand, to devour them and their rosy tips with my mouth! Her petticoats fell between her slightly parted thighs and showed their roundness and beautiful form perfectly as though to provoke my desire the more, desire she must have known was burning me, for she could feel the palpitating of my agitated heart even if a glance of her eyes in another and lower direction did not betray to her the effect her touch and her beauty had on me. She held out one and then the other of her fairy feet, so white and perfect, as though to display them to my eager eyes. The soft and delicious perfume which only emanates from a woman in her youth, stole in fragrant clouds over my face, and her abundant wavy hair fell like silk against my cheek. Was she mad? That was the tormenting thought which would spring up between my hand and the glowing charms it longed to seize!

For some few moments we sat in silence. Then I felt her hand creep up under my white jacket and toy with the buttons to which my braces were fastened behind. She undid one side of my braces and as she did so said, 'I saw you this morning! You were in a dak *gharry* and I just caught a glimpse of you.'

Her hand began to work at the other button. What the deuce was she up to?

'Oh yes!' I said, looking into her twinkling eyes and returning the starry glances which shot from them, 'and I saw you too! I had been fast asleep, and just as I opened my eyes my sight fell upon you and I –'

She had unbuttoned my braces behind, and now stole her hand round and laid it, back up, on the top of my thigh.

'And you what?' said she, gently sliding her extended fingers down over the inside of my thigh: she was within a nail's breadth of the side of my prick which was now standing furiously!

'Oh!' I exclaimed, 'I thought I had never seen such a lovely face and figure in the world!'

The fingertips actually touched Johnnie! She slightly pressed them against him, and looking at me again with the sweetest smile, said: 'Did you really! Well! I'm glad you did, for do you know what I thought, when I saw you lying inside the *gharry*?'

'No, dear!'

'Well! I thought that I would not mind if I had been travelling with such a fine-looking, handsome young man!'

Then after a short pause she continued: 'So you think me well made?' and she glanced down proudly on her swelling breast.

'Indeed I do!' I exclaimed, quite unable to restrain myself any longer. 'I don't know when I ever saw such a lovely bosom as this, and such tempting, luscious bubbies!' and I slipped my hand into her bosom and seized a glowing globe and as I pressed it gently and squeezed the hard little nipple between my fingers, I kissed the loving upturned mouth which was presented to me.

'Ah!' she cried, 'who gave you leave to do that? Well! Exchange is no robbery and I will have something nice of yours to feel for myself, too!'

Her nimble fingers had my trousers unbuttoned, my braces undone in front too, and with a whisk of her hand she had my shirt out, and with it my burning, maddened prick, of which she took immediate and instant possession.

'Ah!' she cried. 'Ah! oh! what a beauty! How handsome! bell-topped! and so big! Isn't he just about stiff! He's like a bar of iron! and what fine big balls you've got! My beautiful man! Oh! How I would like to empty them for you! Oh! you'll have me now! Won't you? Do! Do! oh I feel that I could come so nicely if you only would!'

Would I have her? Why! Gods in heaven! how could a mortal man brimful of health, strength, youth and energy like myself, receive such an appeal to his ears and senses, and not comply, even if the fair petitioner were not half nor quarter as beautiful as this lascivious and exquisite creature, whose hands were manipulating the most tenderly sensitive parts which man possesses. For all reply I gently pulled her on her back; she still kept a firm but voluptuous hold on her possessions as I turned up her petticoat and chemise. Gliding my burning hand over the smooth surface of her ivory thigh, I uncovered, I think, the most luscious cunt I have ever seen or felt in my life! Never had my hand reposed on so voluptuous and full a motte! Never had my finger probed a charm so full of life and so soft outside, so smooth and velvety inside, as it did now. That this most perfect cunt, and the domain around and above it, were in my possession! I was eager to get between her lovely thighs, to snatch my almost painfully strained prick from her hands and bury it up to its balls, and further, in this melting charm, but she stopped me. With her face and bosom flushed, her eyes dancing in her head, and a voice choked with the greatest excitement she cried: 'Let us put on our skins first!'

I was standing before her, my prick at an angle of at least seventy degrees, my balls and groins aching, for the most vigorous action had set in and my reservoirs had already been filled to the utmost they could hold. I felt I must either have this beautiful wild girl or burst!

'What do you mean?' I gasped.

'I'll show you! See!'

And in a moment she had, as it were, jumped out of her clothes, and stood, all naked and glowing, and radiant with a beauty fed by all that is voluptuous and erotic, before me.

In a moment – or perhaps a little longer, for I had boots and socks as well as coat, shirt and trousers to take off, but at all events, in a brace of shakes – I was as naked as she! I can shut my eyes now and there before me see this exquisitely formed creature, surely quite the equal of the beautiful Mademoiselle de Maupin, standing in all her radiant nudity before me. That form so purely perfect, so inimitably graceful, those matchless limbs! That bosom with its hills of living snow topped with rosy fire and that more than voluptuous motte, a perfect 'hill of Venus' clothed with the richest dark bushes of curly hair, sloping rapidly down, like a triangle standing on its point, until its two sides, folding in, formed the deep soft-looking inside line which proclaimed the very perfection of a goddess-like cunt. The only thing which slightly marred this perfect galaxy of beauty was the occurrence of some slight wrinkles which, like fine lines, crossed the otherwise perfect plain of her fair belly, that exquisite belly with its dimpling navel!

Gods! I rushed at this lovely creature, and in another moment I was on top of her, between her wide-opened thighs and resting on her beautiful bosom. How elastic did her beautiful bubbies feel against my chest and how soft,

how inexpressibly delicious, did her cunt feel, as inch by
inch I buried Johnnie in it, until my motte jammed against
hers and my balls hung, or rather squeezed, against her
lovely white bottom and I could get in no further. And
what a woman to have! Every movement of mine brought
forth an exclamation of delight from her! To hear her you
would have imagined it was the very first time her senses
had been powerfully excited from their very foundation!
Her hands were never still, they promenaded over me,
from the back of my head to the intimate limits of my body
to which they could reach. She was simply perfect in the art
of giving and receiving pleasure. Every transport of mine
was returned with interest. Every mad thrust met with a
corresponding buck which had the effect of taking my
prick in to its extreme root! And she seemed to do nothing
but come or spend! I had heard of a woman 'coming' thirteen or fourteen times during one fuck, but this woman
seemed to do nothing else from beginning to end. But it
was not until I had arrived at the exciting, furious, ardent,
almost violent, short digs, that I knew to what an intense
degree my Venus enjoyed pleasure! I thought she was in a
fit! She almost screamed! She gurgled in her throat! She
half crushed me in her arms, and putting her feet on my
behind, she pressed me to her motte, at the end, with a
power I should never have thought she possessed. Oh! the
relief! the exquisite delight of that spend on my part! I
inundated her, and she felt the spouting torrents of my love
darting in hot quick jets and striking against the deep-set
part of her almost maddened cunt! She seized my mouth
with hers, and shot her tongue into it as far as she could,

touching my throat, whilst her whole body from head to heel literally quivered with the tremendous excitement she was in! Never in my life had I such a fuck! Oh! why is there no better word to express what is really heaven upon earth?

The tempest past, we lay in one another's arms, tenderly gazing into one another's eyes. We were too breathless to speak at first. I could feel her belly heaving against mine, and her throbbing cunnie clasped my prick as though it were another hand, whilst her motte leaped and bounded! As I looked into that angelic face, and drank in the intense beauty of it, I believed this to be no abandoned woman but rather Venus herself whom I held thus clasped in my arms, and whose tender and voluptuous thighs encircled mine! I could have wished that she had held her peace and let me dream that I was the much desired Adonis, and she my persistent, longing Venus, and that I had at length complied with her amorous wishes and found the heaven in her arms of which, before I entered her matchless cunt, I had no notion! But my airy fancies were dispelled by her saying: 'You are a good poke and no mistake! Oh! You know how to fuck! No fellow ever fucks like that without he has been taught!'

'Yes!' I said, pressing her in my arms and kissing the ruby lips which had just spoken so coarsely, albeit truly and pointedly. 'I have been well trained! I had good lessons in my boyhood, and I have always tried to practise them as often as possible!'

'Ah!' she said, 'I thought so! You do the heel and toe better than any man I've ever had, and I've had, I dare say, many more men than you've had women!'

Frank and how!

'What do you mean by heel and toe, my pet?'

'Oh! Don't you know? You do it at any rate! and splendidly! Heel and toe is to begin each stroke at the very beginning and end it at the very end. Just give me one long stroke now!' I did so. I withdrew until my prick was all but out of her panting cunnie, and then gently but firmly drove it home, as far and as deep as I could, and then I rested again on her belly.

'There,' she cried, 'that's it! You almost pull it out, but not quite, and never stop short in your thrusts, but send your prick home, with a sharp rap of your balls against my bottom! That's what's good!'

And she appeared to smack her lips involuntarily.

At length I withdrew and my fairest nymph at once commenced a most minute examination of that part of me and its appendages which had pleased her so much. Everything was, according to her, absolutely perfect, and if I were to believe her there had not passed under her observation so noble and handsome a prick, and such beautiful well-balanced balls as I had. That she was the mistress of my balls especially pleased her! She said they were so big! She was sure they must be full of spend, and she intended, she told me, to empty them before she would consent to my leaving Nowshera!

This first sacrifice simply whetted our appetites, and still more inflamed with the minute examination of one another's charms, we fell to again, and writhed in the delicious agonies of another amorous combat! It was about two o'clock before I left her, and we had not been at any time more than ten minutes 'out of action'. The more I had of this exquisite creature, the more I longed to have her. I was fresh, young, strong, vigorous, and it was nearly two months (a long time for me) since I had last indulged in the delights of Cyprian pleasures. No wonder my Venus was pleased with me, and called my performance a perfect feast.

They say that love destroys appetite for food. Perhaps it does when it is love unrequited, but I give you my word, dear reader, that I was ravenous for my tiffin after my morning's work. I was really glad to get something to eat. What with the heat of the combat we had been through and the parching effect of the terrible hot winds blowing, I was dried up, as far as my mouth was concerned, though far from being so as regards the proceeds of my balls. I never felt so fit for woman as I did that day, and I never probably have had so much fucking with so little loss of physical force. Doubtless my steady married life with its regular hours, regular meals and regular, never excessive, sacrifices on the altar of Venus had much to do with the steady power I felt so strong in me, but over and above that was the fact of my new lady love being extraordinarily beautiful and voluptuously lascivious, and the erotic excitement raised in me, was, of course, great in proportion to the cause which gave birth to it. In spite of my hunger for food, I would certainly have remained with her on that most congenial of beds and have revelled on in her joyous arms and filled her with more of the quintessence of my manly vigour, but she told me she always slept in the afternoon, was hungry herself, and wanted my force to be expended between her lovely thighs that night for the solace of her liveliest of cunts!

Whilst the *khansama* was laying the table, I saw a note addressed to me leaning against the wall, on the mantelpiece (for in northern India the winters are sharp enough to render a fire not only pleasant but sometimes quite necessary), and taking it and opening it, wondering who the writer could be as I was perfectly unknown in this part of the world, I found it to be from my young officer friend who had quit Nowshera that morning. It ran thus:

> Dear Devereaux – In the room next to yours is one of the loveliest of women and best of pokes! *Verbum sap.*!
> Yours, J. C.
> PS – Don't offer her any rupees or you will offend her mortally, but if you are inclined to have her, and I think you will be on seeing her, just tell her so and you won't have to ask twice.

Ah! Dear young chap, now I understand why you were so reticent this morning and did not like to tell me that I had a lady for my next-door neighbour! Well! Poor girl! I am afraid that you must be put down as one of the 'irregulars', although it is a shame to think ill of one who has given me the first few hours of real delight since I left home!

These thoughts naturally brought my beloved little wife into my recollection and I was somewhat staggered to feel I should so completely have forgotten her and my marital vows! But I was altogether too full of desire. Desire only just whetted and crying for more! More! I was in fact half

mad with what some call lust and others love and, wife or
no wife, nothing short of death would, or should, prevent
my fucking that heavenly girl again and again until I really
could not raise a stand. I longed for evening. I burnt for
night. I ate my tiffin like a ravenous tiger, hungry for food,
but thirsting for the sweet savour of the blood of a victim
I knew to be within easy reach. Tiffin put away, I lit a
cheroot, and began wandering round and round my room,
glancing impatiently at the door which closed the communication between it and that of my supposedly now sleeping Venus, and like a Wellington I wished and prayed – not
for night and Blücher but for night and her awakening!
Suddenly it struck me as very funny that were some catastrophe to separate this girl and me, neither of us would be
able to say who the other was! We had not exchanged
names. My young friend the officer who signed his initials
J. C. had not told me. I did not even know his name though
he knew mine, probably from seeing it painted on my baggage. Of a surety, this lovely Venus must have a history, and
I resolved to try and get her to give me her version of it,
from which no doubt I could make out what was true and
what was invention – for that she would tell me the exact
truth I hardly expected. Oh! when would she awake?

Should I go and peep and see? By Jupiter, I would –

Throwing away the fresh cheroot I had lighted, I crept,
in my stockinged feet, to her *chick*, and pulled it slightly
open, and there on the bed, fast asleep, I saw my lovely
enslaver. She had simply put on a petticoat and was lying
on her back with her hands clasped under her shapely
head, her arms bent in a charming position, opened out,

showing the little growth of hair under the armpit, hair the same in tint, but not so rich in colour, as that magnificent bush I had moistened so liberally, aided by her own offerings, this morning; her bosom, with its two priceless breasts, so beautifully placed, so round, polished and firm, indeed her entire body down to her slender waist, was altogether nude! One knee, that next to me, was bent, the small graceful foot planted on the bedclothes, each gem of a toe straight and separated from its neighbour in a way that would have charmed the most fastidious sculptor that ever lived, whilst the other leg, bare from the groin downwards, was extended at full length, the lovely foot which terminated it resting against the edge of the bed, so that her thighs, those lovely voluptuous and maddening thighs, were parted! Gods! could I remain outside while so much beauty was freely displayed and I could feast my burning eyes upon it whilst its lovely owner slept?.

I went gently and noiselessly in, and passing round to the other side of the bed, so that my shadow might not fall on that exquisite form and hide the light, already softened by the *chick,* from it, I gazed in silent rapture on the beautiful girl who had made me enjoy the bliss of the Mohammedan's heaven in her voluptuous embraces that forenoon. How lovely was her sleep! Who, looking on that face so pure in all its lines, so innocent in all its expressions, could imagine that in that soul there burned the fire of an unquenchable Cytherian furnace? Who, looking on those matchless breasts, could imagine that lovers innumerable had pressed them with lascivious hand or lip, and been supported by them when they trembled in the agonies and the delight of having her? The fair broad plane of her belly was still hidden by the upper portion of her petticoats, but the fine lines, which I had noticed when she 'put on her skin', had told me the tale that perhaps more than once it had been the breeding place of little beings, who, cast in such a beauteous mould, must needs be as beautiful as their lovely mother! Who, gazing in the girlish face and looking at those virginal breasts which seemed as if they had never been disturbed by pent-up milk and whose rosebud-like nipples seemed never to have been sucked by the cherry lips of babies, could connect such charms with the pains, the cares and duties of maternity? No! surely, like the fair houris of Mohammed's paradise, she must have been created for the fulfilment of pleasure only, not for the consequences of the kiss of love! But the wrinkles told a different tale, and I should like to examine them more closely. It would be easy to do if only they were exposed; all that I had to do was to lift, gently so as not to disturb her sleep, that part of her petticoat which still hid her there, and lay the garment back upon her waist.

With a hand trembling with excitement, I did so! Lo! my nymph was almost as naked as she was born! God of gods! What a blaze of exciting beauty! I had uncovered the sweet belly to look at the wrinkles, but my eye was captured before it lifted its gaze so high! As the bird is caught in the snare surrounding the luscious bait exposed to it, so were my eyes entangled in the meshes of that glorious forest-like bush growing on that voluptuous motte and shading a cunt the like of which for freshness, beauty and all that excites desire could not have existed in anybody but the great Mother of Love, Venus herself. It seemed to me impossible that this beauteous portal to the realms of bliss could have been invaded by so many worshippers as her speech of the morning had led me to believe. It looked far from having been hard used. What grand full lips it had. How sweetly it was placed. How pretty did the fine, dark hairs which crossed it look against the whiteness of the skin, whose infoldings formed that deep enticing line. What a perfect forest overshadowed it, and how divine were the slopes of that glorious hill, the perfect little mountain, which led down the sweet descent to the deep vale between her thighs, and ended in that glowing grotto in which love delighted to hide his blushing head and shed the hot tears of his exulting joy.

But what is that? What is that little ruby tip I see beginning to protrude, near the upper meeting of those exquisite lips which open slightly showing the pearly mouth! She moves. See! I think she must be dreaming! She slightly closes the bent leg towards that one outstretched! It is her most sensitive clitoris, as I live! See! It grows more and more! and by the gods! it actually moves in little jerks, just like an excited prick standing stiff and mad at the thoughts of hot desire!

I gazed at the tranquil face of the sleeping beauty; her lips moved and her mouth opened slightly showing the pearly teeth! Her bosom seemed to expand, her breasts to swell: they rose and fell more rapidly than they had been doing before this evident dream of love, fulfilled or about to be, invaded the soft heart of this perfect priestess of Venus! Ah! her bubbies do move! Their rosebuds swell out, they stand, each like an eager sentinel perched on the snowy tip of his own mountain, watching for the loving foe who is to invade this dreaming girl in a soft and sharp and hot encounter.

Again those thighs close on one another. Heavens! again they open to show the domain of love, excited, moving, leaping, actually leaping! That glittering ruby clitoris is evidently striving to feel the manly prick of which my charmer dreams. Why not turn the dream into a sweet and luscious reality?

I do not hesitate. I swiftly strip and in a moment I am as naked as I had been that morning, but I would like to see whether, as when I raped my cousin Emily, my second love, I could actually get into this sleeping girl before she woke to find me in her glowing cunt.

So I gently got over the thigh next to me and, with knees between hers, supported myself upon my hands, one on each side of her, while, stretching out my legs backward, I kept my eyes fixed on the sweet and burning cunnie I intended to invade. I lowered my body until I brought the head and point of my agitated and jerking prick exactly opposite its lower half, and then I manoeuvred it in!

Gods! The voluptuousness of that moment! I could see myself penetrating that seat of love and luxury! I could feel the cap fall back from the tingling head of my prick and fold behind its broad purple shoulders! For a moment I glanced at her face to see if she had perceived the gallant theft I was making of her secret jewel! No! She was asleep, but in the excitement of an erotic dream! Little by little I pressed in further and further, only withdrawing to give her more pleasure. I am nearly all in – her thick and lofty bush hides the last inch or so of my prick from my eyes, our hairs commingle, my balls nudge her and she wakes with a start!

In a moment her eyes met mine with that keen, almost wild glance, which had so impressed me when I saw her out of the *gharry*, but in a moment they changed and beamed with pleasure and affectionate caresses.

'Ah! Is it you?' she cried. 'I was dreaming of you! You darling man to wake me so sweetly!'

Some burning kisses, some close, close hugs, some little exclamations of delight, and then breast to breast, belly to belly, mouth to mouth, we play for the ninth or tenth time, I really don't know which, that same excited tune which had sounded all that morning so melodiously to our ravished senses. Heel and toe, as she called it, and other delicious movements mingled every part, then hot, quick, thrilling short digs and the torrents of two volcanoes of love burst forth simultaneously and mingled their lava floods in the hot recesses buried below the sylvan slopes of the hill of Venus.

The *ghurry* or gong, on which the non-commissioned officers of the guard sound the hour of the day in India, rang five o'clock. We had been in intense action nearly a whole hour, and my charming beauty was for the fifteenth time examining what she called my 'wonderful' prick and balls – wonderful, because the first showed no symptoms of fatigue, and the second no sign of exhaustion or depletion.

'I don't believe this can be a proper prick at all!' said she feeling it, pressing it, and kissing its impudent-looking head, first on one side and then on the other.

'Why?' I asked laughing.

'Because it's always stiff as a poker – always standing!'

'That is because it admires your delicious cunt so much, my darling, and it is always in a hurry to get back into it after it has been taken out!'

'Well! I never saw one like it before! All other men that I have had always grew soft and limp after the second go if not the first – and generally took a good deal of coaxing to get to stand again, unless one gave them lots of time! But yours! I never, never, met one like it! It will give me a lot of trouble, I can see, to take all the starch out of it!'

'Oh! but I can assure you, my most lovely girl, that with ordinary women I am just as you describe the men you have known. I can assure you it must be your extraordinary beauty which has such a powerful effect upon me! Come!' I continued, opening my arms and thighs, 'Come and lie on top of me and let me kiss you to death!'

Enraptured by the lavish, but not unmerited, praise of her beauty, she threw herself, with a cry of delight, on top of me, and my prick found a sweet resting place between our respective bellies. She took and gave me the sweetest kisses, murmuring little words of love and passion like a cat purring, until I was just going to propose that she should put her thighs outside mine, and let me have her *à la* St George, when a sudden idea seemed to strike her. She raised herself on her hand and asked me: 'I say! Have you reported your arrival to the station staff officer?'

What an idea! Fancy talking of such commonplace things just as I was about to propose the most delicious thing a woman can have from a man, the very poetry of life and love! I could not but think of Mrs Shandy asking her husband, when he was in the middle of that operation which resulted in Tristram nine months later, whether he had wound up the clock.

'My dear girl!' I cried. 'Bother the station staff officer and all his reports. Come! I am hungry for another sweet go! I want this cunt!' and I slipped my hand under her belly and between her thighs, and my middle finger into her palpitating cunnie.

'No!' she said, forcefully pushing my invading hand away. 'No! Not one more fuck until you have gone and reported yourself! Ah! you don't know the regulations, I see! But I do! I have not been in India all these years without learning what they are, and Major Searle, the brigade major here, is a perfect beast and devil! You may depend upon it, he knows you are here, and he would be only too delighted to get a chance of sitting on you, and he will be able to do so if you don't report yourself before dark. Remember you got here early this morning!'

I tried to convince her that I did not care a fig for Major Searle and all the Bengal regulations to boot! I said I was on duty, the post of honour being between her lovely thighs and my Johnnie anxious to go his rounds of her darling cunnie, and I did not think I could properly quit my duty in her body to go and perform another which would do quite well enough tomorrow, by which time, in all probability, Johnnie would have come off guard and would require a rest from his labours! But it was of no use; she declared I did not know my man, she told me a great deal more, from which it was very plain that something unpleasant had occurred between herself and Major Searle, and that it really did matter very much, to herself if not to me, that I should report my arrival, and do so at once.

Never did man more unwillingly do anything than I did, when, in obedience to my lovely tyrant's commands, I dressed and walked out to find the house of the brigade major. I know other men will not believe me or give me credit when I say that I felt as if I had not had one single fuck since I left England. That my balls and groin ached and I had all the sensations of a man who is soon about to have the fuck he has most looked forward to, for which he has lived chastely and kept himself in reserve in order to enjoy more that for which he burns, I can only state as a fact, and let others believe or not as they like. Certain it is, that there are times when either from length of abstinence, or the way in which a woman affects him, a man exhibits far greater power in the fields of Venus than at other times. Let me imitate Théophile Gautier, and request my readers, male and female, to remember that special time, when the former had that splendid night, and the latter had the active, big, strong lover, the best of all she ever had as far as fucking goes.

In this state I walked over to the bungalow which was pointed out to me as that of the brigade major. I was so far fortunate that I met him just as he was going out for a walk before dinner with his smooth English terrier.

'May I ask whether you are Major Searle, the brigade major, sir?'

'Yes, I am!'

'I should have come earlier to report my arrival, sir, but I have travelled so far in dak *gharries* that I have been lying down all day, and it was so very hot when I got up that I have deferred my coming to report myself until now.'

'And who may you be, sir?'

'I am Captain Charles Devereaux, of the First East Folk Regiment of Infantry, and I am on my way to Cherat to join my battalion on promotion.'

'Oh! indeed! How do you do, Captain Devereaux! I am sorry that I did not know you at first! Will you come in or are you inclined for a little stroll? Will you come over to the mess of the 130th and let me introduce you to the officers? I am afraid you won't get to Cherat quite so soon as you may wish; every blessed machine with wheels has been ordered for a week to come, so that if I were offered *lakhs* [thousands] of rupees I could not get you a conveyance here – besides which the road from Publi to Shakkote, at the foot of the hill, is rutted and bad for anything heavier than an *ekka* [one-horse native carriage], and you would have to go up the hill to Cherat either on foot or on horseback when you got there.'

The whole manner of the man changed when he found I was an officer, and what was more a captain, i.e. just one grade below himself in rank. Had I been a subaltern, he might have kept up a higher degree of *hauteur*.

At first I thought my new acquaintance rather an agreeable man. He spoke affably and pleasantly. He asked me about my voyage, my stay in Bombay and journey up country. He spoke about the war which would practically come to an end when the Khandahar expedition had blown Ayub Khan and the conquerors of the ill-fated Marwand to the four winds of heaven; then he returned to the subject of Nowshera, the dak bungalow and its inmates. He spoke of my well-known (as far as her most secret charms were concerned but otherwise perfectly unknown) mistress and commenced a series of very subtle questions, which, from their very guardedness, showed me that there was one person, and one circumstance, which he was approaching like a cunning cat stalking a sparrow, taking every cover as a guard as he crept up to it. I remembered the evident repugnance my new love had shown when speaking of Major Searle, and I fenced his questions until at last he asked me openly: 'Have you seen a woman, a rather lady-like person, in the bungalow?'

'I have seen one lady,' I replied, 'but there may be more than that for all I know in the house; I have not been over it, so I cannot tell if the one I have seen is the person you refer to.'

'Well!' said he, 'let me warn you that the woman I refer to is the wife of a non-commissioned officer – she is very pretty, and, I regret to say, about the most abandoned woman in India, if not in the whole world. She must be suffering from nymphomania, for she cannot see a man without she asks him to have her, and as she is really lovely to look at it is quite on the cards that if she asks a young man, fresh out from England like you, he might accept the proposition, and think that he had fallen in with a very

good thing indeed – but – pardon me – let me finish – the
penalty for adultery with a European woman in India is
two years' imprisonment and a fine of two thousand
rupees, and expulsion from India of the woman herself.
Already the woman I speak of has rendered herself liable to
expulsion hundreds of times; no one has as yet informed
against her, but her conduct at Peshawar has been so
scandalous and indecent that proceedings will most likely
be taken against her. A strict watch – of which she is not
aware – is being kept on her, and some unfortunate fellow,
say yourself, for you are young and no doubt do not dislike
the ladies – ha! ha! ha! – might find himself a victim of her
lust, for lust it is and nothing else.'

'Well! Major Searle,' I replied, 'I am a married man and
so I hope less liable to temptation from the path of duty
than the unfortunate bachelor. Many thanks, however, for
your timely warning, for of course I know that, married or
single, a man may become the victim of his passions, especially when taken off his guard by a pretty woman!'

'Ah! You speak truly!' he replied, 'and I can tell you that
this wretched creature is as lovely as a houri, and as lustful
as the most able whore in Babylon.'

I had not lived so long a life in the worship of Venus
without having seen a good deal of the hidden springs of
men's minds, and I came to the conclusion that this tirade
of friend Major Searle's was not altogether spoken on the
side of virtue, or caution, but that it was a kind of warning, 'Don't you touch that woman, she is my preserve,
and no one hunts in the forest between her thighs but
myself!'

Our arrival at the mess brought the conversation to a close. Like most messes of regiments which have been some time in India, this one was composed of a nice set of generally hospitable officers, all more or less languid from a long residence in a hot and unhealthy climate. They were also too much accustomed to seeing new faces, through the men going to or returning from Afghanistan, to be very greatly interested in me, but they were cordial and kind, made me drink a couple of pegs, asked me to dinner the next night, which happened to be their guest night, and begged me to consider myself an honorary member of their mess so long as I should remain in Nowshera.

I would willingly have excused myself from accepting their kind invitation to dinner, because I was so infatuated with my charming girl in the dak bungalow that the thought of being out of reach of her brilliant charms was purgatory to me, and my senses, but Major Searle was there, and his eyes were on me, and I felt that if my surmises as to the relations between himself and my lovely woman were correct, I had better ward off any suspicion on his part by cordially accepting the invitation, which I accordingly did with all the warmth I could muster. This seemed to relieve the major, for he turned and chatted with another officer. They asked Searle whether he would come and meet me at dinner, but he said he had some work to do tomorrow evening, but if he could find time he would gladly come and rattle the balls about at a game of billiards later in the evening.

After waiting a decent time I said I would go and have a look about whilst daylight lasted, and Searle proposed to accompany me. The man bored and bothered me and I wished him in hell, for my ideas about him began to become very jealous. I thought it extremely likely that he had fucked my charmer, indeed I was certain he had, but I could not suffer him to continue to do so whilst I was in Nowshera. I meant to keep her delicious cunt for myself, she had offered it to me, and I was its present master and entitled to remain so! I knew of the law and of the fine of which he had spoken, and they did not frighten me (as like all Draconian laws, it was seldom it was put in force), but I could not hide from myself that a jealous man, especially one who was something of a brute, would be able to interfere very sadly with such a liaison as I had now on hand, and make it very uncomfortable for the woman too. I had the sense, however, to try and keep my feelings under control and be as agreeable as possible. Our walk was a very simple and short one, for it was straight from the mess to the dak bungalow, whither Searle, as if unconsciously, led the way. I offered him a peg but he declined, as he said the liquor in the bungalow was vile, which was true, and they had no ice. Neither had the mess, then. Ice was unknown beyond Jhelum. But the mess had the simple means, so easily used whilst the hot, dry winds last, of cooling liquids by placing bottles in baskets of wet straw, in a position where the wind blows upon them. The rapid evaporation soon causes the temperature of the bottles to fall very low, and ice is not wanted. I did not know or had forgotten this, but I very soon had it put into practice by the *khansama*, and that very night and every day following I had cool drinks.

We sat on the verandah until it was dark. The gallant major never referred to my connection, whose brilliant and piercing eyes I felt darting their rays at us from behind the *chick,* and whose ears I was sure were drinking in every word. Then Searle went, only referring to his important conversation with the warning words: 'Don't forget what I told you!'

'All right, major. Many thanks. Good-night.'

When it was certain that he was gone, my lady glided on to the verandah and occupied the chair that Searle had sat in.

'What has that brute been telling you about me?' she asked, her voice quivering with passion.

I gave her an exact account of all that had passed between us, and when I told her, though in much softened language, about the way he had spoken of her, she rose to her feet and walked up and down the verandah in a towering rage – like an infuriated tiger.

'The black-livered blackguard!' she exclaimed. 'Oh! truly a nice man to preach continence and virtue! I should like to know who drove his wife to the hills to become the real whore she is! Yes! she is a whore if you like! She asks money from her men! It's five hundred rupees a night to have her, it is! I never yet asked a man for a pice, and I would not take one, or a million, as payment! If I do fuck, I fuck for pleasure, and because I like my lover! But I hate a cad! and if ever there was a cad in this world, it is Major Searle,' and she spat on the floor in token of her disgust for him!

I used all my arts of gentle persuasion to try and calm her down, and at length succeeded. She told me that Searle had never had her with her permission.

I propose, but not just at present, to take you, my patient readers, into my confidence, and tell you what were the adventures of her amorous life, but before doing so I must explain how the abhorred attentions of Major Searle were put a complete end to and how Lizzie Wilson rid herself of a man who had been her plague for some years.

I had hired a native servant as my factotum when I stayed in Lahore *en route* for my destination at Cherat; a capable man he was, and one who had an eye to business, for whether he was married or not I do not know, but he brought a very fine young native woman with him and, as the reader will hear, her talents were not thrown away at Cherat – although for myself I had far finer game to follow than was afforded by Mrs Soubratie's brown skin and somewhat mellow charms. Though no more than twenty she had gone the way of almost all Indian women and her bosom had begun to flow so that her bubbies, otherwise fine and plump, hung in a despondent manner. Such defects, however, are so common that they are little heeded by the British officers or soldiers, who whet their appetite on the fine, juicy cunt, rather than on other personal graces of the dame who affords them pleasure.

Soubratie, hearing I was going to mess, got out my nice, new, clean, white mess clothes, and himself gorgeously adorned and armed with a lantern, saw me safely across the compound, ankle deep in dust, to the mess of the regiment, there to partake of the generous hospitality of the glorious 130th. Is it any use to describe the ante-room, with its swinging punkahs, chairs, tables and pictures, carpets, books, newspapers, trophies of the chase, etc., etc. Shall I tell how the staff and self-important adjutant welcomed me in a proper and decent style; how the colonel seemed to inspect me; how the other officers, whom I had not yet met, greeted me with a polite 'glad to see you' from their lips, and 'I wonder what the devil kind of a fellow you are' glance from their eyes. Most regiments are alike; when you have seen one you have seen all. The English officer is undoubtedly a fearful 'stick' and of all weary humdrum lives, mess life is the most dreary. Along with the air of *ennui* and lassitude, however, there is a wicked, devil-may-care current, which forms the pith of an officer's life, and I knew well that when a good dinner had been eaten, a good share of fairly good wine drunk, and cigars and pegs had become the evening fare, I should hear a great deal more than I was likely to at the dinner table, where propriety and stiffness more or less ruled the roost. Accordingly, I was now regaled with old stories of the war, tales of savagery and cowardly cruelty on the part of the Afghans, with an occasional growl at the generals and authorities who, it seemed, must have been incompetent to a degree or far more significant results would have accrued from the valour of the British troops. I knew how to discount all this, and listened with interest, more or less affected, to my new friends' views.

But the 'cloth off the table', brought a subject which is always congenial to the fore. Woman, lovely woman, began to be discussed. My young acquaintance J. C.'s statement as to the complete absence of women from Tommy Atkins' quarters in Afghanistan and the consequent immense

demand for cunts on his return to civilisation and comfort
was immediately confirmed. In those days (it has been very
recently altered) the regulations obliged a certain number
of native girls to be especially engaged for the services of
each regiment, and these ladies of the camp accompanied
their regiment wherever it marched in India, just as much
a part and parcel of it as the colonel, adjutant and quar-
termaster. But Tommy likes variety as well as other people,
and in every place where there is a bazaar or shops there
are establishments for ladies of pleasure and these latter
earn a good many four-anna bits which should by rights
find their way into the pockets of the proper regimental
whores. The recent influx of troops into Peshawar from
Afghanistan had created an enormous demand for cunts,
and Nowshera, Attock, even Rawalpindi, Umballa and
other places had been denuded of 'polls' who gathered like
birds of carrion where the carcass lay. This was a great
grievance for the officers of the gallant 130th, who were
almost as badly off for women as they had been when they
had been at Lellabad and at Lundi Kotal, at which latter
place a Gurkha soldier who had got a bad case of clap from
some native woman was universally spoken of as the
'Lucky Gurkha!' Not because of the clap, *bien entendre,* but
because, though he suffered afterwards, he had managed to
secure for himself a pleasure so uncommon, under the
circumstances, that it seemed like water a thousand miles
distant to a traveller lost in the great Sahara!

Once the subject of love and women was started
rolling the tongues of those who had been most reticent
during dinner were set wagging, and I found a most

entertaining host in the fat, pudgy, double-chinned major, who seemed to take a fancy to me. He proposed that we should adjourn outside where the band of the regiment was performing some operatic airs and lively dance music, and there we sat, in those voluptuous Madras long arm-chairs, enjoying whatever coolness there was in the air, the sounds of the suggestive music and the brilliancy of the myriad bright stars which glittered overhead, literally like 'diamonds in the sky'.

'Searle, our brigade major, said he would come later this evening,' said the major, 'but I rather think he won't.'

'Why?' I asked.

'Because he is cunt-struck with a very pretty little woman in the dak bungalow.'

This I guessed was a shot to me.

'Indeed! Well! I hope he will succeed and get his greens! Poor chap!'

'Oh! Do you! Well! We were all saying that it was a dammed shame, because we had made up our minds that you were surely in her good graces yourself, and we thought it mean of Searle to try and cut in whilst you were out! ha! ha! ha!'

'Oh!' I said quietly, 'but I am a married man, major, and have just left my wife, and do not go in for that sort of thing! So, as far as I am concerned, Major Searle is welcome to the lady if he can persuade her to grant him her favours.'

'Well! But Searle is a married man himself, Devereaux!'

'Oh! I dare say! I don't mean to imply that a married man is impervious to the charms of other women because he is married. I am not straitlaced, and I dare say should be quite as liable as anybody else to have a woman who was not my wife, but you know I have not been married long enough to be tired of my wife, and I have not been long enough away from her to feel any inclination to commit adultery yet!'

'Well! Searle is married – but he's a brute! Yet I somehow pity the poor devil too! I don't know how it is, but he and his wife, a devilish fine woman, a perfect Venus in her way, don't get on altogether well; in fact she has left him!'

'Oh! my! do you say so?'

'Yes! Now mind you, Devereaux, you must not give me as your authority, but I can tell you that he treated that poor woman like hell, half killing her with a blow from the side of his hairbrush; devilish nearly smashed her skull, you know, and after that she left him, and went and set up on her own account at Ramsket.'

I am sure my dear readers are amused at my assuming the air of a thoroughly moral young husband still contented with the breasts of his spouse, as Solomon, I think it is, tells us we ought to be, but of course I was not going to amuse my new friend, or indeed any others, with tales which somehow spread so wonderfully quickly, and in rapidly widening circles, until they reach the ears of those we would least wish to hear them. Really and truly, my heart and conscience pricked me when this conversation brought to mind my beloved little Louie, and I thought of her in her lovely bed, perhaps weeping in sad silence as she prayed for the safety, welfare and quick return home of one whom she loved so dearly, who made her joyous by day and gave her rapturous fun at night, her husband, and the darling father of her angel baby girl. But alas! the spirit is willing and the flesh weak, as I have remarked before, and the weakness of the flesh exceeds the strength of the spirit all too often.

But the conversation was bearing directly on a subject which was becoming interesting to me since I had seen Searle and heard Lizzie's indignant remark that his wife was a regular whore, whose price for her charms was, however, uncommonly high. I did not mind what my fat major said about Searle's designs on Lizzie that evening, because Lizzie would have to have been a most unaccountably stupid deceiver if she had merely expressed abhorrence of him to blind me! No, I felt certain the abhorrence was real and true, and I had no fear that I should find that she had afforded him a retreat, either hospitable or the reverse, in her sweet cunt when I got home to her again.

'How do you mean "set up on her own account", major?' said I.

'Oh! hum! well! look here, bend your head a little nearer to me! I don't want to talk too loudly! Well! she is – that is, any fellow almost, who cares to give her a cool five hundred rupees, can have her.'

'What!' said I in well-affected incredulous tones, 'you want to persuade me that an officer's wife, a lady like Mrs Searle must be, has actually done such a monstrous, not to say such an idiotic thing, as not only to leave her husband, a thing I cannot understand, but to set up as a whore, and in such a place as Ramsket? Surely, major, you are mistaken! Remember! we are told to believe nothing we hear and only half of what we see!'

'I know! I know!' said he, still as calmly as if he were Moses laying down the law, 'but look here, Devereaux, you won't tell me I am a liar if I say the proof of the pudding is in the eating, and that my proof of what I say is that I, Jack Stone, have had Mrs Searle, and paid for my game! Yes, sir! Rupees five hundred did Jack Stone pay Mrs Searle for a night in Mrs Searle's bed.'

'Goodness, and you have actually –'

'I have actually fucked her, sir! and fucked her well! and a damned fine poke she is too, I can tell you, and well worth the five hundred she asks for the fun. Such a damned fine poke is she that Jack Stone, who is not a rich man but must lay up for a rainy day, has put three times five hundred rupees away in the bank of Simla, and means to lodge them some day soon in the bank of Ramsket, of which the banker and sole proprietress is Mrs Searle, the bank itself being her goloptious cunt, between her goloptious thighs. Did you mark that, young man!'

'And does Searle know this?' I asked, still incredulous.

'What? that I have had his wife?'

'No, not that you in particular have had her, but that she is had by other men, and for money paid down on the nail.'

'Know it! of course he does! It's her way of paying him off for his brutal conduct to her, to drive him nuts by writing and telling him how nicely she is dragging his name through the mud.'

'Then why does he not divorce her?' I cried indignantly, for I felt that it was monstrous for a wife, no matter what her grievance might be, to behave in such an outrageous manner.

'Ah! – but sink your voice a little lower, Devereaux, not that all this is not perfectly well known by our fellows, but about the divorce. Well, you see, if what I have heard is true, a divorce is the last thing Searle can get, or would care to ask for, no matter how much he might wish it could be managed.

'Certain little things would come out at the trial, and he might find himself not only minus a wife whom he hates, but also minus his liberty and what remains of his honour, and I don't think anyone would care to become a convict, even to rid himself of his wife!'

'What little things?' asked I, quite bitten with curiosity.

'Oh! Searle was a long time in Persia before he married, and he got the Persian taste for boys! Sodomy, you know!' And the modest major sank his voice to a whisper. 'Sodomy! he tried to get Mrs Searle to acquire a taste for it herself, but she, like a proper woman, indignantly refused to comply. It might have stopped there, but one night Searle, full of zeal and brandy, actually ravished his poor wife's – hem – hem – hem, well! – bum! and from that day she hated him – quite naturally, I think! Then, of course, she gave him the nag, nag, rough side of her tongue, until he nearly killed her, as I told you, in his passion. Then she went and set up at Ramsket.'

'But,' said I, horrified to hear such a disgusting story, so loathsome on either side, 'how is it she can demand such enormous sums for what I expect equally good returns can be got almost anywhere in India!'

'Oh! but you don't know. First of all, Mrs Searle is in society – she is, I suppose, the most beautiful woman in India, if not in all Asia!'

'In society!'

'Yes! bless you! you don't understand. Now come! You, who have seen the world at home! Have you not heard how Mrs So and So is suspected of poking, and yet you have met her every night at the best houses? Have you not seen common or fast women, who dare to do what your own wife or sister dare not, and nobody says more than that they are fast? Do you suppose you know what women actually do poke, and those who only get the credit for it? It is just the same with Mrs Searle. She lives in a pretty little bungalow, some three miles deep in the hills of Ramsket; she calls it Honeysuckle Lodge, but the funny fellows call it Cunnie Fuckle Lodge. Ha! ha! ha! and she has named the hill it is on Mount Venus; she stays there all the hot weather; in the cold weather she goes to Lucknow or Mteerut or Agra or Benares or wherever she likes. No fellow has her without an introduction. The Viceroy is damned spoony on her, and that is sufficient to keep the fashionable people quiet. People suspect, people know, but people pretend to think it impossible that the quiet lady, living in a little bungalow, away from all the world, minding her garden and her flowers, is anything but a poor, persecuted wife whose husband is a brute!'

'Oh! that is it! So to have her you must get an introduction?'

'Yes! Without that you might as well cry for the moon!'

'And how is it to be managed?' I asked out of simple curiosity, for I had no notion of having Mrs Searle, but I was interested in this curious story of which I did not know how much to believe or how much to discredit.

'Ha! ha! ha! Devereaux! I fancy you are beginning to think whether you can find five hundred rupees for yourself, eh?'

'Not a bit!' said I indignantly, 'I have no idea of such a thing, but simply asked out of curiosity!'

'Well!' said the pudgy little major, puffing his cheroot hard as it had nearly gone out, 'no harm to tell you, anyhow! You can get an introduction from any man who has had her! I could give you one for instance. See! This is how I had her. I had heard of Mrs Searle and had, like everybody else, heard funny reports about her, which, like I see you do now, I only half believed. Well! I did not then know she lived at Ramsket, but chance made me pitch upon that place to spend three weeks' leave in during the hot weather of '75. The Viceroy and his staff were spending the time there also, and every-body was wondering why he chose Ramsket instead of Naini Tal. There is reason in everything and Mrs Searle was his reason, no doubt. However, without being too long winded, I met Lord Henry Broadford, the Assistant Military Secretary, you know. Broadford was at school with me, and is a damned good fellow. One day, soon after I went to Ramsket, I was standing talking to Broadford, when the finest, handsomest woman I had ever seen walked by, and Broadford took off his hat and smiled, and she bowed. She looked full at me as I took off my hat and, by George, sir! she made my heart thump in my bosom, she was so lovely. When she was out of earshot I said, "Harry, who is your friend? By God, she is a clinker and no mistake!"

' "Don't you know," says he, "why that is the famous Mrs Searle."

' "Is it," says I. Then I asked him if he knew whether it was true she poked, as people said.

'Broadford looked at me and grinned and said: "Would you like to know for certain, Stone?"

'And I said, "Yes."

' "Well," says he, "the most certain way is to poke her yourself, for you might not believe me if I told you that I was in bed with her up to five o'clock this morning!"

' "I don't believe you, you beggar!" said I, "you are laughing at me."

' "All right!" says he, "have you five hundred rupees to lose on a bet?"

' "Well!" I hesitated; five hundred is a large sum and the subject was not worth it.

'Seeing me hesitate, he said, "Well, would you give five hundred rupees to have Mrs Searle yourself, Jack?"

' "Yes," said I, plump as could be.

' "Then come along with me," said Broadford.

'Well, we went to my hotel, and there Broadford made me write a cheque, and get five one-hundred-rupee notes from the native banker, new and crisp, in exchange. Then he made me write a letter addressed to Mrs Searle, in which I asked her might I come and take dinner with her on such and such a day? naming the day. I was more than half afraid the fellow was humbugging me, but he pulled out a case from his pocket, and showed me a lovely photo in it of a stark-naked lady, cunt and all complete, and, says he, "Mrs Searle gives one of these to each of her lovers, and she gave me this this morning; see, her name, date and the number of times I had her last night!" Well, I looked at the photo, and sure enough there was no mistaking it was the lady I had just seen, besides which I remembered having seen photos of her taken in the plains.

'By God! sir! the sight of such lovely charms settled my hash. I told Broadford that he would have to bear the brunt if anything went wrong. He swore all would be right, and after I had signed my name to the note to Mrs Searle, he added his initials and "WTBF?"

' "What does that mean?" I asked.

' " "Will there be fuck?' of course!" Well, this done, I put the five good crisp notes in the letter, and we went to the post office, registered it, and then I began to think I had been made a fool of. But it was all right. The day afterwards I got a registered letter. It was from Mrs Searle. In it were my five notes. She said she was very sorry but that she did not think she could have the pleasure of my company at dinner for another ten days, would I write again in about a week's time, if that would suit me, and she would be sure not to disappoint me. I rushed off, found Broadford, and nearly had a fit of apoplexy from excitement. By his advice I waited some eight days, then sent another letter, and again enclosed the notes, and I added after my own signature, WTBF? Next came a letter by hand. It said, "My dear Jack", this time. It invited me to dine the next evening at eight and ended with "Matilda Searle. TWBF." '

'And did you go?'

'Oh! What a question! Of course I did. By God, sir! I was simply bursting. Even now I can hardly tell my story with any degree of quiet! Well, I went; I was received by her in an awfully pretty little drawing room, most beautifully furnished and bristling with knick-knacks, mirrors, pictures and everything that can make a room handsome and elegant. The floor was covered with carpet into which one's feet sank as one walked on it. Mrs Searle was sitting reading when I arrived, and as soon as the bearer had gone out of the room she came and took my hand, shook it, and then kissed me! I was so excited; I felt such a sense of false shame, that at first I was like a stuck pig! But she quickly put me at my ease, sat on the sofa, made me sit next to her, jammed her knee against mine and, whilst asking me where, how and when I had known Lord Henry Broadford, showed off her splendid shoulders and magnificent bosom. I had been awfully randy on my way there, I had been randy all the days I had been waiting for her, but I was so knocked over by the elegance I saw on my first arrival that I declare, if the truth were told, I felt inclined to run away. But little by little, as I got to see the woman I was going to have, as I began to hear her talk as if we were quite old chums, and at her touch – the contact of her hand on mine, to say nothing of the kisses which from time to time she gave me – I began to pluck up courage. So by way of showing her I was no fool but expected something, I offered to put my hand on her bosom, and take hold of one of her glorious bubbies, of which I saw nearly half over her dress. But she laughed and said it was not time for that yet, that when we had dined, and I had had my smoke, we would go to bed, where I should find her all I could wish for, and where I should have the fullest liberty, so long as I did not exceed the bounds which every honest man observed who had a woman.

Well! I kissed her and begged her pardon. I had a rosebud in my buttonhole, and she took it out and said, "See, I place your rose where you shall be!" and she put it between her bubbies and said, "there it is, a rose among the lilies, but that is all of you I can allow at present to be there." Well, sir! we had a splendid dinner. In spite of my impatience I did justice to a rattling good feed, and afterwards she made me smoke a cigar, and when it was nearly done she said she would go and undress, and that when I heard a little bell ring, I was to go to her bedroom which she had already pointed out to me. Soon I heard the bell and I went. Oh! I was delighted! By God, sir! I have had many fine women, but I never saw one who was a patch on Mrs Searle when undressed. She had on a quite transparent kind of nightgown, which covered her from neck to heels. It had no sleeves, and her arms were something splendid. Her bubbies looked more enticing covered with this transparent stuff, than when I saw them bare. Her nipples looked like strawberries, red and luscious. I would have been able to see her cunt, but all the whole of the way, from her chin to her feet, there was a broad rose-coloured ribbon, which fell exactly over it, so that I could only see the fringe of hair on either side where it passed over her bush. I declare, Devereaux, I cannot describe the night I had with her, for it would drive you wild and you would be trying to slip into that woman at the dak bungalow, and it would never do, you being, as you say, a married man, but I never – never – never had such a glorious fucking in my life. It is true I was five years younger than I am now, and as I keep a pretty little piece of brown meat, and have my regular greens twice a week, I might not be able to do as good a turn now, as I did then, but I had that woman eight solid times, sir, seven times before I went to sleep, and once in the morning. She said herself that she did not expect it of me at first sight, as she said I was too fat, and fat men were bad pokes as a rule. When I went away after breakfast she gave me a case like the one Broadford had shown me, and told me not to open it until I got home, and she told me she relied on me not to show it to anyone, unless I thought them a fit fellow for her to have. I'll show it to you now! Ha! Bearer! *Kitmutgar! koi, hai!'* and the excited major shouted to the servants, one of whom came. By his orders the major's bearer brought a little writing dispatch-box, and from this he took a small case, some six inches by four in size, and then, giving me a nudge, he walked to the ante-room of the mess, which was deserted, and showed me a very well-executed photo of a perfectly naked woman. On the back of the photo was written: *From M. Searle to Jack Stone – 15 June 1875 – 8.*

'Now!' said the major, 'any time you would like to have that woman, you drop me a line and I will give you the necessary introduction.'

I thanked him heartily, but I must say I did not feel tempted to give five hundred rupees for the favours of any woman, just then, and mentally I made comparisons between my Lizzie and Mrs Searle which were not favourable to the latter, though, according to the photo, she was certainly a fine woman.

Then, after smoking another cigar, and drinking a couple more pegs and talking Mrs Searle and fuck generally,

I left to go home, and I looked forward to returning to Lizzie and getting rid of some of the hot blood which was running in a desperately excited manner through my throbbing veins, for the little major's conversation had been the reverse of cooling.

It was very nearly midnight when I reached the bungalow and there was not a light in the place. The stars had shown in the road fairly well, but the verandah and rooms, on my side at least, were pitch dark. I imagined that Lizzie must have grown tired of waiting up for me and taken the opportunity of getting a good sleep before I came home, since it was highly likely that, after a good mess dinner and quantities of generous wine, I would be rather lively and keen and put her into that condition too.

Full of this idea, and determined if possible to give her a surprise sweet-awakening by getting into her whilst she slept, I stole on tiptoe towards my room, to undress there and then join her in her 'naked bed'. But as I crossed the verandah something white gleamed on one side and, on looking, I saw it was Lizzie, sitting in my easy chair, apparently, from her position, asleep. I stole up behind her and bending over her I kissed her soft cheek, at the same time stealing my hand into her glorious bosom, and caressing her warm, swelling, elastic bubbies, which always gave me such delight to feel. Oh! What nice things good bubbies are to feel!

'Ah! is that you, Charlie, dear! I must have been half asleep,' she said.

'Yes! darling!' I said softly, still pressing the delightful globes in my hand, one after the other, and kissing the sweet mouth turned up towards me.

Lizzie seemed to enjoy my caresses, for she merely returned my kisses and patted my face lightly with her hand. I found that although she was still dressed, her clothes were loose on her, and that I could pass my hand between the band and her waist, and her beautiful skin felt so soft, so satiny, so smooth, it delighted me as though I had never felt it before. From her bosom I descended until I reached the pretty plain of her lovely belly and here I let my roving hand wander from side to side as it gradually crept lower and lower until it reached the upper fringe of the glorious bush which so splendidly adorned her dome-like motte, and then I threaded my way through this pathless forest until I reached the spot where the infold formed the precious and voluptuous deep line of her delicious cunt. I passed my middle finger in the groove, just tipping the awakened and slippery little clitoris, until I reached the entrance to the rich depths I sought for.

Lizzie said nothing; my left hand, which was over the bosom, felt the breast rise a little more tumultuously, and my arm bore a slightly increased strain as she leaned her head back upon it, but that was all. It was so dreamy, so exquisite, that I stood in that position, caressing the warm moist cunt, kissing the cherry lips with little caresses of mine, as if I were a dove billing its mate.

Suddenly a change seemed to come over me. I was no longer in India; it was no longer Lizzie whose charms I was master of, but my own beloved little beautiful wife. I remembered how, on the third night of our blissful and heavenly honeymoon, she had preceded me to bed; how it was the month of July, and the night was warm and balmy, the scent of the blossoming lime trees filling the air with its sweet aroma. I had given my Louie ten minutes to undress and perform those necessary little acts to make her comfortable for the night, which no young married woman likes to do in the presence of her husband, and then I had gone up to follow her into the bed, my beautiful heaven, in which I expected to find her, a luscious feast for my still ardent and excited and quite uncloyed desire. But when I went to the room she was still dressed. She was seated at the open window, reclining back into her chair. There were no candles. The stars were shining brightly but softly; the heavy masses of foliage on the trees loomed dark against the skies, and there was silence outside, except the occasional rustling of the leaves as the amorous zephyrs kissed the heads of the trees they loved, and the poetry of the moment filled me with a degree of tenderness and love I had not experienced in a similar manner since Louie and I had been made one at God's holy altar. Like Lizzie, she had only half turned to accept my kisses, with a little question as to whether it was me – as though it could be anyone else! – as I had glided my happy hand into her so lately virgin bosom, and caressed the swelling globes which it had so delighted me on my wedding night to find did exist in truth and reality, beautiful, round, firm, polished, elastic and rose-crowned; for Louie had been so jealous of those exquisite beauties, that even when I had seen her dressed for the evening, in her low-necked gown, not one line of the lovely hemispheres did she show, and I had to imagine beauties to exist where my fancy painted them; and I had prayed I might find she really had sweet bubbies; for alas!

how often is man deceived in his expectations as to the physique of his beloved bride. Neither of us spoke; we were too happy; and over her beautiful bosom my wanton hand had descended, until, finding her waistband loosened, it had explored the sweet pastures of silvery belly and crossed the rough surface of the mount of Venus; as my finger pressed in Cupid's furrow, the lovely little clitoris, ever on the watch, had sprung up to salute it with a moist and eager kiss; a thrill, which I could feel, passed over my Louie's form, and as she felt the strong middle finger bury itself in the hot depths of her velvety cunt, she had pressed my face to her burning cheeks, and murmured, 'My man! Oh! my beloved man!'

Full of overflowing sentiment, which this entrancing quiet and this voluptuous scene of love and passion had inspired me with, I quite forgot where I was, and whom I was caressing. I kissed Lizzie rapturously and I murmured in a voice which must have quivered with deep emotion, 'Oh! my darling! my own, own, darling.'

Lizzie started. She disengaged my hands and, standing up, she exclaimed in a voice which sounded strange to me, so different was it from her ordinary tone, 'Charlie! Charlie! Don't speak to me like that! Don't! there's a good fellow!'

'Oh! Lizzie! what have I done?' I said in alarm.

'Oh! you must not speak to me like that! You know you don't love me, Charlie dear. You don't love me like you do your wife, and if you did it would only make me unhappy. Oh! Charlie! the one thing which would take away the only pleasure I have in life, would be to know that some man really and truly loved me. I could not leave my husband and live with him, and I must have a man as often as I can. You don't understand. When a woman has led the life I have she can't steady down unless some illness puts an end to all feeling of desire in her. She must go on as she is till death, or at least till decay of all her bodily powers. Confess now, it was not Lizzie Wilson you were speaking to but your wife!'

'Well, Lizzie, dearest!' I said, quite thunderstruck with her vehemence and her outcry against love, 'I won't tell you a lie. I did for the moment forget where I was. It was this way – but sit down darling – and I will tell you truly.' She did so, and still standing over her, and again possessing myself of the sweet charms between her thighs, to which she admitted me full rights as a true friend but not as an earnest and passionate lover, I told her about the scene of which I have given my readers a faint notion, as regards the delicious commingling of the adoration of the heart and the worship of the senses.

When I had finished Lizzie heaved a prodigious sigh and said: 'Charlie! Take my advice and don't be too long sending home for that true wife of yours! She will keep you from harm out here, and it is not right, it would be a cruel shame to condemn her to pass the life of a nun whilst you are amusing yourself in India, fucking to your heart's content women who do not deserve such delight. For, mark my words, you are not the kind of man to go without women, nor will you find a station where there are not women, pretty and fine, who will not leave you alone – they will be as eager to have you as you will be to have them. Yes! believe me, if ever a man was formed to strike a woman's fancy it is you. Send for your wife, for otherwise some mischief will be brewed, and you may be made to repent that you left her at home.'

These words, spoken with great earnestness, struck me very forcibly. It seemed also so like Satan rebuking sin that I could hardly help feeling amused. After a pause of a second or two, during which I gently stroked the sweet cunt under my hand, I said: 'All right, Lizzie! I believe you are quite right! I will send for my wife as soon as you advise, but come in, there's a darling, and let us enjoy the fleeting hour. It seems like ages since I last had my prick in this sweetest, softest, juiciest little cunt of yours!'

To this she replied, 'Searle has been here tonight.'

My goodness! All my blood ran cold. I felt now as if my Louie, in answer to my prayer to come to bed, so that I might enjoy her loveliness, told me, 'Too late, my dear, So and So has just been fucking me and I'm not inclined for any more!'

'Searle!' I exclaimed, snatching my hand away from under her clothes. 'Searle! Oh! Lizzie! and did you let him have you?'

'I did not say that he had me, Charlie, so you need not get into a fit of jealousy, you silly boy! No! If there is one man in the world to whom I would forever say no, it is Searle; but he was here all the same.'

I breathed. Somehow Lizzie had grown dear to me, she had been so nice, such a splendid fuck, and so tender towards me in spite of her disclaimer of love.

'What did he want, Lizzie?'

'What you say you do now, Charlie! But oh! we had such a row! I declare it has given me quite a headache! Oh! Searle! you . . . cursed beast!'

'And what did he do or say Lizzie! Tell me!'

'Well, you had hardly got across the road before Searle, who had apparently been watching for you to go, sneaked on to the verandah around the corner, and asked if I had got his note. Now I had received a note from him which I had kept to myself, and which I had not shown you, dear, for I did not want to make you jealous; a fine production it is, too, and a very useful one for me, I can tell you. I think he must have been either drunk or mad when he wrote it, for he could not have written a more damning piece of evidence against himself if he had tried to do it in his sober senses. Oh! Mrs Searle would give a cartful of her rupees to have it, for she could then get the divorce she longs for. Plenty of good fellows are ready to marry her if she could get divorced, and I know she has often said she would be glad to give up her present life; but Searle knows this, and his only revenge against her is to behave so prudently as not to give her any chance. If ever he has a woman it is so on the sly that no one knows it. Well, he has written down in black and white that he has had me – and since Mrs Searle left him, too. Let's light a candle and I'll show you the letter!'

Full of curiosity and rather astonished to find how the truth comes out, for I had certainly understood Lizzie to say that Searle had never had her, nor ever should have her by her permission, I went for my candle and lit it. Lizzie then took the precious letter out of her pocket and gave it to me to read.

It commenced with prayers and entreaties to let him come and have her whilst I was at mess. It said that he knew well that I did nothing all day and night but fuck her, that by this time she must be tired of me and at least that a little of her accustomed change of diet would be agreeable. From prayers, it went to using threats. Her husband's regiment was at Peshawar, now with a newly appointed colonel who was death on adultery and fornication, and he had given out that the first time he found any of it going on amongst the married women of his regiment, he would set the penal laws on the subject in force and that he (Searle) had plenty of evidence which would put me (Devereaux) into prison and send her out of the country branded as an unchaste woman, a whore and an adulteress, and that unless she admitted him to her embraces he would help the colonel to make good his word. Then came more prayers and more earnest entreaties – then offers of a thousand rupees (twice what his own wife charged) – jewellery, anything, if she would but consent, and then in a postscript, he boasted that he had already fucked her, at Agra, on an occasion when, stunned by a fall from an over-thrown *gharry*, she had been carried into his bungalow, and seeing who she was, and determined not to lose the precious opportunity, he had raped her in her unconscious state, and enjoyed the 'wealth of her voluptuous cunt' – he actually used these last words.

'The intense blackguard,' I exclaimed, moved to great wrath by the reading of this precious epistle.

'You may say so, Charlie! But now hear what the brute did. At first he asked had I got his letter. I said yes. Then he asked me in a wheedling tone would I consent and let him have me. I said not for all the thousand rupees in India, that he was too loathsome a brute for me to touch with the end of a barge-pole, let alone take in my arms. Then he began to threaten me with our new colonel, saying that I could not get away from here now unless he, Searle, gave me an order for a *gharry,* that everything like a cart with wheels was engaged for the next ten days, and that long before that time was over the regiment would be on the march from Peshawar to Muttra, and that the colonel, finding me here instead of at Muttra, where he had ordered me to go, would be furious, and he, Searle, would take the opportunity then of telling him why I stopped at Nowshera, namely, to have three separate officers who stayed here, two on their way down country, and one on his way to join his battalion at Cherat, and he would tell who these officers were, and it would go hard on them, each of them would lose two thousand rupees or get two years' imprisonment, and "then they will have good reason to curse you for being a damned little bitch, for why should you condemn them to these fines and punishment when by letting me have you for an hour or two you can prevent any harm arising, and I will keep my word if you don't . . ." and he got more and more angry.

'I told him I would see him damned before I would let him touch me, and I dared him to report me, or you or the others, and I reminded him of what he had said in his let-ter, and how completely I would cover myself, and you, and others by it, and I advised him to go away quietly or I would call the *khansama.* That put him in as complete a passion as ever I saw a man. He rushed at me and swore he would have me. I put myself like a shot behind a chair. He stopped for a moment, unbuttoned his trousers, pulled out his prick, which was in a furious state, and then rushed at me again. I shouted for the *khansama*, but Searle did not mind. He seized me around the waist, and lifted me off the floor, and ran with me into my room, dashing the *chick* down as he lunged into it. But I was not going to be ravished without making the best defence I could. I got my ten nails well into his cheeks, and scrawned them down as hard as I could. I could see and feel the blood spurting. Searle yelled and cursed, swore and called me the most awful, dreadful names. I gave him as good a clawing as I could, but he got me down on the bed, pulled my petticoats up to his face, and lay on top of me with all his weight, trying to get his knees between mine. But I kept my thighs locked hard; although he pounded with his knees on my thighs, and nearly choked me with his hand on my throat, he could not get between them. I could feel the tip of his prick banging against my motte like a bar of iron, but he never once got it nearer my cunt than that. At last, finding that he could not manage to make me open my legs to him that way, he began to put his hand between my thighs, and to pinch me most frightfully. Oh! he gave me dreadful pinches. I am sure I am all black and blue, but his weight was off me now, I was able to scream; and I yelled. I called out murder! murder! help! help! as loud as I could, and at the same time I tried to get hold of his balls, so as to crush them if I could, but he managed to keep them out of my reach, whilst he pinched, scratched and beat my thighs as though he would tear them to pieces. But before my fast failing strength left me, help came. Two young civilians came in today from Peshawar, whilst you were dressing for the mess, and got a room on the other side of the bungalow. They at last heard my screams, and came running to see what was the matter. When Searle saw them he ordered them out of the room, saying that I was his wife, and that he had a right to treat me as he liked; but I tried to get out of his clutches, and I implored the young men to save me, and I said that Searle was not my husband and was trying to rape me. The young men then ordered him off my bed, and as he did not obey, one of them pulled him off. Then Searle went for him, for he was blind mad with rage and passion, but the young man was pretty cool, and he gave Searle a most dreadful blow in the face with his fist – oh! I was so delighted to hear it – it made him stagger and the blood spurt from his nose. But Searle seemed really like a lunatic. He rushed again at the young man, and hit him several nasty blows, so that the second one came to his friend's assistance. I urged the two on and Searle got a thrashing, I can tell you! Still he would not quit. By this time the *khansama*, the principal coolies, your servant Soubratie and everyone belonging to the bungalow had come. I could not help continuing to scream. Everybody went for Searle, and at last he was turned out of the house yelling and fighting like a wild beast. Some soldiers came running off the road, and at first, seeing who Searle was, wanted to help him, but the young men told them what he had done, and apparently they don't love Searle at the barracks, for these men joined in beating him, and upon my word I began to get frightened. I thought they would kill him between them all. Oh! the row was tremendous. Presently down came the picket from the barracks; the soldiers seeing them ran away. Searle was lying on the ground, a crowd around him; some men had torches alight, and the *khansama* had got a lantern, and you never saw such a group as they formed. The young men who had helped to save me from being ravished explained the whole matter to the NCO of the picket, and as Searle's trousers were open, and his prick showing, though no longer stiff and standing, he understood the whole thing. Searle, though hardly able to breathe, wanted them to take the young men prisoner, but the NCO begged them to go away, and persuaded him to let himself be carried home, for he could not walk. Oh! Charlie! it made me so sick and ill! I don't know how I have been able to tell you so much – my head is splitting, and I feel all pounded to death by that brute.'

I leave my readers to appreciate the state of anger and disgust towards Searle which this vivid narrative of poor Lizzie's produced. Oh! I had come home hoping for such a sweet night of delightful fucking, but it was plain that that was out of the question, and indeed, all desire, other than for vengeance on Searle, had gone out of my head. Lizzie looked very ill, when I came to examine her by the light of the candle, and I begged her to go to bed.

'Yes, dear!' she said. 'It is the best place for me, but oh! Charlie dear! I am afraid I cannot have you tonight! Poor boy! I am sure you came home expecting to have some grand fucking, and I am so grieved to disappoint you, but I feel too sick!'

'You poor darling girl!' I cried. 'I had hoped, as you say, to have some more delicious fucks with you tonight, but of course it cannot come off now. Come to bed and let me help you to undress.'

She did as I asked her. I undressed her and was shocked to find the state she was in. Her throat was bruised a little but her poor thighs were one mass of contusions, all scored by the fingernails of the monster who had attacked her. I kissed them, 'to make them well', and poor Lizzie smiled faintly and kissed me, and then lay down and begged me to leave her alone. But hardly had she put her head on the pillow than she called out that she was going to be sick.

'Oh! Charlie! Help me to my bathroom!'

But I ran and got her a *chillumchee* [brass basin] and brought it to her, and she, poor creature, was deadly sick. I held her burning forehead in my hands and did all I could to comfort her, and to assist, and at last, completely exhausted, she sank back and her whole appearance alarmed me. When I came home she was fairly cool, but now she was the colour of a penny, and her skin was hot, parched and burning. I guessed she had a fever and the suddenness of the attack alarmed me. All that night I tended her, keeping her well covered up to induce perspiration, and from time to time gave her water to drink for which she moaned. Nobody who has not watched a sickbed under circumstances somewhat similar can tell how tedious, how weary, such a watch is, especially when, as in my case, the watcher is ignorant of what he ought to do, and has to go

by instinct, as it were. At length, just as the morning began
to break, Lizzie seemed to fall into a sound sleep. Her
breathing was more regular and easy, her colour was more
natural, and – blessed be heaven – her skin was again cool
and moist. It was evident that the strength of the attack
had passed.

Satisfied that Lizzie was really in a healthful sleep, I got
myself a cool peg, and then going back to the bedside I sat
down in my chair, leaned my head against her pillow and
fell into a sound sleep myself. How long I slept I do not
know but I was at length awakened by Soubratie, who
touched me and murmured that sickening: 'Sa–hib!
S–a–a–hib!' in my ear with which your native servant
always rouses you.

'What is it?' said I, raising my heavy head.

'Major Stone, sahib! Outside on verandah! Wanting see
master!' replied Soubratie who spoke English like a native.

'Major Stone! Oh! yes! all right! Tell him I will be with
him in a moment, Soubratie.'

'Yes, sahib!'

I felt desperately tired and not in a pleasant humour at
having my much needed rest broken. However, after a
yawn or two, and an anxious glance at poor Lizzie, who
seemed to have quite regained her ordinary appearance
and to be having a really sound and refreshing sleep, I
tightened the strings of my pyjamas, and went on to the
verandah, where I heard the footsteps of my friend the
major as he moved about somewhat impatiently. Seeing
me come from Lizzie's room in sleeping costume, he put
up his hands in mock deprecation and said, *sotto voce*: 'Oh!

Oh–h–h! Captain Devereaux! Oh–h–h!' and he put on such a comical look I could not help smiling.

'Not so fast, major, please! Appearances may be against me, but I think I can give a satisfactory explanation. The lady who lives in that room was most dreadfully ill last night and I, out of pure charity, have been nursing her!'

'In your nightshirt and pyjamas, exactly! I expect she required a little cordial administered by an enema, only in front instead of behind, and required your services and elixir! Oh! Devereaux! it won't do, my boy, but Jack Stone is not the man to preach; still he would like his friends to be frank with him, so, Devereaux, you may as well tell the truth and confess that, full of my description of Mrs Searle, and the splendid night I had between her plump white thighs, you came home and spent, I hope, as good a night with the fair lady in there! Confess now!'

'Quite wrong, major, I can assure you! I plead guilty to having been much moved and stirred by your voluptuous narrative, and as human nature is frail, I dare say might have spent such a night as you believe, only that the lady was, as I said, fearfully ill, and all owing to that blackguardly brute Searle, too!'

'Ah!' said the major, 'that is just what I have come to enquire about. Look here, Devereaux, there is a devil of a row on. Searle was brought home last night between seven and eight o'clock, whilst we were at mess, with five or six ribs broken, his right leg broken above the ankle, his nose smashed flat, his front teeth driven down his throat, and battered, cut and bruised all over. In fact, the doctor hardly expects him to pull through, he is so fearfully weak, and so completely smashed to bits. The corporal of the picket reports that hearing a disturbance going on in the dak bungalow, he doubled his men down and caught sight of two men of the 130th running away, and hearing loud voices in the bungalow compound, he found a crowd of natives and two civilians, Europeans, standing round the brigade major, who was lying on the ground, all doubled up, and from what he could gather there was a woman at the bottom of it, but he could give no clear account of what had happened, or how it had happened, or anything. Well, the colonel is, of course, much put about. We none of us love Searle, who is a sulky brute, if a good officer, but a brigade major can't be half killed without a row being made about it, so he has sent me to try and find out all about it and as I guessed you would very likely have heard something, I came first to you.'

I then gave the gallant major a succinct account of the whole business, as told me by Lizzie. I had to undergo some unmerciful chaffing from Stone about her, and found it impossible to hide from him the truth about my relations with her. But he promised to be mum, and, as he said, there was no need for my name to be mentioned at all in the business, at all events at present, and perhaps not at all, as I was not at the bungalow when Searle was there but at the mess, luckily for me!

Armed with his news, and quite interested how it was that Lizzie should have had such violent ill usage, and should have passed through such a terrible scene, he returned to make his report to his colonel, and about four o'clock he sent me a note, or chit as it is called in India, to say that the colonel had agreed to hush the whole matter up, and simply report Major Searle on the sick list, and him – Jack Stone – acting station staff officer. He went on by saying that the sooner the parties were out of Nowshera the better, and he advised me to prepare Lizzie for a start; he would order a dak *gharry* for her as soon as one could be got, and a couple of *ekkas* for me, the *ekka* being the only wheeled vehicle which could run on such a road as there was from Publi to Shakkote.

Meanwhile, after Stone had gone, I returned to my post beside poor Lizzie. I watched her for a short time and presently she woke; seeing me still there, and neither shaven nor dressed, she rightly concluded that I had not been to bed all night.

'Oh! Charlie! how kind! how good of you! How can I ever repay you!'

'By getting well as quick as you can, my Lizzie. And then –'

'Ah! Won't I just! If I was kind before I will be doubly kind now! But I am all right! I had a bad go of fever last night, and my poor legs are stiff and sore, but I am well! If I only had some quinine, now would be the time to take it, just to keep off a second attack of fever.'

I had purchased a bottle of this invaluable powder at Bombay, and I ran and got it, and gave her the quantity she said would be right, in a glass of water.

'There,' she said, having made a wry face as the bitter dose ran down her throat, 'now something to eat, for I feel faint for want of food and I am hungry. You see I was bad, my Charlie, but I think it was more fright than anything else.'

I had, when I left her to go and get my peg that morning and before I went to sleep, called Soubratie and ordered him to prepare and have ready whenever it might be called for, some strong beef tea, and this I had brought, hot and refreshing, to Lizzie, who was really moved at this additional proof of my care and devotion to her.

'Oh! Charlie! If all men were only like you!' she exclaimed, and the soft tears of gratitude rolled down her lovely cheeks. I kissed them off and she put my hand on one of her swelling breasts, saying: 'There! my Charlie! I would let you have me this morning if I could, but I feel too weak for that. I dare say when I have had another good sleep I shall be better, and then darling, we will fuck, won't we!'

I laughed and said we would and put her hand, in my turn, on my bunch of charms, and showed her how greatly fatigue and watching had reduced the strength and vigour of what the most ardent battles between her shapely thighs had failed to subdue. Poor Lizzie! She looked so disappointed! But as her little hand toyed with my limp prick and played with my relaxed balls, fresh life came, and to her joy she succeeded in raising a perfect standard, to be planted as soon as possible in the keeping of her fort. But both of us were wearied and tired out, and I told her she should go to sleep, and that I would go to my own bed and sleep too, for I was dead tired, and with more sweet kisses and caresses she turned on her side and was soon asleep. I then left her and going to my own room threw myself on my much needed couch, in the cool breeze of the swinging punkah, and was soon sound asleep.

Whilst Lizzie and I are thus *hors de combat*, it will, I think, be a good time to tell my dear readers her early history, and I will endeavour to keep her words as nearly as possible. So, gentle readers, imagine that Lizzie and I are either seated on the verandah, after our dinner, or are in or rather on the bed together, whilst she tells her artless tale, certain portions of which she and I illustrated by very suggestive action when either her memory added fuel to the amorous passion which made her blood boil or my wanton fancy stirred all the man in me.

'Well, Charlie, I was born and bred in Canterbury. My earliest recollections are all associated with that dear old place, and for the first thirteen years of my life I never left it. My mother is the only parent I can remember. My mother was a dressmaker by trade and custom was good. She never seemed in want of money, whether she had work or not; on the other hand, though we had an honest plenty in our house, there were no luxuries, nothing for mere show, except perhaps in one of the rooms kept for ladies to try their dresses on, where she had some little knick-knacks for appearance's sake. As a child I used to think that a splendid room, and wonder if anyone else had as fine things as my mother had! So you must understand we had a sunny, warm house, good food, good plain clothes, good beds, in fact, everything which was required for real comfort, but nothing superfluous.

'My mother kept no servant, that is, no one actually lived in the house as such; an old charwoman came every morning and did what scrubbing and cleaning was required. My mother and I did light dusting, made our beds, etc., and cooked our simple meals. Until I was twelve years old I went to school, and as I was pretty quick, I learnt perhaps more there than girls usually do. And there, too, I formed acquaintances among the other girls, and as our conversations were not always about lessons and sums, apples or lollipops, I gathered some information about the relations of the sexes, about lovers and their ways, which I did not repeat to my mother. However, what I did learn in this way in no respect had any effect upon me or my morals. I knew I had a little cunnie, and that I should have babies one of these days, and that I should have regular monthly illnesses. I believed that I should marry, and when I did, I believed that my husband would put his 'thing' into my 'little thing' and that in time I should have a child, as I saw all married women do, but although girls used to talk about these matters, there was never any reference to the vast delight to be found in fucking. We were all too young to know more than something vague and undefined. But before I was thirteen my mother withdrew me from school, not only because I was growing very tall for my age, but because my bosom began to form, and two lovely little doves of breasts to push out on either side of my chest. With what pride and pleasure did I see them grow. Even my mother, when she bathed me regularly every Saturday in a tub before I went to bed, remarked on them, and said to me one day, "Lizzie, you will have a perfect bosom. I don't remember ever seeing prettier or better placed breasts, or any which looked to be so quick growing." And

I would notice her eye give a quick look down at my cunnie, and I guessed she was looking to see if my hair there was beginning to sprout. But my bubbies were a good bit grown before any came. However, the hair and my menses came almost together. First there was a profusion of little black-looking points all over what you call my motte, Charlie, and hairs grew from them very rapidly, so quickly indeed that by the day I was thirteen I had quite a nice bush which I could twine round my finger. My cunnie, too, underwent a marked change. It seemed to grow fatter and become more formed. I can hardly explain, but I am sure you must have noticed similar changes in your prick and balls when your bush began to grow. You may say, then, that as far as outward appearances were concerned, I was quite a woman at thirteen and I had a fair amount of flesh on my bones, a lovely bosom, a nice waist, fine swelling hips, good thighs and very pretty feet and ankles. I was too well formed altogether for short dresses, and my mother made me some long ones, in which I used to admire myself in the tall glass in the trying-on room. Still although I certainly did admire myself, it never entered my head to court the admiration of men. I had not, as yet, felt the least spark of desire, and if, as I dare say she did, my mother watched to see any signs of coquetry or flirting in me, she saw none, for there were none to be seen. However, I was much nearer the realisation of the hidden stores of pleasure I had within me, than either she or I was aware of.

'At the back of our house was a longish bit of garden, say something like fifty or sixty feet long, by thirty or forty feet wide. This garden was my mother's pride, for she raised early potatoes, and all kinds of vegetables in it for our use, besides plenty of pretty and sweet flowers, so that we always had nice vegetables for dinner, and nosegays for our table and mantelpiece. At the end of the garden was a lane on the side of which was a row of stables where the officers of the cavalry used to keep their private horses. I used to be very fond of leaning against our little wicket to see those beautiful horses, all bridled and saddled, being taken to their masters for exercise. Sometimes the officers themselves came to have a look at the stables, but they paid no attention to me, so I was quite accustomed to looking on without being spoken to. About August, however, when I was a little more than three months older than thirteen, some stables, which had been empty, were taken by an officer who had three beautiful horses. I was curious to see who this officer was, for he was new, and so one evening I was watching for him, hoping he would come, when I saw a tall, slight, but a fine and very handsome young officer in undress uniform, stable jacket, breeches, long boots and spurs, and his gold-laced cap well on one side and far back on his head, come walking at a smart pace down the lane, smacking his boot every now and then with his riding whip and looking right and left, as if he were taking everything in and that everything was new to him.

'He looked at me, too, and gave me a good stare, and then he saw the stable beside me, muttered something to himself, looked at me again, and with a little mock salute with his whip he turned into the stable. Then I knew that that was the new officer. There was something about him which took my fancy at once. He seemed so different from the others I had seen. They had always looked so heavy and black about the face, and altogether as if nothing was worth noticing on either side of them; whilst my new officer was so trim and jaunty, so pretty and nice looking, and he had actually smiled at me, and shown me that he had seen me. I felt quite a flutter when he made his little mock salute, and half drew back from the gate I was leaning on, but I did not go away. I wanted to see him again, so I stayed. Presently out he came, talking to the groom, then the groom went back into the stable. The young officer looked up the lane and down the lane whilst he pulled on his gloves, then, seeing me, he came playfully towards me, made me a little bow, smiled, and saying, "Good evening, Polly. A nice evening this," he turned and walked rapidly away. A new flutter again came into my bosom. I know I looked wistfully after him, and was delighted when, turning his head, he looked back at me from a little distance, and again waved his whip at me. Poor little fool that I was! I had fallen in love and I did not know it! But so it was!

'Well, evening after evening this young officer and I met this way. Nothing more than what I have described passed between us. If an evening came and he did not appear, I used to feel so grieved. I missed him dreadfully. I found out that his name was the Honourable Charles Vincent, and that he was a captain in the Hussars. I heard the grooms speak and that was how I knew; besides, all his horses had a big C. V. worked in white letters on their clothing.

'Did I tell you that at the end of our garden, in the corner and next the road, was a little old shed without any door? No? Well, there was and I had planted honeysuckle and clematis and a climbing rose against it and as a school-girl used to love to learn my lessons there, when it was fine, warm weather. The honeysuckle and rose and other climbing plants had grown very well, and the dirty old shed was transformed by them into quite an elegant bower.

'One evening my handsome officer did not come as usual. I was vexed and sorry, for I did love seeing him, and he always seemed to look for me. I heard his groom talking to the men in the next stable, saying he wondered the captain did not come, that the bay mare was sick and he had told his master of it. So I knew my hero was coming. I went into my bower and sat down and listened and peeped through the chink into the lane. Soon the grooms all went away but one, and that was Captain Vincent's. At last he seemed to be altogether out of patience, and I heard him swear and talk to himself, saying he would be damned if he would stay any longer; he would go and get his glass, and then he would come back. So he locked the stable and put the key into his pocket and went off.

'Well, I waited and waited! At last I heard the footstep I knew so well, and with a heart beating as if I had really expected and ardently wished for a lover, I went out and stood as usual at the gate. The sun was setting and all the lane was in shadow. Captain Vincent came walking quickly, saw me, smiled as usual, saying, "Good evening, Polly!", and tried the door of his stable. Finding it locked he kicked at it, so, as I knew there was no one in there, I called out,

"Sir, the groom waited for you, and after a while said that he must get his glass, but that he would come back."

' "Oh! did he, Polly? Thank you, my dear!" and then coming near me he went on, "How long ago was it that the groom went?"

' "Oh!" said I, guessing, for the time had seemed dreadfully long to me while waiting, "about three quarters of an hour, I should say, sir."

' "Three quarters of an hour," the captain exclaimed, looking at his watch, "well, then he should be along soon now, I should think. And how are you, Polly? I see you here every day. What a pretty hand! What a lovely girl you are, Polly! I declare I must marry you! Will you marry me, Polly, if I ask you?"

'Well, of course I was a little fool, but I could not help being pleased beyond measure at his admiration, though it was quite plain to me that his question about marriage was only a joke.

' "Oh! sir!" said I, "don't be making fun of me! You know I cannot marry you, sir!"

' "Well," said he, "at any rate you could give me a kiss, child, could you not, Polly?"

'I felt my face burning. It was just what I was longing for. Oh! I cannot tell you how I had longed to be taken notice of by him. I looked around carefully, and seeing no one in sight, I said: "If you are quick, sir, because someone might see and then there would be talk."

'The words were hardly out of my mouth before the gallant and eager captain had his lips to mine, and gave me such a kiss as I had never had before in my life, a kiss which seemed to go right through my body down to my very feet!

' "Polly!" said he, in a low voice, "could I come into your summerhouse after I have seen my horses and chat with you a little while?"

'I knew there might be a little chance of mother seeing him, so I said quickly and with a palpitating heart, "Yes sir! I'll go in now, and wait, and you can come in when you are ready, but please don't stand there talking to me – for fear – you know!"

' "I understand," said he, his eyes blazing as they looked into mine, and he turned away and walked a little down the lane, in the direction the groom had gone. I went into the "summerhouse", as he called it, and stood watching at the chink. Oh! how my heart beat! Would he kiss me again! How I wished the groom would come, for if I stayed out too long my mother might call for me to come in. At last the groom came and the captain and he had some little talk, but no quarrel. I think I prevented that, for I am sure Captain Vincent was angry when he found his man had not waited for him, but now he was certainly glad. He did not stay long in the stable. He and the groom came out together, and walked away down the lane. Oh! what a pang I felt! Was he not coming then? How cruel! how cruel! I could not help it, I sat down and began to cry and sob, and all of a sudden there was my lover, inside the little house. He had come back as quick as he could, and had only walked the groom out of the lane to get rid of him. I sprang up as he came in, and he saw I had been cry-ing, and he sat down and pulled me on his knee, and with one arm around my waist and his right hand on my bosom, he gave me, oh! hundreds of kisses! He seemed quite excited, and I was simply beside myself with happiness and joy.

' "Oh! Polly!" he said, "do you know I've been longing to kiss you ever since I first saw you; you are the very prettiest, loveliest girl I ever saw."

'I could only smile. It was rather dark now in the little house, but I could see him clearly enough. He kissed my face all over, and my neck too, and his hand closed over the bubbie it was nearest. I liked it too much to tell him to take it off, but I knew he ought not to have done that. All the time he was kissing me he called me his pet, his little dove, his lovely little darling, and so forth, and I stroked his hair and gave him sweet kisses too.

'At last he said, "How old are you, Polly?"

' "My name is not Polly, sir! It's Lizzie!"

' "Well! How old are you, Lizzie? Sixteen? Seventeen?"

' "Sixteen! Seventeen!" I replied. "No, sir! I am thirteen!"

' "Why Poll – that is, Lizzie, you must be more than thirteen! Who ever saw so fine a girl as you only thirteen?"

' "Well, sir," I said laughing, "I really am only thirteen!"

'He looked at me; he put his hand on my other bubbie and gave it a delightful squeeze, as if feeling it, and then he replaced his hand on its old place on the first bubbie.

' "Then," said he, "I expect this, these rather, are only padding!"

' "What?" said I.

' "Why! these bub – these – what do you call them? Your bosom, Poll – that is, Lizzie!"

' "Indeed, sir," said I indignantly, "there is no padding about me. I do not require padding! Not I, indeed!"

' "Oh!" said he, laughing, "but, Poll – that is, Lizzie! – I wish I could remember your name, my pet! No girl of thirteen has such fine, well-developed bubbies as these!" and he pressed them again and again. "They are much too fine for a girl of thirteen! You must be older than you think!"

' "No indeed, sir! I know I am only thirteen!"

' "Well! Then I don't believe these are real! They must be padding, Poll – that is, Lizzie!"

'I was vexed. Why should he be so persistent? Why should he believe that my breasts were not good flesh and blood but only padding? So I said, "If you think I am only made up, sir, please don't feel them any more!"

' "But," said he, "Polly – Lizzie, I don't say that they are not real, the fact is, I don't know what to think. There is a mistake somewhere, but don't be angry, my pet! Come – kiss!"

'Those delicious kisses! Those delightful pressures of his hands!

' "Lizzie, let me put my hand inside your dress!"

'And so saying he began to pull at the front of my bodice which was fastened by hooks and eyes. They bothered him and he grew so dreadfully impatient that I, who was quite as anxious that he should be certain that I was not padded as he was to feel my bubbies that he found so nice through my clothes, at last pushed his too eager hands away and undid the obstinate front which opposed him.

' "There!" said I laughing, "you can get your hand in now, but there is still a petticoat inside to unbutton."

'But the petticoat gave him little trouble, and as if he were snatching for a prize which would escape him if he was not very quick, he thrust his strong but gentle hand between my shift and stays, and closed it over the firm little globe he found there.

' "Oh!" he exclaimed, making a kind of sipping noise with his lips as if he were taking something hot to drink, "Oh! Lizzie! Polly! Lizzie! what a splendid little bubbie, and what a smooth little nipple! Let me feel the other one now!"

'And he reversed his hand and pushed it on to my right breast, which he went mad over like he had the other. The effect on him was wonderful. I cannot describe my sensations to you, Charlie, because you, being a man, cannot understand what a girl feels when her breasts are so nicely handled by a man as mine were then, but a kind of all-overish feeling came over me. I felt that I wanted to put my arms around my lover and clasp him to me! It felt that there was something more that I wanted from him; a something which I could only get by pressing my body to him as close, close, as possible, but in the position I was, with his arm raised up and his hand pushing at my bosom, I could not think of folding him in my embrace. All I could do, I did. I put my arm round his neck and pulled his face down to mine, and kissed his mouth with a passionate energy which put him into a still greater ferment. "Undo your collar, Lizzie! Oh! I must see and must kiss those splendid little gems of bubbies."

'Oh! how his voice thrilled through me! I felt as if I trembled all over and his voice trembled also. It was passion, desire, love which had seized both of us. One knew its meaning well! – the other – myself – was still in a state of ignorance very soon to be cleared away.

'I did not hesitate to obey him. I undid my collar, and he, pulling my dress wide open and off my shoulders and bosom, poured a torrent of kisses on my swelling breasts and I – oh! – I leant back, supported by his strong arm, and gave myself and my thrilling bubbies to him to do with as he liked. It was beyond description. How his mouth flew from mount to mount. How his lips climbed each hill, and his teeth seized each little ticklesome nipple in its turn, and his hot breath descended into the valley between my breasts, and swept down over my body until my waistband stopped its further progress. But oh, whilst his lips were so busy, his right hand, in my lap, pressing between my thighs, was producing ravages in another part of my body. I felt inclined at first to resist, not because I did not like it, but because I felt a feeling of shame rise in me, almost stronger than the intense sensation of pleasure his moving fingers gave me.

' "Ah!" said I.

' "What, darling!" How he said that one word, "darling", as if his soul breathed it from his heart of hearts.

' "Oh! don't put your hand there, sir!"

' "Oh! yes! yes! yes! oh! my delicious Polly Lizzie. What is your name? I must! Oh! Lizzie, I shall not be happy now until I have had you! You know what that means, don't you, darling? Say you will let me have you? Won't you?"

'Well, I didn't know exactly, but I began to guess that love, marriage and the "putting of his big thing into my little thing", as the girls said talking of husbands and wives, were all very intimately connected and the pleasure the proximity of his fingers caused in my melting little cunnie made me think that the "putting" must be something heavenly – and I was right!

'I don't know whether I said "yes" or "no" to his question but he acted as if I had said "yes" anyhow! For he suddenly put his hand under my dress, and before I could say "Scissors!" he had it as high as it could go between my thighs, at the same time pressing me to him and kissing my mouth. My drawers, that came up to the waist in front, offered a slight obstacle, but his eager and nimble fingers found their way in! Oh! the delicious sensation of those fingers as they caressed my cunnie! and the ravishing feel of the one which he pushed in deep between its glad lips. I no longer attempted to prevent his doing what he liked. It was much too delicious. I opened my thighs a little more, and whilst he sucked my mouth with long burning kisses that finger went in and out, every movement giving me more and more exquisite pleasure until at last a throb, a thrill! a kind of jump seemed to pass through cunt, motte, belly and all of me, and my lover exclaimed, "Ah! ah! oh! Lizzie, darling! I have made you spend!"

'Then for a moment he took his hand from between my thighs and I felt him doing something to himself. In a voice shaking with emotion and excitement he said, "Where is your hand, Lizzie? Give me your hand!"

'He took it and put it on what felt like a great big thick stick, thicker than a broom handle, and hot and awfully hard, except for the outside, which felt like velvet, and which was loose and moveable. It was so big that I could hardly get my fingers round it. The very feel of it, however, made my brain whirl round. "What is this?" I gasped.

' "It is me! Lizzie! it's me. It is my – my – my prick! Don't you know, darling, darling, Lizzie – that is what fits in here!" He had his finger moving in my cunnie again, setting me wilder still. "Let me put it in, darling Lizzie! It would kill me if you said no!"

' "Oh!" I gasped, for I could hardly speak, "you can't do it, sir! It is much, much too big!" and as I spoke I felt the curious, soft and elastic head which crowned his powerful weapon.

'For a reply my lover put me off his knee on to the seat, jumped up, undid his braces, pulled down his trousers, pulled up his shirt and I had an astonished glimpse of what looked like an enormous white bar, with a red tip, growing out of a perfect forest of black hair.

'Before I could either speak or resist, my impatient Charles, as he made me call him, pulled up my dress, petticoats and all, and pulled me on his knees, so that I had one leg on either side, then, whilst he drew the lower part of my body towards him, he made me lean back. I had to bend my knees to do so, and stand on the tips of my toes, whilst he was seated on the very edge of the seat. Oh! what a shock of delicious pleasure I received and how astonished I was when I felt that he had pulled me right on to what he called his prick, and that with a little kind of pop it had gone right into my cunt.

'Except for quickly, over and over again, "my darling! my darling!" he said nothing, and as for me I was too much in heaven to think of speaking. To support myself, however, I had to put my arms around his neck, and I hung back so as to give myself to him as nature taught me to do.

'Charles did not make any attempt to take my maidenhead then. He wished to allure me by giving me nothing but pleasure, and oh! he succeeded! He pushed his big prick in until my maidenhead prevented further ingress and then he pulled it back until it was almost out, and each time he did so I felt my cunt open and its lips slip over his vast head. Again I felt that exquisite spasm, and Charlie cried out that he had made me "spend" again, but soon he got powerfully agitated, his movements grew quicker and quicker, his thrusts more energetic, until all of a sudden he crushed me to his bosom, keeping his prick in my cunt, as deep as he could, and I felt that he was pouring something in hot, quick jets into me! It made me "spend" again, and then I felt something hot running all down my thighs, inside my drawers, and that all my bush and that part of me was inundated with something which had come from him. I felt almost inclined to faint with the inexpressible pleasure I felt, when all of a sudden I heard, "Lizzie! Liz–z–zie!"

' "Who is that calling you?" said Charles, quickly putting me off him and pushing my clothes down whilst at the same time he jumped up, tucked away that thrilling thing of his, which he had called his prick, and arranged his clothes as best he could.

' "Oh!" I cried, feeling dreadfully guilty and frightened, "It's mother!"

' "Well," said Charlie, giving me a hurried kiss, "don't be frightened; fasten your dress – call out that you are coming!"

' "I'm coming, mother!" I cried.

' "Come then, child!" was the answer as my mother went indoors.

'My lover peered through the tangled honeysuckle which hung over the hole I called my "window" and saw her go in. Then he took me in his arms and hugged and kissed me, and taking my left hand he put it on his huge, stiff prick, which was standing inside his drawers all up his belly, under the front buttons of his trousers, and put his right hand between my thighs, and pressing my throbbing cunnie, he kissed me again and again, and begged me to meet him the next evening at the same time, but to be careful not to let my mother notice anything strange in my behaviour and appearance. I promised, gave his delightful prick one more tender squeeze, and ran happy, but still nervous, to the house.

'After I had gone up to undress for the night I made a minute examination of my naked self. So I was a beautiful girl, was I? I had better bubbies than most other girls and my little cunt was a perfect gem! If only Charles could come to me in bed! How perfect it would be! He would do to me all night long what he had done to me in the summerhouse! But he was coming again next evening! I would try and get to sleep as fast as I could and dream of him.

'But sleep would not come. I was too excited. I found myself putting my finger into my cunnie as deep as I could, and pushing it in and out, as Charlie did his, but his finger was so much bigger than mine, it had given me more pleasure, and as for his prick, oh! was it possible so huge a thing could by any possible means all fit into my cunt? I could not believe it and yet he had told me it could. Why did it not all go in then this evening? Perhaps it was because he was so hurried! It might require more time. It was ever so long before I did sleep, and then, alas, I was disappointed! I did not dream of my lover or anything else.

'Well, the next day did seem long! But I took the greatest pains to seem quite myself, though I felt I had undergone a tremendous change. I did not feel like the little girl who only looked for her admired young officer to be happy at the bare sight of him. I now expected, wanted, desired much more! And I got it! For, although when he came and found me seated in the little house, he at first did nothing more than kiss me, and feel my bubbies and cunnie through my dress, because as he said my mother was so near it would be dangerous if I were in such a state of undress that I could not run out at once when she called, and meet and divert her from the summerhouse, yet, little by little, he grew more and more excited; he did not, indeed, open the bosom of my dress, but he put his hand under my petticoats, and caught hold of my cunnie and set it mad with his caressing fingers, and I, in my turn, felt his iron-stiff prick, until at last he said, "I think, Lizzie, we must have just one poke," and he asked me would I like to get his "man" out. Oh! would I not! I at once commenced unbuttoning his trousers and I got my hand in and pulled away his shirt and oh! the delight of getting that splendid big, hot thing in my grasp! and Charlie, delighted too, told me to be careful but to feel his balls, telling me how to get at them and I did! The darlings! How nice they felt! Like two fine eggs in a bag of velvet! and then he pulled down his drawers and again took me on his knees, and I had the same delight of feeling his prick just popping its big hard head in and out of my cunnie and of spending, and the quick thrusts and his almost groans of pleasure, and the hot quick jets of spend he poured into and all over my excited cunt! This time we were not interrupted by my mother, and whilst he held me, still with his prick in me, he asked me, "Lizzie, will you come and sleep with me? It would be so grand to be both in our skins in a nice warm bed! and then I could have you properly. I can't do it here. All of my prick ought to go inside you, but I cannot get half nor a quarter of it in."

' "Oh! I should like it, but how can I ever sleep with you, my dear Charlie?"

' "Oh! you must come away with me, of course! Tomorrow! Meet me here and I will take you to Dover. We will spend a week there! Well, will you come, Lizzie?"

'It seemed impossible. The idea of running away from home was so new to me and at first I could hardly bear the thought of it, but Charlie easily persuaded me; but what his persuasive voice said in words his still more persuasive prick said in eloquent silence to my eager little cunt! Oh! my cunt was on Charlie's side.

'I said I would do whatever he liked, and just what he told me. So, still keeping me in this delicious position, on him, he told me to get what few things I required, and to bring them during the next day, when I could best do so unobserved by my mother, and put them in the summer-house, and to be sure to have my best dress and best hat and to bring all I had best, because I should travel as his wife, and I must look very nice indeed as his wife should. Then he said he would not come for me before nine o'clock, and I must manage to be quite ready. He wanted to know whether I should find it difficult to get out of the house so late, as, if so, we must make another plan. But I knew I could do it easily, and I did so long, long for the time to come. I assured him I would be quite ready, and as nicely dressed as he could wish for – my mother being a dressmaker and I being a good "model", she always had me well dressed, saying I was her walking advertisement.

'So, after a night of almost complete sleeplessness and what seemed an eternity of waiting, the fated hour came. I carried out Charlie's instructions. I took, bit by bit, the things I required, and hid them in the summerhouse, and when Charlie came he found me dressed and ready. I had changed my clothes and left those I usually wore every day on the seat, where my mother found them a few hours later. I was in such a ferment of mind and body that I have a most indistinct recollection of how we left the little summerhouse. I left it a virgin, not quite a chaste one it is true, and when I came back I was one no more! Heigh oh!

'Well, I remember things more distinctly from the time Charlie put me into a first-class carriage, and followed me when he had seen my portmanteaus into the baggage van. There was only one other occupant, an old gentleman, who had evidently travelled from London. He took off his spectacles to look at me, and seemed so satisfied that I was worth looking at that he hardly once took his eyes off me until we reached Dover. It irritated me more than I can tell, being so stared at, but it amused Charlie immensely and he gave me sly little nudges from time to time and whispered in my ear that I had made a new conquest.

'However, I kept quiet, though I would have loved to say something pert to the old gentleman. The fact was that my nerves were strung to such a pitch of excitement that I often wonder my brain was not turned. We went to the Ship Hotel, which, of course you know, is close to the pier at Dover, and Charlie took a private sitting room and a double-bedded sleeping room, and put himself down in the visitors' book as Captain Charles Vincent and me as his wife, with the Honourable before our names.

'I felt very nervous indeed. Everyone seemed to look very hard at me. In my heart I said to myself, "They know." But at last we went upstairs to our sitting room. There Charlie took me in his arms and gave me, as he said, all the kisses and fond caresses and passionate embraces he would have given me in the train had not the horrid old gentleman been there. He took off my hat and cloak and went back a few steps to admire me, as he said, and when he had looked me over for a moment he ran up and again clasped me in his arms, saying, "Oh! Lizzie! I have never seen you so well dressed before. You look as perfect a lady as could be, and only thirteen, my darling. This swelling bosom, these lovely bubbies and those splendid hips don't belong to a child of thirteen, but to one of nineteen or twenty; and your beautiful, really beautiful face, though delightfully young looking, is by no means that of a child!" and he kissed and petted and fondled me, and put his naughty, delightful hand between my thighs, and I began to lose all the nervousness I had, and leaned against him with a heart brimful of love and affection; and desire made me throb all over.

'Charlie insisted on our having some supper, and we had a bottle of champagne. I did not feel in the least hungry and I told him so, but he said he was certain I had eaten nothing all day. He confessed it had been the same with him, and unless we ate and drank we should have no strength to support us during the night. "If you think you are going to get a wink of sleep before four o'clock, and perhaps at all tonight, you are vastly mistaken my Lizzie darling," and his eyes poured forth volumes of dazzling light into mine.

'Before we had our supper brought Charlie had given me two rings; I have them both now. Here they are where he first put them. A wedding ring and a keeper with pearls, diamonds and rubies. This was my mock marriage and real honeymoon. I was afterwards really married with the same ring and that marriage was followed by a mock honeymoon. It was well he did this, for we were waited on by a handsome and pert maid, and several times I noticed her eyes fixed on my hands as if to see whether I carried the outward and respectable mark of matrimony. I wonder how many similar rings Charlie had given to other girls? He was a great ravisher of maidens. A great hand at seduction in all its phases – a perfect hunter after women – and I was only one of a great number who had passed from virginity to womanhood through the gates of his arms, for, like my last Charlie, my first Charlie began cunt-hunting very young and being, like you, handsome, well furnished with the necessary weapons and rich, he scored far more successes than failures. He always said I was the gem of all he had had, and that he found me by accident. Certainly he had no trouble with me, for like a ripe peach, I fell the moment his fingers touched me.

'Well! after supper the maid wanted to know whether she should assist me to undress when I went to bed, and Charlie answered for me, saying that I was obliged but I should not require her services that night, and he added that we were not to be disturbed in the morning, as we had come a long journey, and would probably sleep it out. The girl, I could see, struggled to suppress a smile. I was too plainly very recently married, if married at all, and I think she saw well enough that our night would not be passed in sleep! I know I blushed! I could not help it. As she left the room I caught her running her eye over Charlie, and unless I am mistaken, she thought she would willingly change places with me, and take her chances of getting any sleep in Charlie's bed.

'And now I am very near the end of the life of my poor little maidenhead which died before I was fourteen. Few perish quite so early, but I am afraid, at least in that class of life in which I was born, few survive fifteen or sixteen. There are too many opportunities for such girls to get rid of these little pests! – I had just found that I had one only to see or rather to feel it disappear forever.

'Charlie, as soon as the maid was gone, begged me to go to bed! Now it is strange but true, and I think it is natural, that eager as I was to be had, delighted at the idea of being in bed with him, knowing the pleasure I had already had from his sweet prick, even so the "bed" rather alarmed me. I would willingly have put it off, but Charlie begged and besought me not to delay his happiness and mine too, and feeling a little like a real virgin bride, no doubt, I suffered him to lead me to our room. "Now darling! darling!" cried Charlie, "I must go and take half a dozen whiffs of a cigar and see who is in the house, so as to find out if there is anyone I had better keep you hidden from. I won't be long. You unfasten your clothes but don't take them off. I will be your maid tonight – and – your man too!"

'"Oh! Charlie! don't be long! Don't leave me all by myself!"

'"No one will come and eat you, my pet! Besides," said he smiling, "you may like to find yourself alone for a few minutes."

'I understood I did require it very much, and I said no more to detain him. I saw the necessary article, and in my mind I thanked my Charlie for his kind thought. It seemed so delicate of him, too, and I felt my heart bound towards him.

'Before I followed his instructions and loosened my clothes, I peeped out of the window. Then suddenly remembering what I had to do, I let the blind fall from my hands and set to work unhooking my dress, and unbuttoning and loosening the strings, and whilst I was doing this my Charlie came in, with quick, eager steps, catching me in his arms, putting one of his thighs between mine and exclaiming, "All right, my Lizzie! There's no one here that knows me or whom I know. Now! my pet! let me undress you! We will put our skins on and have a lovely – oh, a lovely night in that heavenly bed."

'Oh! he was quicker at taking off my clothes than my experience in the summerhouse at home would have made me believe possible. In a brace of shakes he had me naked, all but my chemise, stockings and boots. I thought he would leave me my chemise, but you will see! To take off my boots and stockings, he made me sit down on a chair, and his naughty hands kept on pushing up my chemise, to be out of his way, higher up my thighs than was at all required, and somehow my cunnie would come (as he said) in his way. It was lovely! He tickled me so, he made me laugh – he excited me so, that to pay him out I put my now naked foot between his thighs. At once he took it, and put the sole of it on to his beautiful stiff prick and a thrill like electricity shot all through me. My touch made him hurry up too. Both stockings were off now, and I was going to rise off the chair, but he pushed me back and said he must see my shoulders and bubbies bare! In a moment he had my chemise off my shoulders, so that it lay round my middle; all above it was perfectly naked. With a cry of delight he fell with his mouth on my bosom, kissing, biting, nibbling, whilst he pressed between my thighs and stroked them beneath my chemise with his hands. Then, suddenly rising, he caught me in his arms, pulled me straight up, and, my chemise falling to the floor, he lifted me up, kicked it away, and put me down in front of him as naked as I was born.

' "Oh! Charlie!" I exclaimed, "how could you! Let me have my chemise!" and I put my hands, naturally, over my motte and cunnie, for I felt shame glowing all over me, to be so dreadfully naked in the presence of a man!

' "Oh! my lovely, my beautiful Lizzie! I cannot let you cover up that lovely form and those exquisite charms! Look, girl! Here! Come! Look at yourself in this glass, and say whether you ever saw anything prettier in your life!' And he half pushed, half carried me, a most unwilling victim at that moment, before the long glass in the door of the wardrobe.

'Oh! I can hardly tell you what an impression my own reflection made on me! The moment before I felt as if I were crimson all over, from shame at being completely naked in the presence of Charlie, but now I was so struck with what I saw before me that all feelings of shame vanished and were replaced by a flood of pleasure. I had never seen myself, as a whole, naked in the glass, for I had no such mirror in my own little bedroom at home, and it never struck me to strip myself and see what I was like, when clothed in nothing but my naked charms, with the assistance of the cheval glass in mother's trying-on room. Besides all the surroundings were in favour of my seeing myself to the highest advantage now. The wallpaper of the room was dark, and reflected light badly, so that my figure in the mirror stood out against a dark background and showed up with dazzling whiteness. I could not but admire myself. Mother had often said I was a well-made girl, but she never expatiated much on my figure or my charms. Here I had them all before me, and I was amazed and delighted at the revelation! You, Charlie, have seen me naked and know what I am like now. Well! I was nearly as rounded in form and full in figure and shape of my limbs as now. What perhaps struck me first, most of all, was what a nice unblemished skin I had. Next, how lovely my shoulders and bosom were, how slender my waist, and how beautifully my hips gradually expanded until they were wider than my chest. My pretty little bubbies, well separated, each looking a little away from the other, each perfectly round where it sprang from my bosom, and both tapering in lovely curves until they came to two rosebud points, next caught my delighted eyes. I had never seen them look so lovely as they did now, as they gleamed and shone, apparently whiter than the body from which they grew, as the light flashed upon them. My belly was smooth, broad and dimpled in the centre with a sweet lit-tle navel, like a perfect plain of snow which appeared the more dazzling from the thick growth of hair which curled in dark rich brown locks on the triangle of my motte, gradually growing thinner and less close as it tapered to that point which, receding between my rounded thighs, divided at the spot where my pretty, demure little cunnie commenced to form. I could not see the whole of my cun-nie when I stood upright, for it turned in between my thighs too quickly, so to say, as if it felt that it should hide itself until love demanded it to be displayed by the action of opening my legs. My thighs, knees, calves, ankles and feet next came in for their share of inspection, and by the time I had looked myself over from head to toe, I came to the conclusion that Charlie was right, and that a lover should be permitted to gaze with enraptured eyes on charms of no common class of beauty. Don't think me vain, but I have been too often told that I am beautiful to believe that every man who has seen me naked is and has been a liar.

'Well, whilst I was thus intoxicating myself with my own reflection Charlie was not idle. He had completely stripped himself, and came eagerly up, as naked as myself. He put his arm round my neck, and stood beside me, adding his masculine beauty to the picture I saw in the glass before me.

' "Now, Lizzie! is not that a perfect picture? Don't we make a real handsome couple?"

'I could only respond by putting my arm around his waist and pressing him to my side. His warm body sent a thrill through me, as I felt it in this delicious close contact, and I saw a little ruby and shining point suddenly protrude between the upper lips of my excitable little cunt. Oh! Charlie looked splendid! I took my eyes off myself to gaze at him in wonder and admiration. He looked so powerful, yet so lithe. His shoulders were as broad as mine were narrow, and his hips as narrow as mine were broad. His deep and manly chest contrasted with my more graceful but completely feminine bosom. His arms, long and muscular, seemed perfect models in marble, and every movement on his part showed the firm muscles move under the skin beneath which there was little of that soft fat or flesh which made my limbs and body so pliant and smooth. But naturally, it was his long, stiff, straight, grand-looking prick and the big rough bunch which formed his handsome balls underneath, in their velvety wrinkled bag, which chiefly attracted my burning eyes, for there it was, that truly stalwart prick, pointing up at my face! It seemed a formidable weapon indeed, so strong, so conquering, so irresistible. Its head, of a more or less rosy colour with a suspicion of violet at the edges, was half uncovered, and its almost impudent look amused me as it seemed to scan me with its slit-like little eye on its top. I could see that this splendid weapon was broader and thicker at its base, where it sprang from the forest of hair which clothed my lover's motte, and slightly tapered until it reached its head, where it suddenly widened again only to taper quickly off to a rounded blunt point, where its "eye" was. Charlie took my hands, put one under his balls and the other on his prick and made me feel and press them for a moment. I almost fainted with the thrilling emotion this feeling of him sent through me, and clasping me to him, he pressed himself against me so that his mighty spear-like weapon was closed in between his belly and mine. I could feel its point high above my navel, and I remember wondering whether, supposing he could get it in, I should feel it up inside me as far as that! At the same time I felt certain that to get so huge a volume as that into my tight little cunt would be impossible. I was convinced of that.

'After a few more thrilling caresses on the part of each of us Charlie said, "Now, Lizzie!" and lifting me up in his great strong arms, he carried me like a baby to the other

side of the bed where he laid me down on my back, pulling
the sheets down. Oh! I was inclined to have him! My whole
body panted for him! My bubbies seemed to be swelling
as if they would burst and the little red nipples on them
were as hard as peas and tickling me! As for my cunt, it was
raging! Such a throbbing as went on in it I had never felt
before, not even when he had half fucked me at
Canterbury. I expected him between my thighs, which I
opened for him, but instead of taking his place there at
once, my irritating lover commenced kissing me on the
mouth, cheeks, eyes, ears, throat and all of that part, whilst
his hand wandered over my bosom from bubbie to bubbie,
which he tenderly felt and pressed. He did not seem to be
in half the hurry I was. If his intentions were to drive me
half frantic with desire, to raise up all that was lascivious in
my senses, he certainly succeeded to perfection! But really
he was right. I always think a good preliminary engagement of hands and lips makes a fuck much more delicious
than when one comes to close quarters without any at all.
Charlie's lips descended from my lips to my bosom. He laid
his head between my breasts and turning it from side to
side kissed each bubbie as his lips encountered its warm,
rounded side, and whilst so doing his naughty hand crept,
crept, crept over my belly, down my groin, down my
thighs, up again, all round my motte, then skimmed my
bush with its fingertips, then just touched, but no more,
the line of my cunnie, until I could hardly endure the
almost agonising pleasure he caused me! Then suddenly
he took a firm bite of one breast, and in went his strong
finger, right up to the knuckle, with a bang against my

cunt, and this he repeated, biting, but not hurting, my other bubbie; then, with repeated kisses, his mouth roved over my belly, down one groin, down that thigh, up the other, just like his hand had done, until suddenly he brought it up right to my quivering cunnie, which he almost burnt with his kisses! I could feel his tongue darting at my agitated, excited clitoris, and at last, unable to bear it any longer, I almost screamed to him to leave off that, and give me what I craved for. He turned a dreamy look at me, then suddenly seemed to wake up, as it were.

' "Oh! I nearly forgot!" said he as he ran to the mantel-piece and brought from it what looked like a pot of pomatum. "This is cold cream, my Lizzie! As you have never had all me inside you yet, and your delicious little cunt is as tight as can be, some of this will help us both! Hold the pot, darling, and let me anoint your cunnie Queen of my Prick!"

'He took fingerful after fingerful of the cream, and put so much of its cool substance inside my cunt I thought he meant me to have it all. It was so sweet and cool and pleasant, I liked it for its own sake as much as for the sake of feeling his finger push it as far in as it could.

' "Now," said he, "anoint my prick King of your Sweet Cunt, my Lizzie!' and he turned that awful mad-looking weapon towards me. I took it, close to the root, with my left hand, and with my right I anointed its head; as I stroked the cream down, its hood slipped right off, and gathered behind its spreading shoulders, and here Charlie made me put a great lot of the cream. Then with both hands I, by his directions, put all that remained in the pot on the shaft of his prick, until it shone as though dipped in oil! Oh! the feeling of that prick! I am sure you remember the excitement you must have felt the first time you had a good, free and complete "feel" of a girl, Charlie? Well! think of what I experienced, for that grand prick, those glorious balls, were all mine, to press and caress in perfect freedom for the first time.

'Charlie made me wipe my hands on his curly hair and then, with a triumphant, "Now Lizzie, open your thighs! Now, for heaven and bliss and all that is delicious!" he pushed me on to my back, and was between my willingly opened arms and thighs before I could wink! He made me introduce himself into my cunnie, then he put one hand under my head and the other under my hips and with a slight pressure forced, or, rather, easily slid, his weapon in as far as it had ever gone before. At first, as if careful not to raise any doubts in my mind, he contented himself with toying in and out, as he had done at Canterbury, giving me delicious pleasure, but suddenly he gave a thrust which stopped my breath, and he kept up such a fearful pressure that it began to hurt me not a little but a good deal, I can tell you.

' "Oh! Charlie!" I cried out, "Don't, darling, you are hurting me dreadfully."

'He said nothing, but gave me a kiss; then laid his cheek to mine, and gathered me more firmly than ever in his arms, and again seemed to burst violently into my insides!

'I almost screamed but Charlie would not listen to my entreaties! Again and again did he batter, and at last, with a sickening sensation of rending and tearing, I felt that the obstacle, whatever it was, had gone before his dreadful prick, and that each stroke, each thrust, was carrying it deeper and deeper into my insides! I really feared he had burst my poor little cunnie, and that I should die, in consequence; but, before I could express myself in words, I felt that every atom of that awful prick was buried in me, for I could feel Charlie's balls against me distinctly, and as for our bellies, they were completely pressed together, as well as our mottes! Then Charlie relaxed that tremendous grip on me, and raising his face looked eagerly into mine, and smiled and kissed me and said, "Ah! Lizzie, darling! I hope I did not hurt you very much. You had such a dreadfully tough little maidenhead, and your little cunt is a tight one – so much the better! for you will have the more pleasure! Do I hurt you now, darling?" and he kissed me tenderly.

' "Not now! but oh, Charlie! you don't know how much you did hurt me! I hope you have not done me any harm!"

' "Not a bit," said he laughing. "I am glad it does not hurt you! But now for pleasure, my Lizzie! You lie quite still and let me fuck you quietly and you will see whether you won't forget any pain I gave you."

'Then commenced those splendid, exciting, thrilling, long strokes. Even that very first time I felt great pleasure from them, and afterwards, when all soreness had completely disappeared, every time was like plunging into a new world! My cunt was like a violin, and Charlie's prick like the bow, and every stroke raised the most ravishing melody on the senses that could be experienced or imagined! Oh! I am sure he was right when he said that never was there a girl so plainly brought into the world for fucking and fucking only, as myself! I adore it! I can't live without it! And at times I cannot imagine how any man or woman can pass a day without having it at least once or twice.

'That was how I lost my maidenhead before I knew I had one! Ah! That week at Dover will always be remembered by me as the most exquisite in my life. Charlie was never done! He was so kind too! He took me for long drives, showed me the castle, took me out boating; we laid perfect fairy plans for our future. I was to be his own pet love! I was to live in a sweet little house in London, to have my own carriage and servants and all that I could want, and I should be his darling mistress, almost his wife. Not once did I remember my poor mother, or my duty to her as a child. I declare it seems most terribly selfish – but oh! I was ravished with my lover, and the whole world seemed centred in him! And yet when the test of that cunt-burning love came to be applied, you will see how it stood.

'Yes! Yes! It was an exquisite dream! Such a dream as I have often wished to have again but never in my happiest moments since have been able to approach!

'Well, it was all settled. Charlie's leave would be up now that our six days' honeymoon was spent. We were to have one more blissful night in one another's arms, and oh! how I had learned to love being well fucked! How I had come to appreciate its ravishing joys, its indescribable delights!

'We were, I say, to have one more night at Dover, and then Charlie was to take me to London, leave me in a hotel for a day, get more leave, and come and hunt up a nice little house for me, etc., etc., as he had planned, and I was to be his kept mistress. The idea of returning to Canterbury to my mother had completely faded from my mind. From her arms I had been snatched away to quite another and perfectly different life, and like the brilliant fly, I could no longer think of resuming my life as a grub. The thing was impossible, so impossible that I never gave it a single thought.

'But – ah! there are a good many "buts" in the world, which like stones in the road are apt to upset the steadiest and most courageous – but, the last evening of our stay in the Ship Hotel a note was brought to me, just as I was going to take off my things. Charlie and I had been for a long drive over to the camp at Shorncliffe. A glance at the writing showed me it was from my mother! I dropped on to a chair and Charlie, seeing me look as if I should faint, ran up in alarm.

' "What is it, my darling? Who is this from?"

' "Oh! Charlie," I ejaculated, "it is from my mother!"

' "The devil! What does she want? What business is it of hers, I should like to know, to come interfering?" cried poor Charlie, who forgot that she had every possible business to do so.

' "What does she say?" he went on impatiently, for I had not the courage to open the note but held it in my shaking hand. "Here, girl! give it to me! Let me see what the old – h'm – old lady says. Lizzie, your mother says she is on the pier and asks you to come out for a moment to see her, or she will come in and see you here! You had better go, darling! It would not do to have her kick up a row in here. Will you go with her if she asks you, Lizzie? Tell me! God damn and blast it all! What an unfortunate thing! Lizzie, Lizzie! You must not leave me! I cannot live without you! I must have you! Do you hear?"

'I was drowned in tears and my bosom was torn with sobs. I loved Charlie! Oh! I did! What girl would not love a lover who had adored, worshipped and fucked her as Charlie had me? But on the other hand, I loved my mother too. How dearly I did not know until now. The two affections, the old and the new, wrestled within me. I was at the parting of the ways, and if it had been possible I would have liked to have walked on both of the roads.

' "Oh! Charlie!" I cried, as I threw myself in his arms, "I cannot say! I cannot say! Perhaps mother will tell me that after what I have done she won't have me home again!"

' "And then!" cried poor Charlie eagerly.

' "And then, of course, I would come with you, Charlie."

' "That means if your mother – confound her! – says come home, Lizzie, you will leave me?"

' "Can't I go home with her if she will have me and come to you another time, Charlie dearest?" said I.

' "Well," he cried, "now let us get rid of this uncertainty, Lizzie! Though it rests with you, I fancy! If you had any pluck at all you would send her word that you could not see her!"

' "Then she would come in here, Charlie. You don't know my mother! She is very kind, but if she says she will do a thing, she does it!"

' "By Jove! Yes! I forgot! She would come in here and then there would be a devil of a row! Run! Lizzie! run, and keep her out like a good girl!"

'I dried my eyes, went quickly downstairs, out of the hotel and on to the pier, along which I walked, straining my eyes in the fast gathering darkness to see where my mother could be. At last I saw a figure standing just in front of the recess, and I recognised my mother and flew to her. She received me with open arms, folding me tightly to her bosom, and there we both stood clasped together, and both sobbing as if our hearts would break.

'Charlie, I can't go into the details of that sad meeting. You must spare me and let me only say that my mother did not say one word of upbraiding or scolding; she told me that she had nearly died of fear and sorrow when she found me gone and keeping her wits about her she spread no report, asked nobody about me, but putting two and two together came to the conclusion that if I had gone with anybody it would probably have been an officer of the Hussars. Then she found out that Captain Vincent had his stables behind our house and that he had gone on leave from the very day I had disappeared and accidentally she saw his name and that of his wife in the Dover papers, as being at the Ship. She had found out that he was not married, had come straight to Dover, on a chance had sent the note, hoping that the Honourable Mrs Vincent might be myself, as indeed it was! She said that whatever mischief had been done had been done, and that the only thing to do was not to make it worse by raising a scandal. She told me to go back to Charlie, to stay with him for the night, to manage to return home after dark to Canterbury, where she would meet me and have a cab ready outside the station. Our reserved and quiet way of living had prevented our neighbours noticing my absence, and unless some future event happened nobody need know anything about it.

'All my dreams of a little house in London came to an end. I loved my Charlie, it is true, but it was cunt love more than that of the heart, and my mother easily prevailed on me to give him up.

'Charlie, poor fellow, was overjoyed when he saw me return. He fancied I was coming back for good, and his disappointment was intense and bitter when he knew that I had firmly resolved to return to my own home, and not to go to London with him! but presently when the first bitter draught was swallowed, he said that of all wonderfully wise women he had ever heard of, my mother beat all in getting me back to him for the night.

'Ah! well! I had a quiet and not altogether unhappy life with my mother until I was fifteen. The Hussars had left Canterbury and though I naturally often thought of Charlie, I was rather indignant that he never apparently once tried to see me again. He told me afterwards that he had done all he could think of to get letters to me. Perhaps my mother intercepted them. I never got any of them. I hate the next episode in my life. One day I met a sergeant, dressed in the old and beloved Hussar uniform. I got talking to him, and from talking to walking, and from walking to lovemaking, and from lovemaking to fucking! I could not help it! I wanted a man most dreadfully, and all my cunt's old fire came back at the sight of the Hussar uniform. Of course, I acted deceitfully, and kept all from my mother, who had hoped by trusting me fully to prevent all such action on my part. My new lover was only on furlough. He had not been gone long before I found I was, this time, let in for a baby. My distraction nearly killed me, and all the more because I feared to tell my mother. But time told her. My figure lost its elegant shape and I had to confess – the awful, awful pain of that confession. But true to herself, my mother lost none of her wits. She found out my second seducer, went and saw him, found him to be the master tailor of the regiment, told him what an excellent dressmaker I was, proposed marriage, held out the promise of a fair dowry, her savings for many years – poor mother! – and I was married to Sergeant Thomas Wilson in time to save the legitimacy of my baby. But we did not live happily.

'One day when my husband was out, Charlie came to see me. Oh! I was glad to see him. We had a long explanation and it all ended in his having me on my husband's bed! I was fucked again – joyful thought – by the darling man who had taught me what a sweet thing it was! But hardly had Charlie gone than in came Tom. Going from room to room he saw his own bed tumbled, and then he grinned! He accused me of having had Charlie whom he had met, and of whom he had heard, goodness knows how, and there and then he made me an offer which I accepted. It was that to bring him custom, I should let myself be – admired. He would hear nothing, see nothing, know nothing! I was too unhappy with him not to jump at an offer which would give me back Charlie! All that had to be done was that a suit of clothes should be ordered from time to time, and Charlie ordered at least a dozen. More and more officers followed his example and soon my husband had them all, every one, from colonel to junior lieutenant, on his books, and I had them all as my lovers. I had several children. I only know the father of one for certain, and that was my husband. I think the second was Charlie's, but I am not sure. None lived. That is my story, a sad mixture of happiness and misery, folly on my side and wisdom on my mother's.'

I could not but wonder how it could be that such a sweet countenance could be the seat of a temple in which Venus reigned, not only to the exclusion of all other gods and goddesses, but with more than ordinary power. I must leave my gentle readers to form their own opinions of this lovely wanton, but that there was much good in her I became convinced the more I knew her. At all events it is not for me to throw the stone of condemnation at her. To enjoy a woman and then run her down is not my style. Lizzie must have had a yearning for a purer and a better life, for she was constantly urging me to send for my beloved Louie, warning me that if I did not I should most certainly constantly wander from the path of virtue, and also saying that it was not fair to any woman, especially one who loved her husband, in every sense of that expansive word, to leave her to pine alone. Well, it was my hope that either I should rejoin my Louie in England, or that she should come out to me in India, but the fates were against us.

During the remainder of my stay in Nowshera, I enjoyed my tender Lizzie in all tranquillity and my tender girl readers may be sure that every opportunity was taken, and none lost, of procuring both for her and for myself the most complete pleasure which our active senses could expect. Her poor thighs were still marked by the violence of the brute Searle when I last saw them, but the sweet, sweet cunt between them lost neither beauty nor attraction on that account. To this day I look back upon that week of ardent fucking with regretful delight. I have never yet succeeded in regretting having sinned against heaven and my dearest wife in having broken the seventh commandment with Lizzie. 'Stolen waters are sweet,' saith Solomon, and I, Charles Devereaux, say to that, 'Amen, Amen, verily that is true.'

Our new station staff officer, my good friend Major Stone, got a dak *gharry* for Lizzie and two *ekkas* for me, and we started off on our respective routes on the same day; Lizzie started in the morning and I in the evening, she making for India proper, and I for Shakkote, at the foot of the hills on which Cherat is situated. It was not without a pang on each side that we parted, and we exchanged locks of hair, pulled from our respective bushes. I have hers still and never look at its now somewhat faded curl but that the delicious days and nights I spent in her fair arms at Nowshera come back to my memory with a force that, if she only knew it, adds to the happiness I feel every time I recall the joys I experienced so keenly between her delightful and voluptuous thighs; and my Louie does not lose, I can assure you, by my having been unfaithful with Lizzie!

I took Soubratie with me, leaving 'Mrs Soubratie' to look after my luggage for which her husband was to return when he had seen me safe as far as Shakkote. I heard that she proved the delight of the gallant officers at Nowshera during her husband's absence, and that she brought a big bag full of rupees with her to Cherat, where her charms enabled her to add a good many more to the stock earned by her active and diligent cunt.

Of my journey, of my arrival at Cherat and of the two lovely maidens I found there, who as yet had not known a man, but to whom it was my most happy privilege to communicate the thrilling sensations of soft desire and voluptuous sentiment, I must tell my readers in the chapters which follow.

2

A Position of Trust

I never in my life journeyed in such an uncomfortable conveyance as an *ekka*, and I only hope that none of my fair readers may be subjected to such aches and pains as I had to suffer. But what is an *ekka*? some of my fair readers may ask. I will tell you. It is a two-wheeled conveyance much used in northern India. It has no springs. It has a platform of but three square feet on which you sit as best you can. It is drawn by a small pony. The shafts generally rise so the platform on which you sit generally slopes back. The driver sits on the shafts, and if, as is very likely, he is highly odoriferous, you get the benefit of his evil smell. But that is not all about the *ekka*. It has its good points. It can go almost anywhere. It is light and strong. Many and many a time I have seen one carrying half a dozen natives, who can squat with ease where one European cannot find half room enough for himself. It is a cheap conveyance, and it is generally a most gorgeous one to behold, for from every one of its four corners there rises a pillar of white carved with all the cunning of the Indian carpenter's art. Over this is a dome, generally surmounted by some brass ornament, and the entire *ekka* is painted in the most brilliant colours and ornamented with quaint patterns cut out of brass and hung with little tinkling bells and, in fact, presents the sort of barbaric appearance which pleases the native eye and fancy so much.

Amongst the European soldiers and their wives the *ekka* is known as a Jingling Johnnie, a name which perfectly describes the noise it makes when in motion, for it does nothing but jingle, thus adding to the civilised ear as much torment as its uncomfortable shape and motion do to other parts of his anatomy. Altogether it is not the kind of carriage which I can recommend as forming one of the comforts of Indian travel.

Added to the great discomfort the *ekka* afforded were several others. First the road had been cut to pieces by the thousands of men and carts of all descriptions, including artillery, light and heavy, which for the last two or three years had been constantly pouring along it, over all the road, to and from Afghanistan. It was consequently inches deep in dust as fine as flour. This dust rose during the day and did not settle for hours; it formed a perfect fog which choked the driver, dried up his mouth and filled his eyes and ears, besides covering me from head to foot. Again, how many camels died on the march? I believe they numbered tens, even twenties of thousands. Judging from the stench which hardly without break filled the air between the outskirts of Nowshera and Publi, there must have been a fair proportion of those deceased camels all along the road. As fast as possible the carcasses were either burnt or buried, but enough were left above ground to sicken even the strongest stomach.

I fell fast asleep and did not wake until the *ekka* stopped and I found myself in a little grove of trees close to which was the last military outpost with its guard of native infantry; here I was told I had to dismount as I was at Shakkote.

Towering high above me and looking perfectly unclimbable was a lofty range of mountains whose torn sides testified to the violence with which the rain dashed upon them in its hurry to reach the lower level. Cherat, I was told, was on the very summit, and was some four and a half thousand feet above where I stood; that is higher than Snowdon, the highest mountain I had yet ascended, and these mountains seemed twice as steep. A couple of ponies stood at the door of the shanty, one had a saddle on, the other not. I asked whose ponies these were, and hearing that they had been sent down to meet an officer expected with baggage, I asked no more questions, but at once claimed my right to them, which fortunately was not contested. Mounted on my pony and directing Soubratie to be quick to strap my portmanteau as best he could on the other animal, I told the *syce* or groom who was in charge of my beast to proceed, and show me the way, which the half-naked savage did.

At last, after a perilous ascent, my pony staggering with immense fatigue and the fearful strain the terrible climb had cost him, we reached the top. The pony's trot soon died down into a quiet walk along a very good, well-made path, some five or six feet broad, which followed the edge of the valley, across which I saw facing me a pretty cottage, and good heavens! quite a sweet-looking English lassie, walking with a child, evidently taking her early-morning walk. I therefore encouraged my pony to put on his best paces, and almost as soon as I had caught sight of her, the unknown girl seemed to see me too, for she stopped in her walk and stood looking towards me. I soon got within twenty or thirty yards of her, for the path rounded the end of the valley, at the head of which was the cottage.

The first view I had of her close up, showed me that she was a really pretty girl – not exactly beautiful in the sense that Lizzie Wilson was, but more like my own beloved Louie, sweet, feminine, pretty in every sense. Her cheeks, rounded with health, were coloured like the rose, showing that the climate of Cherat certainly agreed with her. Her skin was perfectly clear; and her lips, those dear lips which were in days yet to come to be so often joined to mine in passionate ecstasy, were of the brightest red, that red that only belongs on the lips of the young, and which my experience has shown me is a sign of a nature tender, passionate and voluptuous. Her throat was beautifully formed, round and full, and her figure was that of a maiden passing from the stage of girlhood to that of womanhood. I could see that although her bosom was not yet fully developed, it was already adorned with two charming little mounds; it was certainly not a pair of empty stays which formed the slight hemispheres on either side, but good, sound, solid flesh. Her waist, though not so tapering as Lizzie's, was sweetly small, and her hips had that generous breadth which announces a fine, beautifully shaped belly, fit couch for any man to repose upon! Repose! Can a man be said to repose when he lies between the thighs of his darling, and fucks her with movements so full of sweetness, of joy, of ardent rapture for both him and her? I know not! – but no matter – my maiden showed two well-shaped little feet and ankles beneath her petticoat, as she stood watching my approach, and a smile began making her eyes alive with a kind expression of welcome, and two bewitching dimples began to form which gave her lovely face the appearance of great sweetness, just such a look as might well take any man by storm who saw it for the first time.

I took off my hat and bowed, and asked this charming girl, 'Can you kindly tell me where I should go to find Colonel Selwyn?'

'Papa is at the orderly room, but he will be home soon. This is our house. I suppose you are Captain Devereaux?'

'Yes! I have only just arrived. I have been travelling all night and I am afraid I am more than dirty, and you must kindly excuse me for venturing to come near you in such a condition. You see I did not know which way to go, but left it to my pony and he brought me to you.'

'Well! Won't you let the *syce* take him, and come in and meet my mother and have a cup of tea? Papa won't be long, I am sure.'

'I am very much obliged to you Miss Selwyn, but I really feel much too grimy and dirty to present myself for the first time to Mrs Selwyn! It would make a bad impression I am sure and I should be sorry for that, for it might perhaps have the effect of her taking a dislike to a man who, since he has seen Miss Selwyn, would wish to be on good terms with her father and mother!'

'Don't talk rubbish!' said this downright little maiden, blushing and looking as pleased as punch. 'My mother will, I am sure, make every allowance, and I am sure you must want a cup of tea or a peg, which perhaps you would prefer. Do come in!'

At this moment a lady, somewhat taller than Miss Selwyn, accompanied by another girl, much the same height as her sister, came to the door of the bungalow, evidently attracted by the voices they heard.

'Oh! mama!' cried my friendly maiden, 'here is Captain Devereaux, just arrived. I have asked him to come in and see you, and have a cup of tea or a peg, but he says he wants to see papa first, and is much too – too – well! dirty! Do make him come in!'

'Hush! Fanny! you let your tongue run away with you too fast! I am glad to see you, Captain Devereaux. I suppose you have had a terrible time at Nowshera during the last week. We heard you were there and could not move on account of the troops returning from the war wanting all the *ekkas* and carts.'

I made my excuse, saying that I considered it my first duty to report myself to the colonel, and that then, after I had made my toilet, I would do myself the honour of calling.

Fanny looked at me with reproachful eyes, as much as to say, 'You might as well have done what I wanted.' The other girl looked at me out of her great lustrous eyes, her mouth smiling slightly, while Mrs Selwyn gave me

directions how to find my way to the orderly room, viz.,
by going back a part of the way I had come until I found a
road leading to the barracks in which all the regimental
offices were situated, about a mile from where we stood.
Making my bow, and thanking Mrs Selwyn, giving the now
pouting Fanny a bright look, as full of thanks as my dust-
filled eyes would permit me, and taking another long look
at the daughter whose name I had not yet learnt, I handed
over my pony to the *syce* and walked along in the direction
I had been told to go.

Before turning the corner I looked back. Fanny was
alone, still standing in front of the house, looking after me.
Her attitude was one of wistfulness. Somehow I felt she
had been snubbed, and I was sorry for her, but glad to find
my lines would be cast amongst people who, at first sight,
seemed to be so lady-like and nice as Mrs Selwyn and her
two daughters. These thoughts rather interfered with my
admiration of the wild and savage beauty of the scenery I
was passing through. Presently, turning a jutting shoulder
of the cliff wall, I saw, perched on a slight eminence above
me, a long, low wooden structure of large proportions,
having an extensive red-tiled roof. Seeing a group of
soldiers in their khaki, or mud-coloured, uniforms standing at the door I guessed this was the building housing the
regimental offices, and passing through the group, I
entered what seemed to be one vast hall with wooden
pillars supporting its roof. The first person I saw proved to
be the paymaster; hearing my name, he welcomed me
warmly enough and showed me whereabouts I should find
Colonel Selwyn, whose office was at the far end of the

building. Thither I proceeded. The colonel was seated at his table dispensing justice. Around him stood officers in uniform, some red, some khaki, some blue, who had to bring up men. I scanned their faces. I knew none of them, and not being in uniform myself, and moreover covered with dust and dirt, I dare say I did not present a very favourable appearance. I waited until the last unhappy 'Tommy' was weighed off and then, advancing to the table, reported myself as Captain Devereaux, just arrived to join the battalion. Colonel Selwyn looked at me with interest for a moment, whilst the hitherto glum and stern-looking faces of the surrounding officers broke into smiles of welcome.

'Ah!' said the colonel, rising, 'glad to see you, Devereaux! I heard you were stuck at Nowshera. You came at an unlucky time when all the conveyances were engaged. I am afraid you had a wretched time of it down there!'

He shook me warmly by the hand, and introduced me to various officers, who did the same, and then, recommending me to go and get a peg before anything else, he asked the others to show me the way to the mess, saying he must himself hurry off home.

I accompanied my new brothers-in-arms, who led the way chatting and laughing and making many enquiries of me, until we reached the miserable shanty, called by courtesy 'the mess'.

I will not go in for a description of each and every officer. Suffice it to say that they were a very fair sample of the officers who form a proportion of every regiment in Her Majesty's Service. The seniors as usual proved to be selfish and greedy. The captains verged on the same state, but the subalterns were, as usual, gay devil-may-care, generous and ever ready to share their pittance with a brother in distress.

First thing I learnt was that, as water was very scarce, it was doubtful if I should get a wash that day; everyone was on an allowance, and my coming was not provided for. The next, that unless I had a *chokidar* [native watchman] neither my property nor my throat would be safe, since it was impossible to keep robbers out of the camp at night.

All this was a strange and by no means welcome contrast to the life I had been so lately leading at Nowshera, where I had the soft and delicious cunt of a perfect Venus to revel in. But as almost always is the case, my lines eventually turned out to be not cast in altogether so bad a mould as first appearances led me to expect.

In a few days I had found a nice little mud bungalow which would hold me. It is true it swarmed with the most formidable-looking and really dangerous centipedes, but I never got bitten by any, so that they only helped to keep me in a pleasant state of excitement, and I killed many of them. What made up for a great deal of the discomfort at Cherat was the delicious, cool and bracing air. I felt invigorated and strengthened by it. I enjoyed to the fullest inhaling it; and the savage grandeur of the scenery added enjoyment to breathing the pure mountain breezes which played upon it.

Soubratie had returned to Nowshera for his wife and my baggage, and it was nearly a fortnight before he returned. It was so difficult getting a cart, he said, he had to stay until Stone could get one for him, but I suspect that the profit arising from Mrs Soubratie's facile charms amongst the officers at Nowshera had much to do with his extra-long delay. I had not mentioned Mrs Soubratie to anybody and indeed hardly thought of her, but I got a most unmerciful chaffing about her the first night of her arrival. A married man! Just from his wife's arms! To engage a woman! It was in vain I endeavoured to defend myself, until I said that, as far as I was concerned, any fellow might have her, that it was my belief she would not be coy! At first my comrades would not believe me, but when they realised that such was indeed the case, their joy was unbounded. Like elsewhere, all the regiment's whores had deserted when the cry for 'cunt' went over the land from Peshawar on the arrival of the troops from Afghanistan and for several months neither officers nor men had enjoyed the sweet solace of a good luscious fuck at Cherat unless, as was the case in a few instances, he happened to be married and his wife was with him.

Mrs Soubratie was allowed no rest. That night she went from tent to tent, from hut to hut, and by morning a dozen officers had once more tasted of that meat of which, until exhausted nature can take no more, man never tires.

There was at this time in Cherat several officers of other corps or regiments in charge of details who had been sent up from Peshawar to recruit their health in our cool and salubrious air. With these gentlemen my story has nothing to do, except that perhaps I should do Mrs Soubratie the justice to tell my gentle readers that her active and much-sought-after cunt drew the coin it loved from their balls, and the coin she liked from their willingly opened purses. But there were two officers of the army medical department whom I must mention more particularly, because the action of one of them unconsciously pushed and almost forced me into that road which ended in pretty Fanny Selwyn's delicious little cunt, whence it branched off into that equally sweet one between her sister Amy's plump white thighs.

The two doctors were Surgeon Major Jardine and Surgeon Lavie. The former was a huge, coarse Scotchman, of low birth and low mind. Coarse in appearance and conversation, he was equally coarse in manners and soul, and I was amazed, after some months had elapsed, to find that he had not only thought of Fanny as a prospective wife, but had actually proposed to her.

He kept good natured and that is about all I can say for him. He was by no means handsome, though he was certainly very big; and in the eyes of some women huge proportions and the appearance of a Hercules strangely outweigh beauty of countenance and elegance of figure. Such women should be cows and consort with bulls.

Lavie was very different. He was a gentleman by birth and education. In mind he was as refined as Jardine was coarse. In manner he was decidedly reserved and shy, not given to much self-assertion, an interested listener and one who, when he did open his lips, spoke to the point. I used to take most pleasant walks with him, and soon he and I became real friends. In fact, Lavie was the quite uncon-scious instrument by which the road leading to the sweet little cunts of Fanny and Amy Selwyn was made, levelled and smoothed for me and along which I travelled almost unconsciously until I innocently arrived whither I was being conveyed.

It must not be supposed that I delayed making my first formal call on Mrs Selwyn and her fair daughters. Indeed I went to see them the second day of my arrival at Cherat, when I had at last succeeded in having a bath and a shave, neither of which feats I had been able to accomplish the day of my arrival.

The colonel was at home also and I saw the entire family. I was charmed with Mrs Selwyn, who was an enchanting woman, still beautiful though, alas! rapidly nearing the grave. She was tall and must always have been slender, and judging from the remains of her now faded charms she must, when young, have been more than ordinarily lovely. Her face had suffered far less ravagement than her person, and she still had most beautiful features and glorious eyes, but her poor bosom, alas! had entirely lost its billowy form, and I can hardly find the words to describe the condition of her body. Curious to say, though she knew she was delicate, and her husband had only too good reason to know it also, neither one seemed to have the remotest idea that her ever increasing emaciation must end in an early death; early, for Mrs Selwyn was not much more than forty years of age. Lavie, when I questioned him about her, would shake his head and say it was of no use hinting anything to the colonel, and that the only time he had ventured to do more than hint, the colonel had got quite angry and told him he was much too inexperienced a doctor to presume to give an opinion, and that all her life Mrs Selwyn had been as she then was, and he was sure she would out-live them all.

Naturally the conversation I had with this family, which was to prove so interesting in every sense to me, when I first called, rambled over a great space, for they knew from my darling Louie's letters, which had reached Cherat before I had, that I must be either married or engaged. I confessed to the former condition, which Mrs Selwyn declared she was delighted to hear. I thought, all the same, that as she had daughters rapidly growing up, she would have been better pleased had she found I had a heart still to be disposed of. Of one matter I was pleased to find that both she and the colonel were entirely ignorant, viz., that there was such a person in the world as Lizzie Wilson. They had, of course, heard that the brigade major at Nowshera had met with some kind of severe accident and was to be sent home as soon as he could be safely moved, and they questioned me about that accident, as it happened, as they knew, during my stay at Nowshera. I told them all I was disposed to allow I might know, stating that the story I heard was that Major Searle, having made himself obnox-ious to the soldiers at Nowshera, had been waylaid and badly beaten by some of them.

'Ah!' said the colonel, 'that accounts for the extraordi-nary reticence on the part of the commanding officer down there! I could get no details of any kind from him, by either heliograph or letter – of course he does not like to publish the fact that his men have been guilty of so gross a breach of discipline as to beat an officer!'

'Fanny! Amy! dears, now run away to your lessons,' said Mrs Selwyn. 'My girls have no governess, Captain Devereaux, the poor things have to learn as best they can. India is a bad country for young children, but I could not leave them at home. We have not money enough to keep two establishments.'

I could see by Fanny's face that she quite understood why she was being sent out of the room, viz., that her mother wished to speak 'secrets', and although, as I afterwards found, she was not always ready to obey an unwelcome order without more or less remonstrance, she on this occasion rose and led the way, followed by Amy and the younger children.

When the room was left to Colonel and Mrs Selwyn and myself, Mrs Selwyn said: 'Whilst you were at Nowshera, Captain Devereaux, did you hear any strange reports about Mrs Searle?'

'Well!' said I hesitatingly, as though not quite willing to enter on any details of scandal, 'I did, but I must say I do not entirely believe what I heard!'

'Then you have heard that she is separated from her husband?'

'Yes!'

'Did you hear anything else?'

'I heard that she was still in India, living at Ramsket, I think it was.'

'Ah! Well, she is as bad a woman as ever drew breath! A disgrace to her sex! I think it scandalous that the government should not force her to leave India! If there is a law which could be brought to bear! But the Viceroy –' and she made an expressive stop.

'Oh my dear!' interposed the colonel, 'you forget to say that if Mrs Searle is no better than she should be, it is on her husband the chief blame should fall!'

'Oh! I know! I know!' exclaimed Mrs Selwyn warmly and with much excitement, 'Oh! Captain Devereaux! I wonder whether you heard what led to the separation?'

'I can't say I did,' said I, telling a most tremendous lie, of course, but curious to see how Mrs Selwyn would reveal to me, as I could see she was dying to do, that Searle had compelled his wife to commit sodomy.

'Well, read the first chapter of Romans and especially that verse alluding to the conduct of certain men towards men! I cannot be more explicit, Captain Devereaux, and as it is my face feels as though it were burning!' and indeed her ordinarily pallid features were crimson, whether with shame or anger I could not well determine.

'I understand perfectly, Mrs Selwyn,' said I, 'and if Mrs Searle has disgraced her husband's name, I think it is hardly more than he can have deserved!'

'But she has disgraced her own, too, Captain Devereaux! Fancy what the natives must think when they see a lady – for she is a lady by birth and education and all – sell her charms to anyone who can afford to pay five hundred rupees for the possession of them – there is only one name for such a woman, and it is not prostitute, but one more vigorous and of course Saxon.'

I soon became a welcome guest at the colonel's house. The family was what we would call 'homely'.

During our married life Louie and I had lived very quietly. It was in bed that we lived a stormy life if anywhere!

Fanny Selwyn, though not to be compared in character with my Louie, did in many ways remind me of her so that I found a charm at the colonel's house which made an invitation to tea always agreeable. On one of those early occasions on which I dined with them, our conversation fell on the advantages of education, and Fanny said, with an accent of great yearning, 'I know I do so wish I had a governess! I shall never be able to teach myself from books without help, and as for teaching a child anything more than their multiplication table and ABC, it is the blind leading the blind.'

'What is your special difficulty, Miss Selwyn?' asked I.

'Oh! everything! But perhaps anything harder than arithmetic beyond the rule of three!'

After dinner I asked her to show me what sums they were she found so difficult, and after a little pressure she brought one of simple fractions. I showed her how simple it was, did one after another for her, and finally pressed her to try her hand at one herself. She did, and though being afraid to express her ignorance, as she said, to her infinite delight she got the right answer. One would have thought I was a perfect god to see the delight of Fanny at what she said was all my doing, and I was so pleased at having been able to give her so much real and innocent pleasure, that the spirit moved me to propose that, as I had so much leisure, I could not do better than come for an hour or so every morning to assist at the lessons if Colonel and Mrs Selwyn had no objection. Mrs Selwyn jumped at the offer, but the colonel hung back a little. Whether this was because he might have thought of Fanny's growing bubbies and consequent approach to an age when desire, easily raised by close and constant communication with a young and lively male, might seize upon her youthful cunnie, even though the young man was married, or rather because he fancied I was generously rushing in on a task of which I should soon grow uneasy and repent having undertaken it, I don't know. But I at any rate stuck to my offer and it was accepted.

At first I had a tremendous amount of chaffing to undergo from my brother officers, who could not understand my motives; some hardly hid their suspicions that I aimed at seducing Fanny and Amy, others looked upon me as a lunatic who did not know how to appreciate the charms of perfect idleness, but I did not mind.

But as for Fanny! She afterwards told me that in those Cherat days she looked upon me as the most wonderful man in the whole world, for I knew everything. Poor little Fanny. The truth was she knew nothing, and my acquirements in the educational line were to her prodigious. It was not marvellous, therefore, that I obtained over her a degree of power which although hardly perceptible to her, existed like the steel hand in the velvet glove. My word of praise or commendation made her joyously happy, a tear would spring in her eyes if I forgot myself and hinted that she really should have done better. It was an association of real and true happiness, undisturbed by the flames of passion but full of affection on either side, the communion, as it were, of beloved brother and dear sister.

The effect on me was very 'purifying'. Little by little I thought more of Fanny and Amy and less of Lizzie Wilson, more of the extraction of the square and cube root than of the matchless cunt of that superbly beautiful Venus; although at times one or the other of my charming pupils, leaning over my shoulder, may have had her rosy cheek, blooming with health and youth, touching mine, her fresh sweet breath mingling with mine, and a rising breast making itself felt against my shoulder, yet, as though fast asleep, my prick remained perfectly quiescent, for his master never once thought of the two blooming little cunts to which he could even then have easily found a way had he been inclined to take advantage of the dear girls' ignorance and inexperience.

Soon the most complete trust was reposed in me by Colonel and Mrs Selwyn, and after hearing 'lessons' I often was permitted to take the girls for a ramble down the wild and beautiful Chapin Gaant, or wherever our fancy led us to stray.

One evening Drs Jardine and Lavie were invited with myself to dinner at the colonel's. Jardine, at that time, as I afterwards learned, was looking forward to asking for Fanny's hand in marriage. I certainly had no idea of it, judging from his demeanour and Fanny's apparent indifference to him that evening as on other occasions. As usual, towards the close of the party, she had come and sat beside me and chatted in her ordinary lively manner. Her mind was fast opening up and receiving new ideas, and a month's tuition had had a great effect upon her. I little knew that Jardine was watching all this with jealous eyes, but on our way home he said: 'You seemed to be all there, Devereaux, this evening.'

'How do you mean, doctor?' said I.

'Why, the little girl seemed to have neither eyes nor ears for anybody but yourself. And you seemed to have her hands comfortably squeezed between your own. Ha! Ha! Ha!' and he gave one of those disagreeable guttural laughs which I so much disliked.

'Look here, Jardine!' said I, rather nettled, 'I can assure you I don't like the way you speak. Miss Selwyn is nothing to me but an amiable little girl to whom I give some lessons which amuse me and I hope instruct her. She is quick and clever and very intent to learn, and it is only natural that she should like to talk about her work to me, when her whole heart is set upon learning.'

'Ah! if you don't teach her any other lessons besides, my boy! What had you to do squeezing her hands, eh?'

'I deny it!' answered I hotly, 'your eyes must have deceived you!'

'Well!' he said, 'perhaps so! But at any rate, Devereaux, you should remember you have a wife of your own and should remember you should not take up too much of the young ladies' attention but leave some chance to us poor bachelors.'

I did not reply. I felt angry and vexed that my innocent attentions should be found fault with by a man who professed to see nothing desirable in a woman above her pelvis.

We were now approaching a row of huts in which lived a number of married women of other regiments who had been sent up from Peshawar out of harm's way until their husbands' regiments had got back from

Afghanistan. Mrs Selwyn, woman-like, had insisted on these married quarters being securely guarded by sentries, whose duties were not only to prevent any 'unauthorised person' from visiting them, but to prevent any woman leaving her hut after dark. This was a source of great irritation to all concerned. The officers wanted the women to fuck, and the women would have been only too glad to be fucked; they had had great times at Peshawar, where they scarcely went a day or a night without experiencing that delight of delights, and where they harvested bags of rupees from their innumerable and ever changing adorers, but here at Cherat they were, as it were, in a nunnery, and they pined for the longed-for prick, and the accompanying rupees.

It was a very dark night, and a kind of drizzle was falling, a most unusual thing. The first sentry, challenged and being answered, allowed us to pass. As we went along the front of the low enclosures before each hut, Jardine said, in a fairly loud voice, 'To think of all these lovely women here, and not a chance of having one of them! I believe they are all bursting with randiness, and would give rupees, instead of asking for them, to be well fucked!'

'Right you are, sir!' came a feminine voice in decidedly Irish tones. 'Right you are, and shall I come with your honour now?'

'By George! Yes! Come along! but we shall have to pass another sentry. Here! Put on my cloak and cap. There! that'll do famously! Now, Lavie! Devereaux! Let the girl walk between you and I'll go in front.' Saying this Jardine put his cap on what I could see was the head of a fine and buxom young woman, though it was too dark to see her features. She buttoned his cloak around her, and without any more ado we four proceeded. Lavie and I carried on a conversation with Jardine in order to deceive the alert sentry we had yet to pass, and soon we had our lass safe from all danger of immediate discovery.

'Now to my hut!' said Jardine, 'you are my property for tonight and this is the way to my hut!'

'Faith, sir!' said she, laughing, 'I'm thinking of taking ye all! I could do it aisy, one after another, and indeed all ye cud do to me tonight wud hardly make up for three months' total abstinence. I've not had a man all that time, and I did not become a married woman for that anyways!' With a laugh we condoled with her, and she continued: 'Oh! it's aisy it wud be for any of us to come up to you gentlemen any and ivery night when there's no moon, but you see there's some so jealous and catankerous! There's women down there,' pointing down towards the 'married quarters', 'who would love to come out on the prowl for officers, but who hate it falling to anyone but themselves! Only for that and the reports suchlike make, there would be half a dozen of us in yer honours' beds ivery night!'

'Well! we are wasting time,' said Jardine impatiently. 'Devereaux, you won't have much chance tonight, so you had better go home and fuck Mrs Soubratie, if you want a woman.'

'Thanks,' said I dryly, 'but I don't think I want any woman. All the same I wish you every pleasure. Goodnight,' and off I went.

Was it virtue? What was it?

Lavie told me next day that Jardine kept Mrs O'Toole until two o'clock, and then passed her on to him, and that so ravenous was she that he was completely *hors de combat* by four, and that but for the distance of my bungalow from the 'married quarters', and the near approach of daybreak, I would have had a visit from the lively woman. I was glad she had not come, for I knew, when put face to face with a nice fresh cunt, I should not have hesitated to fuck it, and Mrs Selwyn would have heard of it, as she did of Jardine and Lavie. This was not the only visit Mrs O'Toole paid the doctors, and they kept it a deep secret from the other officers, but the secret oozed out somehow and Mrs O'Toole was one of the very first women sent down to the plains when Cherat was gradually denuded of all the officers and men of my regiment.

Early in October a telegram came from Peshawar which sent a thrill of joy through the hearts of the Tommies at Cherat, and made the officers feel happy too, but which somewhat displeased Mrs Soubratie. It ran thus, 'Twelve plump, fresh young whores will leave Peshawar for Cherat today.' This was the telegram from the *kotwal* [police-officer] at Peshawar to our regimental *kotwal*. The moment Colonel Selwyn heard of it he telegraphed back, 'Keep the women until I have inspected them.' He did not tell Mrs Selwyn of the nature of his duty, but he told her he had been called for by the general at Peshawar to go down and see him on important business, and he lost no time about it. I only heard of his intended visit to Peshawar after the colonel had actually departed and it made me uneasy. The house was very much exposed, being at the head of the Chapin Gaant, and the robbers had been particularly active lately. It is true the Selwyns had a *chokidar,* which is the way English people in India purchase immunity from the robbers, the *chokidars* being always selected from those tribes or villages in the vicinity which furnish the greatest number of robbers, but there had been many instances lately of theft and in some cases of violence and bloodshed at night, so that my faith in *chokidar*dom was rather shaken. The nights, too, were brilliantly lit by the moon, of which the splendour can hardly be imagined by those who have never seen that luminary in the East.

I knew that from her delicate state of health, Mrs Selwyn could hardly give the colonel much pleasure of nights, if indeed he could ever fuck her at all, and I also knew, from certain little stories the colonel told me in private, that he was as fond of a good juicy cunt as any man. I guessed, therefore, that the news of the twelve plump, fresh young whores of the telegram had brought upon him a flood of desire and that he had gone to Peshawar not only to inspect them but also to try them, and fuck them, and see whether they came up to the description given of them. My suspicions were well founded, for when I went to Peshawar myself, some two months later, the *khansama* at the public bungalow told me that Colonel Selwyn sahib was the finest man he had ever seen, and that he always had four women every night; and Jumali, one of the twelve, told her colleagues that the colonel had at Peshawar fucked her every night during his stay, and took three others, turn by turn. Poor colonel! He had the biggest balls of any man I ever saw, and no wonder if at times his bottled-up emotions burst forth! I believe myself that the sentries guarding the 'married quarters' at Cherat were put there by Mrs Selwyn more as a preventative against the colonel than against the other officers; at any rate, this visit to Peshawar had very nearly fatal consequences for some of the colonel's own family.

The first night I could hardly sleep from ill-defined dread of what might be going on at the far end of the camp, a mile away from me, where the Selwyn house was, and towards morning I rose, whilst the lovely landscape was lighted by the moon only, and walked rapidly until I reached the colonel's house. Everything seemed all right. The *chokidar* was at his post, giving from time to time that horrid cough which they all give, a kind of sentry's 'all's well'. The next two nights succeeding I took the same walk with the same result. But the next night (at the very time the colonel must have been between the dusky thighs of the last but one of the twelve fresh young whores whom he had gone to inspect), I was just turning the corner where the path joined that from which I had first seen pretty Fanny Selwyn, when I heard a sound which made me shiver with apprehension! I thought I could distinguish my name being called upon. I set feet to ground with all my force, and ran as I had never run before! A few minutes brought me to the house, and during those few minutes the fearful shrieks never ceased. It was for me that someone, some girl was calling and – Oh! God! – the shrieks were suddenly stifled just as I got to the verandah! There, on the ground, with his throat cut from ear to ear, his head thrown back and a horrible yawning gap, from which a stream or river of blood was still gushing, separating his chin from his chest, lay the luckless *chokidar,* whose cough had given me such comfort when I heard it on the preceding nights. I trod in his slippery gore before I perceived it but I had no time to lose. The window of what I knew to be Fanny's bedroom was wide open. It was a high lattice window, opening like a door, and the sill of it was no more than two and a half or three feet from the ground. I sprang through it at a bound, and there before me I saw a tawny Afghan struggling between a pair of quivering thighs, completely naked and uncovered, and those thighs and feet and legs I knew to be Fanny's.

For a moment I stood paralysed with horror. The position of the accursed Afghan was exactly that of a man who in fucking a woman has completed the exquisite short digs and is pressing his prick way home while pouring out his burning spunk! His struggles were exactly those of a man under such circumstances, and his whole weight seemed to be resting on the quivering form of the prostrate girl. I could not see her face, but her poor left hand lying motionless and palm upwards told me that she was insensible, if not dead. It was only a moment I stood thus.

Then, with a stifled cry of rage and despair, I rushed at the sacrilegious brute who was thus defiling the temple reared for beings altogether superior to such as him; he had not heard me jump in at the window for the floor was *chaman* [extremely hard lime and mortar] and my shoes had India rubber soles, being, in fact, my lawn-tennis shoes. I seized him by the collar of his coat, and gave one wrench, pulling up so suddenly that he had no time to let go his hold of poor Fanny, but dropped her as soon as he recovered from his surprise. The lifeless manner in which the unfortunate girl fell back with a thud on the bed, her head almost disappearing on the other side of it, gave me a further terrible shock. I was convinced she was dead. But the rotten material of which the burly brute's coat was made, gave with a shrill-sounding tear, and a cloud of stinking dust rushed forth from it as though from the explosion of a musket. Without attempting to attack me in return, and with a stifled cry of alarm, the fiend made for the window. Before he reached it, however, I had hold of his coat again, but could not manage to get close to him, he was so quick, and I could only make a grab at his shoulder as he fled. Again the rotten cloth gave way, this time, however, not quite so quickly, but too quickly to enable me to grasp the man himself. As the garment almost fell off, his blade or long glittering knife fell to the floor; wrenching himself away, the filthy brigand bounded out of the window, dashed across the path and appeared to hurl himself head-foremost down the steep side of the valley. I could hear him crashing and tearing through the bushes, for all was silent as death. Satisfied that not only was the brute gone, but that there were no others hiding near at hand, I turned with a heart full of sickening fear and dread to the bed across which the lifeless form of the unfortunate Fanny was stretched. The verandah outside somewhat darkened the room even in the daytime, but the powerful light of the moon reflected from the ground and the rocky slopes still managed to illuminate the bedchamber, and the small oil lamp, which generally burns all night in every person's room in India, added its feeble rays to show me what looked like the desolation of death!

Fanny's foot just touched the ground. Her pretty legs with such beautiful and slender ankles, the calves round, graceful and well developed, were wide apart, as were her full and really splendid thighs, white as snow and polished as marble.

I could not but see the darling little cunt, for it was looking straight at me, and the light of the little lamp shone full on it showing me that the bush, which topped the rounded, sloping motte above it, was thickest in the centre, and not very rich or abundant. I shivered when I saw that sweet, sweet, cunt, that holy land all smeared with blood, and a thick drop oozing from its lowest point of entrance. My God! My God! She had then been raped, outraged, ravaged! And by a blasted, cursed and never-too-much-damned, stinking, filthy, lousy Afghan. The incredible insolence which could have animated a native, in time of peace and within our own borders, to commit such a crime, astounded me, but I had no time to indulge in thoughts or rather to dwell upon them, for these thoughts rushed through my brain like lightning. I bent over the poor lifeless girl and raised her head. Her eyes were closed, her face looked so pure, so peaceful and though the colour had fled from her cheeks I thought I had never seen Fanny Selwyn look so beautiful. Her lips, slightly parted, showed the rows of pearls which formed her teeth, small, beautiful and perfectly regular. She felt warm. Of course she would be warm, for if life had indeed departed, she could not have been dead five minutes, so rapidly had events passed – though it has, as usual, taken me many words to describe them. Her lovely sylph-like form felt warm to my touch. Oh! how elegant were its lines! How pure, fine and spotless was that satiny skin! How beautiful were those swelling, rising breasts – not yet full grown, but giving promise of one day being more exquisitely beautiful, even, than they were now – the snowy breasts of a nymph of six-teen summers. The little coral beads which surmounted them seemed to me to have more colour in them than they would have shown had death really taken possession of this elegant form. I put my hand on her heart! Oh! thanks be to God, she was not dead! Her heart was beating and firmly too. In an ecstasy of delight, I kissed those mute lips, and could not resist closing my hand, as I was accustomed to do when kissing lovely girls, over the sweet little bubbie near her heart. It was lovely! so firm! so hard! so sweetly filling to the hand. It was an unwarranted liberty, but I could not resist the temptation! But suddenly I thought about the base effects of the deeds of the monster who had ravished her virginity. My eyes glanced again down over the lovely, smooth, dimpled belly, over the delightfully but only slightly forested slopes on the rising hill of Venus, till they travelled along the deep line of her soft little cunt. What if within those so lately virgin portals were lodged the accursed spawn of a loathsome Afghan! What if, as might be the case if she lived, that lovely little belly were to swell to become the source, the mould of a child to be looked upon with horror and dismay! Oh! what should I do! Suddenly the idea struck me to endeavour to prevent such a terrible catastrophe by opening the beauteous gates of the temple and trying to encourage the beastly slime to flow out. No sooner thought of than done. I did not hesitate! I passed my trembling middle finger into that soft little cunt, until my knuckles prevented further ingress. To my inexpressible joy I discovered that Fanny had not been ravished. The close little maidenhead was distinctly there, unbroken, unscathed! I felt it well to make quite sure, and then, withdrawing my finger from the hot depths, delighted to find by its moisture that the aperture was still alive, I once more looked to see if I could discover the source of the blood, if blood it was which covered that lovely cunt. I could not imagine what it could be from, and fearing that perhaps the frightful and agonised shrieks I had heard might have arisen from the torture of some dreadful internal wound, caused by the violence of the ruffian who had assailed her, I parted the hair of her dear little bush to see whether there could be a wound hidden by it, and feeble though the light was by which I worked, it was too easy, alas! (for I love a fine, thick, curly forest to adorn the sacred mount of Venus!) to see every particle of skin under it, and there was not so much as a scratch. On moving about my foot suddenly trod on something soft and flabby: I picked up the object it had encountered and found it to be a cloth covered with blood, and I had hardly to glance at it to recognise the source of all my alarm. Poor Fanny, in fact, had her menses, and the blood I saw was the harmless result. I almost laughed with joy and amusement. But whatever might be the cause of the blood, there could be no doubt that the girl, in such a serious faint, must be in a bad way, and I began to get alarmed on that account.

I had laid her in a more commodious position, hoping she would come to quickly, as I had generally seen women do who had fainted, but she lay so dreadfully motionless. Her moving breasts alone told my eye that she was alive. They rose and fell but through a very small space. Poor, dear little breasts! I caressed them. I pressed them. I gently pinched the little rosebuds. But Fanny's eyes remained hard closed. I passed my hand all over her, over her smooth sides, over her dimpled belly, over the precious motte, down her lovely and beautiful thighs. I even slipped my finger again into her luscious cunt, hoping to awaken her from her torpor, and though I pressed the velvet lips together, and could feel the active little clitoris swelling under my titillations, Fanny felt it not. At last I spied a tumbler on the table, and I sprinkled her face and undulating bosom with the cold water. She moved! Cold had done what warm caresses had failed to do – she opened her glorious eyes, gazed wildly at me for a moment and then shrieked with fear and dreadful alarm. I clasped her in my arms and tenderly pressed her to me, she struggling violently all the while.

'Fanny! Fanny! Miss Selwyn! Fanny dearest,' I cried in imploring and soothing accents, 'it is I! Captain Devereaux! Don't be frightened, there is no one to hurt you now! I hunted that fellow and he has run for his life!'

My voice calmed her somewhat. The poor girl turned her face to my bosom and clutched me wildly, whilst she burst into an agony of weeping and cried aloud like a child. Her convulsive sobs and almost hysterical movements forced her hard little breasts against me, and I could feel them distinctly, although I had my coat and waistcoat on and she was naked. I caressed her, tried to soothe her and she clung all the closer to me. I felt I was a brute, but her nudity, the warmth of her body, her clasped arms, and above all the sympathetic sensations her bubbies caused all over my bosom, made my prick stand with tremendous force. I had no idea of profiting from my situation, but I could not help feeling the delicious excitement of the moment. All the time I kept trying to prevail on Fanny to subdue her emotion of terror. I spoke, I know, in the fondest manner. I was much moved myself, and I found myself calling her My darling! My tender beloved little pet! and similar endearing epithets. Fanny at last seemed to cock her ears and listen. Her sobs grew less violent. She left off crying aloud and turned her face up to mine and I kissed the cherry lips and tried to dry the flowing tears on her cheeks with my mouth. Oh! she liked that!

'Oh! dear Captain Devereaux, you have saved me! How can I ever thank you?'

'By being good now, dear Fanny! By trying to recover your courage and tell me how that brutal Afghan got into your room?'

'Was he an Afghan? I could not see well! I was asleep and suddenly I felt a hand between my thigh ... – on me – somewhere – and when I opened my eyes I saw two natives –'

'Two!' I exclaimed.

'Yes! Two! I am sure of it! There were two; one had his big face close to me – the one who had his hand on me – on me – somewhere! The other had a knife in his hand and was grinning! I could see his teeth! Then I shrieked and tried to jump out of bed, but the man whose hand was – who had his hand on – who had his hand on – who –'

'Yes! darling!' I said, seeing she was embarrassed, 'the man who was attacking you.'

'Yes! He put his hand on my chest and held me down. I hit him in the face, and must have hurt his eye, for he cried out and put his hand to it, and I jumped up, escaped for a moment and began to call out as loud as I could. He reached round for me and caught me, and I felt him tear my nightgown, and he dashed me down on the bed and fell upon me with all his might and seized my throat with his two hands, and I suppose I fainted then, for I remember nothing else. Oh! how did you come here, dear, dear, dear Captain Devereaux?'

All this time the gentle, frightened girl had her arms round me. She did not appear aware that, except for the upper parts of her arms, she was as naked as the day she was born. In fact, although able to talk now, it was plain to me that she had not yet fully realised her exact position. She clung to me with the grasp of the drowning; and this was what was so charming, and yet so dear, as it was like the embrace of a girl who feels the lively and moving prick giving her rapture beyond compare.

'I had been nervous ever since your father went to Peshawar, Miss Selwyn, and every night I have patrolled to satisfy myself that you were safe. I heard your shrieks and that is how I happened to arrive just in the nick of time.'

Fanny raised her head and looked at me with eyes from which love and gratitude both darted most speaking rays.

'Kiss me!' she cried, with passion plainly thrilling through her, 'you are a good fellow!'

I did not wait to be asked twice. I passed my thirsty lips to hers in one long, deep draught, but whilst doing so a question struck me. What had become of the second Afghan? Had this thought not occurred to me, I really don't know what might have happened. I was rapidly losing control over my passions; Fanny was in a glow of more than loving gratitude; a very little pressing and I felt sure she would welcome me between her thighs, and in spite of her 'illness' I should have there and then swept away the charming maidenhead I had discovered to be safe and secure. A standing prick has no conscience, saith the proverb, and as to that, mine was worse than standing! It was in a terrible state of agonised extension and fighting to crack the outer skin!

But that second Afghan!

'Fanny! Did you not say you saw two men? One with a knife?'

'Yes! I certainly did!'

'Where is the second?'

'I don't know! I suppose he must have run away when he saw you.'

'But where to? Your door is shut! There is only one window and I am certain that he could not have got out of that. That man is in the house somewhere.'

It being plain that the second Afghan was not in the room, I insisted on searching the house. It struck me as odd that no one seemed to have been roused by Fanny's shrieks, and yet I had heard them a hundred yards off when I was outside the house. Cursing my folly in delaying when each moment might be precious, and for thinking of how sweet it would be to fuck Fanny, when perhaps Amy might be lying ravished or murdered, I sprang to the door, though poor Fanny did all she could to try and hold me back. She was alarmed at the idea of seeking danger and was frightened for me, but I persisted.

Between her door and her sister's was a passage. But I must first say I had picked up the knife my Afghan had dropped. This I held sword-like in my hand. I opened Amy's bedroom door suddenly and quickly, and there I saw another sight which made me sick with horror. The Afghan was apparently buggering Amy. Apparently? Alas! no! He was actually doing it! And like the other ruffian whom I had so fortunately caught just in time to prevent any real damage being done to the suffering Fanny, this devil's spawn was so intent on his rich enjoyment that he did not at first notice my entry. All took place so rapidly that I cannot attempt to imitate time in my very true history. I dashed at the villain who withdrew his glistening black prick from poor Amy's bottom so suddenly that it made a 'pop' like a cork coming out of a bottle. He reared himself upright, seized a long knife from off the bed, where he had placed it ready for use before he had begun buggering the poor girl, and with a shout of triumphant defiance and the expression of a fiend courting further victory, he rushed at me crying in terms of abuse common to gentle Hindu and savage Afghan alike that he had defiled both my sister's cunt and my mother's cunt, then, passing from the general to the particular, 'I have fucked and buggered your sister – I will now bugger you too!'

In my rage I roared in reply, 'I'll be buggered if you do!' quite an unnecessary piece of bad language on my part. I now found what a mistake I had made in not holding my knife dagger-wise instead of as a sword, for before I could make any attempt to stab my huge antagonist he had his knife twice in me, once in my left shoulder and once in my breast. He was trying to stab me down to the heart through the shoulder, and had I not sprung back, his second stab would have succeeded. As it was he cut me terribly all down the left breast. I, however, caught my knife well into his left side and turned hard. Fanny, screaming at the top of her voice, had fled the moment she saw this second devil, and all the time the combat lasted I could hear the hills and rocky caverns resounding with her shrill shrieks, for she had gone to the open window and was literally hysterical. Meanwhile the burly and really immense Afghan was getting the better of me. He was far more accustomed to using the dagger than I was, who had never fought with one in my life. He stabbed me many times, but fortunately, chiefly in the left arm, though I caught some fearful rips in the chest like the first one. I began to fight at random, for I felt bewildered by his extraordinary activity and lightning-like blows which I had to ward off as best I could or avoid by jumping from side to side like a cat, but at last a lucky and desperate stab from me laid the red brute lifeless at my feet. I had struck him an upward blow in the stomach, and the keen knife, having penetrated his clothes and outer flesh, had passed, as through a pat of butter, up to the hilt into his body and transfixed his heart. He lay on the floor a moment writhing and trampling with his feet, and then he gave a dreadful gasp or two and died! To the last his fierce eyes seemed to bore deadly hatred into mine, and I could not help shuddering, even in victory, at the terrible escape I had had.

At first I was overcome with faintness and fatigue. I could hear Fanny yelling but could not go to her assistance. I sat on the bed next to the motionless Amy and panted; I did not feel my wounds much, but they made me sick. Poor Amy was lying on her face, which I could not see. She was stark naked. Her arms were tied behind her back, her elbows being made to meet. Bandages, also fastened behind, passed apparently over her face and confined her rich flowing locks at the back of her head. I had not time, nor spirit, to fall to admiring her lovely form, but to this day I see those rich full hips and those beautiful hemispheres, between which was that back entrance so lately defiled by the beastly Afghan's black prick. At last, somewhat recovered, I began with hands trembling with fatigue and excitement to try and undo the bandages. They were knotted too tightly, however, and I had to use the knife I held to cut them, and wherever I touched her the blood streamed from me on to her fair white skin, until she looked as if she were weltering in her own gore; but at last I suceeded, and got the arms free, and the bandage off her face, then putting my hands under her, I turned her on her back. In so doing I unconsciously grasped two full and firm bubbies which adorned her bosom far more richly than Fanny's did hers, for, though some eighteen months younger than her sister, Amy was more 'grown up' in body than Fanny. I was in an agony to know if the Afghan's brutal boast was true. Had he fucked as well as he had undoubtedly buggered the unfortunate girl? Hardly noticing then the fact that the bush which curled all over the plump and well-shaped motte under my eyes was far thicker and more grown than on Fanny's, I slipped an enquiring finger into the palpitating and sweet little cunt, feeling sick at heart with dread and apprehension! Oh! joy! she had not been fucked. Her dear little maidenhead was intact. Buggered she had been, but not ravished.

Full of this good and important discovery, I ran to Fanny, whose voice was hoarse, and implored her to go to her sister's assistance. Already I could hear voices of men running up the steep path which led from the bazaar in the valley on the other side of the house, and fearing lest, in their zeal to help, a number might break in and discover the two girls naked as they were, I implored Fanny to put on her petticoats and to go and cover Amy. But Fanny had quite lost all self-possession. She indeed went to Amy's room, but on seeing her naked, bleeding and apparently dead, and the gory carcass of the slain Afghan lying on the floor in a lake of blood, she rushed out again, screaming and crying like one demented.

I ran to the door in time to prevent the *kotwal* from letting any of his men climb in through the window, and I begged him to set guards round the house, to remain where he was, and to send at once for Dr Lavie and the picket of the regiment. Satisfied that my orders were being carried out, and that though bursting with curiosity neither *kotwal* nor *peons* would try to get inside the house, I went to Fanny who was crouched in one corner of the room, and endeavoured to assuage her fears, telling her that Amy was only in a faint, and that it was my blood and not hers which covered her body. The poor girl had received so many shocks to her nerves that at first it was almost impossible to rouse her to her senses, or make her understand that her sister must be attended to. I called her attention to the chattering and hubbub outside, and I really was anxious to get her out of the room, for I could hear the remarks made to each newcomer and the ughs! and ohs! with which each one saluted the dead body of the murdered and unfortunate *chokidar*.

I wished this piece of news not to get to Fanny's ears yet awhile, and at last I persuaded her to go and look after Amy. I threw a dark blanket over the bloody corpse of the abominable Afghan, and Fanny, with visible shudders, picked her way over the blood-spattered floor. She did not seem to appreciate that she was, to all intents and purposes, naked. The Afghan had not, as the one in Amy's case had done, torn her nightdress completely off her. He had rent it from top to bottom in front, and Fanny still had her sleeves on her arms, short sleeves which permitted her arms to be almost entirely seen.

Perhaps feeling the fluttering remnants of her night-dress made her think that she was covered, but as a matter of fact I saw (and as I saw I admired, and as I admired I desired) the whole of her body in front, and she looked bewitching, with her eyes wildly glancing about and her sweet little bubbies rising and falling rapidly as her bosom expanded and contracted with her quick breathing. Her pretty motte, pushing out a little into a perfect cushion, rapidly narrowed to the point where the plump little gem of a cunt showed its deep and tempting line. Her bush was not thick enough to permit me yet to see that line which is visible when a naked girl stands upright and is not conscious that she is displaying her secret charm of charms to an admiring man, and when she sat down beside her completely naked sister I could compare cunts, and fancy which one would give me the greater pleasure to fuck.

Goodness! what strange thoughts do get in a man's mind at inopportune moments! I was perfectly conscious that what I had to do was to relieve Amy, and further search the house, and yet there I was debating those two lovely girls' cunts in my mind, and comparing their bubbies, their forms and their thighs.

I got Fanny the water and bade her sprinkle Amy, and I begged her again to be quick and put something on, for, 'You are perfectly naked, my dear girl!'

'Oh! What does it matter? What does it matter?' she said, bursting into tears again. 'I feel as if I should die!'

'But look, Fanny darling, you must not give in so! Remember, you are a lady and a soldier's daughter, and be brave! That's right, dry your tears. I have sent for Dr Lavie and expect him here. But quick and bring Amy around. She breathes all right,' I added, laying my two hands on her lovely bubbies. 'Sprinkle her well! That's right! She will soon be all right! Then cover her up in bed and get in with her. You have not been half so badly used as she has!'

'How?' asked Fanny, in a voice of surprise.

'She was gagged by that ruffian,' I said, pointing to the dead Afghan under the blanket, 'and he had tied her arms behind her, and I don't know what else he may have done.'

Fanny had been long enough in India to have learnt all about the theory of fucking, even if she had not been old enough before leaving England to know it in that happy land.

She burst out, 'Oh! poor, poor, Amy! Oh! Captain Devereaux, what shall we do? What shall we do?'

I understood her cry.

'Don't be alarmed, dearest Fanny. I don't think the ruffian did any wicked deed that will leave bad results. But I am sure Amy must have fought, and perhaps got badly bruised and hurt.'

I could not tell her that I had actually seen the Afghan's prick in Amy's bottom up to his beastly balls, and Fanny had run away too soon to have seen it herself, and she knew nothing of sodomy at that time. I persuaded her to be brave whilst I went and visited the rooms, saying that I felt sure no other Afghans were in the house, but I would first make sure. Before going, however, I called in the *kotwal,* and posted some of his men in the passage, shutting Amy's door so that no curious eye could see the naked girls.

The first room I visited was the colonel's bedroom. There was Mrs Selwyn apparently fast asleep. I tried in vain to rouse her. I opened her eyes and the immensely distended pupils told me the reason for her torpor. Opium! Drugged! There had been premeditation, and there must be a traitor, or a traitress, in the house.

I next went to what was called the nursery. There Mabel, a fine girl about twelve or thirteen, slept with the younger children, and an *ayah* ought to have been there also. But there was no *ayah*!

Mabel was awake, crying and sobbing. She gave a little shriek as I came into the room, but the moment she saw me, she sprang out of bed in such a hurry and in such disorder that although there was but the feeble little light, burnt as I have said by everybody at night, I not only saw her sweet little cunt to perfection, but could see that already a downy growth was shading the motte, which promised to be beautiful when the season for collecting the ripe fruit from the garden of Venus duly arrived. Mentally I ejaculated to myself, 'I seem to be destined to see all the fuckable Selwyn cunts tonight.' For Mabel could certainly have taken me then, young as she was. I knew the measure of a cunt which would admit my prick by this time. However, let me proceed.

Mabel, delighted to see me and not, as she feared, an ogre or a robber, flew into my arms and hurt my left one and my chest wounds so much that I could not refrain from calling out. She started back and roared when she saw her nightdress all covered with blood. I had great difficulty in pacifying her, but got her back into bed, where I kissed her and begged her to stay quiet. I told her how the robbers had come, and I had killed one, after being wounded myself, and that everybody was safe and sound, and that I would tell her more in the morning. She was a biddable girl and really was very quiet, lying down and promising to be good. I examined the two other children and found them in the same state of stupor as Mrs Selwyn. Evidently they had been drugged and the whole thing was a plot. The *ayah*'s absence assured me of this. Had she run away to give the alarm, help would have come long before, but the *kotwal* had told me that it was Fanny's unearthly screams that had aroused the bazaar. It seemed plain to me that the mission of those two Afghans had been to rape, perhaps to bugger also, Fanny, Amy and Mabel, and that Mrs Selwyn and the two younger children had been drugged to prevent their adding any outcry in case of a squalling match on the part of poor Fanny and her sisters whilst they were being raped, etc. The man I had killed had done his work better than the fool who took Fanny, for he had commenced by gagging Amy, who could not utter a sound, even whilst she was being buggered, poor child! Had she not been gagged, I would have heard her when I was trying to bring Fanny around and perhaps poor Amy might have been spared. I went back to Amy's room, but dreadfully sick, ill and in pain. She expressed her gratitude more by her eyes than by her voice and she put up her sweet face so imploringly to be kissed that I bent down, though it hurt me to do so, and gave her some warm kisses on her trembling lips. Then bidding Fanny to remain where she was, in bed with Amy, I went to see whether there was any sign of Lavie and the picket.

I had not to wait long. But during the interval the *kotwal* told me that three of the colonel's house servants were lying dead in the go-downs of the outhouses, viz., the cook, the bearer and the sweeper, and that the *chuprassy* [office-messenger] could not live long, having been repeatedly stabbed, and two children had their throats cut. It was a fearful massacre and I could hardly believe that two men could have done it. There must have been more, but I only saw two and no one lived to tell the entire story of this ferocious attack.

Soon the regular beat of drilled and disciplined men was heard as the picket came as quick as they could up the steep ascent from the bazaar, and jolly little Crean, the wild sprig from the Green Isle, and Lavie both appeared. In as few words as possible I put them in possession of the facts. Lavie instantly sent off for his stomach pump, which he had not brought, not expecting he would require that implement. Crean set his sentries and scoured the bushes and rocks but found nothing new. The bodies of the slain were put in one outhouse by themselves, and as soon as Lavie said the young ladies could bear it, the party entered their room and carried off the huge carcass of the dead Afghan. He was an enormous man, and I shuddered for poor Amy's bottom when I saw the immense size of his now dead, limp and hideous prick! No wonder it fitted tight and made a 'pop' when he had suddenly pulled it out of her unhappy behind! I had determined not to tell Lavie what I had seen that prick doing, but left him to suppose that I had arrived just in time to prevent a rape.

Then, and not till then, did I let him see the state I was in.

Dear reader, have you ever been wounded? If you have, you will remember how sickening it was when the skilful surgeon dressed your wounds. Mine were not dangerous, except one where the knife had just penetrated inside my ribs, but they grew necessarily painful as they got uncovered and the clothes were pulled, no matter how gently, away from them. Lavie insisted on my going to bed in Fanny's room. He said I must remain perfectly quiet and drink nothing but water (for I was dying of thirst and longed for a peg), for fear of inflammation setting in. Luckily, I had lost so much blood that unless I did something foolish there was little fear of my getting into a bad state from inflammation; still, it was wisest to take every precaution.

The state I was in, I wondered how my prick could have stood so exorbitantly stiff such a short time since, whilst I was toying with Fanny's cunt, trying to bring her to, for now it felt as if it would never stand again! I felt so deadly weak. The excitement was over and the reaction had set in. I blamed myself, for I thought that had I had my wits about me I would have left Fanny's cunt alone and visited the other rooms first, and then in all probability poor Amy would never have been buggered. I wondered, did she know she had been? Or did a merciful heaven render her insensible before the brutal Afghan defiled her bottom with his beastly prick? I hoped the latter. I wondered at Fanny; I thought she would have been more heroic, but I made due allowance for her, and oh! she did look so lovely, and so did Amy, when they were both naked! And what a charming little cunt Mabel had too! And so on, and so on, until I fell into a kind of delirious sleep from which I did not awake for several days.

I remember that awakening very vividly. It was bright daylight. The window was open, as well as the door of the room, and the sweet cool air blew gently in upon me in the most refreshing manner, sometimes mingled with loud laughter which came rolling up the hillside from the busy bazaar. The twelve fine young whores had arrived, and I dare say I heard the happy laughter of some of the Tommies waiting anxiously for their turn for a jolly good fuck. I heard of this event from my young friend Crean, who told me later that Jumali was really an AI poke, and a splendid and very pretty woman. In fact, Jumali was the favourite of all those useful and graceful women. It was she who, I afterwards heard at Peshawar, had always commenced the night with the colonel to be followed by three or four of the other fresh and plump ones. Ah! that 'inspection' cost the colonel dear, and might have cost him more than it did. Poor Amy! Poor Amy!

Well, then, I woke up, and at first wondered where I could be, but my arm in a sling, and a feeling of painful stiffness all over me, quickly recalled my wandering memory. There was someone in my room. I could hear him or her gently stirring on the chair, but I could not see who it was. I called out in a weak voice, 'Is anyone there?'

'Oh! Captain Devereaux! Are you all right then? Do you know me?' cried the sprightly Fanny, who came swiftly and smiling to my bedside, looking as fresh as a rose and as neat as usual, for Fanny was a very tidy girl at all times.

'Know you!' I cried in surprise, 'of course I know you, Fanny dear!'

'Mama! Mama! Papa! Come Captain Devereaux is not silly now. Come! Come!' she cried, running out of the bedroom.

Mrs Selwyn soon came as fast as her weakness would permit her, for the deadly narcotic which had been administered to her had made her exceedingly ill, and this was the first day she had left her bed since the events which I have, I fear, so feebly described, took place. At first she could not speak from emotion. The tears rose to her eyes and sought along the lashes a place to roll forth, which at last they did. She took my unbound hand in both of hers and pressed it, and at length finding her voice, said, with much emotion and very slowly, 'Oh! Captain Devereaux! Captain Devereaux! What do we not owe you?'

'Nothing at all, dear Mrs Selwyn.'

'Nothing! Oh no! We owe you everything, the lives and honour of our girls! We can never repay you!' and without another word she bent down and kissed me, letting her tears fall upon my cheeks.

I could not but feel moved. Fanny stood by looking on with a mixture of amusement and apprehension on her face. Very comical. She was evidently amused at her mother kissing me, but why she should be apprehensive I could not tell. At all events she said nervously, 'He does not call me Louie now, mama!'

'Why! Did I call you that?' said I.

'Oh yes! You seemed to think I was your wife! You would insist that I should come to bed! You said you wanted me very badly, and I do not know what other rubbish.'

'Well! Fanny! That shows that Captain Devereaux loves his wife and that his only thoughts were on her when he was delirious!'

'Was I delirious?' I asked in amazement.

'I should think you were,' said Fanny, bursting into almost uncontrollable laughter. 'The things you said to me! You would have it I was your wife!'

'Ah, me!' said Mrs Selwyn. 'I never saw your wife, Captain Devereaux, but I never in my life wished a man not to be a married man as I wish you were not!'

'Because then he would marry me!' laughed Fanny.

There was a little awkward pause which I ended by saying, 'And I should have got a good and very lovely wife in that case, Fanny!'

Fanny blushed and looked more than pleased. Her eyes assumed that look which at times gave them the appearance of speaking love and affection.

'Ah now!' said I, laughing, 'if I were only a Mohammedan and you another, Fanny, I could marry you now! But you see we have the misfortune to be Christians.'

'Worse luck,' said Fanny with a sigh.

'Well!' said Mrs Selwyn, 'I can only say that if it could be a pleasure to a mother to give her daughter to a man, it would have indeed been a pleasure to me to give Fanny to you, Captain Devereaux, for you have deserved her.'

'And who can tell,' said Fanny, innocently and quite unconscious of the sense of her words, 'but he may have me yet!'

'Come, Fanny! Captain Devereaux's beef tea. I can see he is tired. We have been talking too much to him and Dr Lavie will be furious with us if he finds it out.'

The colonel here entered the room. He looked the picture of misery and woe. His conscience smote him. He knew that the young man lying prostrate and unable to move before him on his daughter's bed was in that condition owing to his lust. Poor man! He knew that a number of innocent persons had gone to their doom for the same cause, and that his wife and one daughter were still ill from effects springing from the same cause. I took his grieved appearance to be simply that of sympathy, but as he wrung my hand, he said quietly to me, 'Devereaux, I owe all to you and you owe all to me!'

'How, colonel?'

'I owe you the honour and lives of my girls – and – I ought never to have gone to Peshawar!' and he drew his hand across his eyes and groaned heavily.

Presently he added, 'Lavie tells me it will be some little time before you are strong enough to resume your duties, and that he would like to see you in your own quarters which are nearer to him, but he allows that you will be better in a house where you can be nursed and looked after, so you will remain here till you are quite well and strong again.'

'Thanks very much, colonel. I hope, however, I shall soon be all right. How is Amy?' I added, 'I have not seen her.'

'She is still in bed, poor girl!' said the colonel. 'The attack made on her had a very curious and I am sorry to say a serious effect. She has had a recurrence of an ailment which attacked her as a baby.'

'There! Never mind,' said Mrs Selwyn, 'never mind what is the matter with Amy. Captain Devereaux will be contented with knowing she has received a shock – not to be wondered at – and is still very low and depressed. Come, Fanny! get Captain Devereaux his tiffin!' and mother and daughter both left the room.

'It is a most singular thing,' said the colonel, looking carefully out of the door before he spoke, 'but poor Amy as a baby had a relaxed sphincter and – you understand? And it has come on again. Lavie says it is most unusual, but hopes to get her all right again so long as she is not allowed to pass anything but liquid. You understand?'

I felt inclined to burst with laughter, only I was so weak, and I remembered that my amusement arose from poor Amy's having been buggered.

'But, colonel, what could have brought it on now?'

'Lavie says shock, only shock.'

My goodness! I had noticed the peculiarity in the colonel before, viz., a determination not to see, or want of power, perhaps, to see, things as they were. He knew as well as, perhaps better than, I did, how addicted Afghans are to sodomy. Another man would have at once suspected this relaxation of the sphincter in poor Amy to be due to her having been buggered, but, like the ostrich, the colonel buried his head in the sand of obstinacy, and refused to see what was apparent. He did not wish to think a daughter of his could be buggered, therefore she had not been buggered. That is all.

Lavie, too, questioned me very closely as to what I saw the Afghan do when I caught him with Amy.

'Now, Lavie,' said I, 'I don't know what you expect to hear, but let me tell you this, the light in her room was very dim, I could not see very well. The moment I saw him, he seemed to see me, and we were hard at it trying to kill one another immediately!'

'You could tell me more, Devereaux, I am certain. I see I must tell you what I fear happened. Poor Amy has the sphincter of her – her – anus ruptured – at least, I say it is ruptured. Jardine says it is only unnaturally distended. If it is ruptured, an operation will be necessary. If Jardine is right none may be wanted. I should feel myself on safe ground if I knew for a certainty that she was buggered, for then the state of her anus would be explained. The colonel says, however, that as a child Amy always had a weak sphincter; even so, some violence must have brought it on so badly again.'

'Lavie, you are a gentleman, and I can trust you, but don't let it go any further, don't even tell Jardine, for it may be one of the unhappiest things that can happen to poor Amy to have the truth known. She was buggered and completely buggered too! The blasted Afghan's prick was buried in her arse as deep as his balls and he roared at me that he had buggered her and would bugger me too!'

'I thought so,' said Lavie, gravely. 'I knew I was right. I am certain it is rupture and not abnormal distention of the sphincter. But I am afraid, Devereaux, that the mischief has been done. Nobody, of course, knows for certain, but everybody in the whole camp believes that Amy was buggered, and the men are ready to kill every Afghan that comes in. Most unfortunately, the lessons you have been giving to the girls come in so handy for a joke, too. It was young Crean who started it when Jardine said he was not sure but that Amy had been buggered. Says Crean, "Then she is BA, Buggered Amy! Oh! ho! Now we can chaff Devereaux and congratulate him on one of his pupils having taken her degree." '

When I was well enough an official enquiry was held and, briefly, these were the facts which were elicited.

The soldiers were, on arrival at Cherat, warned that if they ever went shooting on the mountainsides, they must always be in parties of five or six. If fewer in number, they might be attacked; if greater, it might alarm the natives. But the whores had deserted, and the only fucking the men could get as such was at the danger of their own lives and those of the obliging women they could from time to time find herding goats and cattle. It appeared that two parties of six men each, making a total of twelve, met accidentally at a lonely place in the glen, in which were two fine young Afghan lassies in charge of some cattle. The offer of a rupee from each man made the maidens joyful and they willingly earned twelve rupees each, for each man had each girl turn about. The girls returned delighted to their village and the Tommies came back to camp much relieved.

The promise had been given of more rupees for more fucking, but alas, the promise never could be fulfilled. Somehow or other the tribesmen found it out. The inevitable consequence for the poor unfortunate girls was that their noses had been cut off and, thus mutilated, they had been paraded before the assembled men, women and children; then they had been slowly burned to death. Moreover – these poor girls having been considered to have been virgins – a desperate vengeance was to be taken on the English at Cherat. It was a pity that Mrs Selwyn should have engaged her *ayah* at Peshawar, where she had gone to meet her husband on his return from the war. This *ayah* had Afghan blood in her veins and Mrs Selwyn made a mortal enemy of her by boxing her ears for some impertinence or slackness of duty.

This happened just about the time when the irate tribesmen were looking out for English virgins to rape. Fanny, Amy and Mabel were the only fuckable girls in Cherat, and the *ayah,* knowing what was happening, plotted with the tribesmen to give these poor innocents into their hands at the first opportunity. When Colonel Selwyn went to inspect the whores, the consequences were what I have endeavoured to narrate. It goes without saying that the *ayah* disappeared and was never heard of again. But for the fortunate circumstance of my having that extreme feeling of uneasiness, all three girls would certainly have been raped, buggered and perhaps killed too; as it was, only poor Amy was buggered.

It is curious how events hang one upon another. The flight of the *ayah* necessitated the hiring of another, and Mrs Selwyn engaged, on the recommendation of a lady of Peshawar, a woman whom I felt certain she never would have entertained had she seen her first, for Sugdaya was the most lovely native woman I ever saw. Mrs Selwyn knew that owing to her own weak health and consequent inability to give the colonel those satisfying nights of really succulent fucking which keep married men chaste and quiet, a man of his passionate temperament must feel desire at times press him immensely. To admit so tempting a piece of flesh as Sugdaya into her house was therefore rash to a degree, but once done it was impossible to undo. Sugdaya was modest in demeanour and assiduously avoided the colonel, devoting herself to her duty to Mrs Selwyn and the Misses *baba* [term of affectionate respect for the children of the family], and in fact becoming Mrs Selwyn's right hand.

3

Captain Devereaux Bows to the Inevitable

At last came the longed-for orders. We were to start to march in December to Rawalpindi, there take the train – the line having been opened as far as that now – and then proceed to one of the nicest stations in Bengal – Fackabad.

If I had time I should like to describe this march in detail, for marching in India is truly delightful, but I can only tell of two incidents of which the first affected relations between Colonel Selwyn and myself, and the second raised me to heaven only to plunge me down into hell. Let me explain.

The first night of the march we encamped at Shakkote at the foot of the hill. Lavie and I, who were inseparable, went for a stroll and did not get back to camp until after dark. Going to my tent I met Soubratie outside who made me a mysterious sign and told me in a whisper that the colonel sahib was asleep on my bed.

Out of curiosity and wondering why he should have chosen my bed instead of his own, I gently and in spite of Soubratie went and peeped. My camp lantern was dimly burning, turned down as low as possible where it stood on the ground, but there was light enough for me to see that a man was on my bed between the thighs of a woman and fucking her deliciously. I could not see their faces, but I could see their bottoms and such an enormous pair of balls hanging and quite hiding any part of the cunt which might otherwise, perhaps, have been seen when the prick to which they belonged was drawn out of it as far as could be before the next home thrust, that had not Soubratie told me it was the colonel, I should have guessed it was he. I could not resist it. I went straight in as though I had expected nothing. The poor colonel looked up, blurted something, and I roared with laughter!

'I really beg your pardon, colonel! I did not know you were here! Never mind, I won't say a word and I won't disturb you.' And before he could say anything I left the tent.

By and by out he came. I made as if I didn't wish to see him, but taking me by the arm he said, 'Devereaux, Devereaux, I must offer you a thousand apologies! For God's sake don't tell anybody! My dear boy, if your wife were as delicate as mine, you would understand how impossible I find it to go without a woman. Don't betray me, Devereaux! Don't! It would kill Mrs Selwyn! I can't help it but she would not understand. Oh! boy, speak!'

'Of course I won't tell, colonel. But why on earth do you look at Mrs Soubratie when you have such a lovely *ayah* in Sugdaya?'

'Because, my boy, take my advice, if you ever fuck a woman who is not your wife, don't let her be one of your own household. Now! if you would like to fuck Sugdaya yourself, you are welcome. Would you?'

'My dear colonel, I am really very greatly obliged, very greatly indeed, but I think I lost too much blood up the hill there to feel the want of a woman again before my wife joins me.'

'Well! If you do – you know – Sugdaya or any other – remember,' said the colonel.

I am sure he did not intend to include Fanny or Amy in the 'any other'.

On the third day of our march we arrived at Nowshera. How my heart beat at seeing the familiar dak bungalow, once the very temple of Venus, in which I had officiated as her high priest, and had offered so many sacrifices to her with joy and thanksgiving in her favoured shrine between the fair Lizzie Wilson's voluptuous and beautiful thighs. I was tired with the march – not that the distance we had taken was at all excessive but I had not yet recovered my strength after the tremendous blood-letting at Cherat. Lavie had marched with me. The colonel and his family, attended by Jardine, had gone ahead, and sat on the very verandah where the struggle between Lizzie and Searle had taken place. They looked at us as we marched by with the regiment to the camp ground behind the bungalow, between it and the Kabul river. Amy and Mrs Selwyn had each been brought in a *dhoolie* or palanquin, and Jardine and the colonel kept Fanny company.

In the evening after I had strolled to the banks of the river, from visiting which I had been withheld on my first stay by the superior attractions of Lizzie's delightful cunt,

I got back to my tent where I found Soubratie mounting guard again, and he told me with a grin that the colonel sahib was there speaking to his woman in master's tent. I went and peeped in very quietly and had the felicity of see-ing the colonel without his coat or trousers on, lying beside Mrs Soubratie, whose fine, fat brown cunt he was manip-ulating with his hand while she was grasping those balls so remarkable for their colossal size. Evidently the interested pair were making ready for a second assault and soon I saw this accomplished. The colonel, evidently, enjoyed himself very much and judging from the little feminine ripple of laughter which from time to time issued from Mrs Soubratie, she likewise profited by the nice titillation which her admirer's very full-sized prick was occasioning her. Soon came the vigorous short digs and then the final hard squeeze home, which told me in eloquent silence that the colonel was inundating the shrine with the oil of his man-hood; then, withdrawing his prick from its hot retreat, he lay down panting for a few minutes and after a little while got up and commenced dressing his nether limbs. Had I seen this good performance some weeks earlier before I had been so disabled by my wounds I should have been driven nearly frantic and have had my own prick in such a state of alarming stiffness and fury, that I should probably have waited to see the colonel safe out of the tent, and then gone in myself and in spite of Mrs Soubratie's big hands, which always spoiled any idea of fucking her that came into my mind at Cherat, where I had at the time no other available cunt, I should have gone in and had a round or two with her then and there, and worked off the extra effervescence of my feelings. But now! Oh! It was sickening to me! Not a stir came in my prick. Not a ghost of a stand. Not even a ripple.

But ah! during the next day, during the next evening, a delightful and most cheerful change in this respect came over me! If any medical man should happen to read this exact narrative of my feelings and history he may be able to account for it, but I cannot, at least I cannot give scientific reasons, which no doubt he can and will to any enquiring soul. Well, the next morning I got a nice little note from Fanny:

Dear Captain Devereaux – Mama wants to know why you are making yourself such a stranger. We have caught hardly even a glimpse of you for a long time now. Will you come and dine with us tonight? It will be an early dinner, at six, because we have to get up early tomorrow morning for the march. Do come!
    Yours always affectionately,
    Fanny Selwyn

I sent back a little note accepting, feeling a strange beating of my heart, for Fanny had grown much too dear to me and the reader knows why I did not cultivate her love more ardently than I did.

Meanwhile honest Jack Stone had been to see me and told me that the unfortunate Searle had died of cholera on his way to Bombay.

Stone was dreadfully anxious that I should not add fuel to the flames as regards reports about Mrs Searle and her establishment at Honeysuckle Lodge and the reason for this became apparent to me some years later, when I met him and a lady whom he introduced to me at Brighton as Mrs Stone. This lady's features struck me as being somehow familiar to me, and on racking my brains I remembered they were extremely like those of the naked lady in the photograph he had shown me on that eventful night when Searle had tried to ravish Lizzie Wilson. The gallant Jack had made Mrs Searle an honest woman again in the sight of the world, and had gained an equally honest right for himself to fuck her whenever he liked without having to pay five hundred rupees for that grand pleasure. She seemed a fine voluptuous creature with decidedly large, well-formed bubbies, and I dare say old Jack had many goloptious nights between her goloptious thighs, fucking her goloptious cunt, as he had expressed it.

It was not without still further heart stirrings that I found the Selwyns occupying my old room in the bungalow as their sitting room and using what had been Lizzie Wilson's room as a bedroom for the girls and children. The door which communicated between the two rooms was open, and there, as I sat beside Fanny at dinner, I saw the very bedstead on which I had so often fucked the beautiful Lizzie with rapture indescribable. As I looked at it and revolved past scenes in my mind, Fanny caught the direction of my eyes.

'That is my bed,' said she innocently.

'Is it?' I replied mechanically.

Oh! What had come over me that the sight of that bedstead did not make my prick rage? I am sure I was dull and stupid at dinner. The colonel, however, was in high glee and I knew why.

The poor man had at last outwitted his careful wife and obtained the much-longed-for fuckable cunt. So he was beaming and overflowing with anecdote. I let him talk and behaved as a respectful listener, only occasionally replying to some question Fanny put from time to time, hoping to bring on one of our old free and unconstrained conversations. The way she stuck to me all that evening touched me. Instead of being offended at my obstinate silence she came and sat next to me on the verandah, where I smoked cheroot after cheroot, listening to the colonel's continual chatter until at last Mrs Selwyn, with a warning that it was growing late, carried him off to bed, leaving me with Fanny alone.

'What is the matter with you, dear Captain Devereaux?' at last she said, laying her gentle little hand on mine. 'You have hardly spoken one word to me since you came. I am afraid the march is too much for you and you feel done up.'

'Well! Fanny, I do but I don't know that it is exactly the march. I can't quite tell you what it is, but I have never been myself since that fierce night of the Afghan.'

'Ah! Mama says she is sure that has something to do with you being so gloomy. Why should you be? If I had killed an Afghan under such circumstances I should be so proud there would be no holding me.'

'Ah! Fanny dear, before that night I was a man. I had power, force, strength, but ever since I have felt that I have none left – no power – do you understand?'

'Power? What do you mean by power?'

'That which makes a man acceptable to his wife, dear!'

'Oh!'

Did Fanny understand? I fancied she did; after a little silence she said, 'Do you know I had such a funny – such a nice dream about you last night! I dreamt it three times – but I am afraid – that is, I don't believe it can ever come true for all that.'

'What was it?'

'I dreamt that you came whilst I was asleep in that room and woke me just like the Afghan did – only more gently – you woke me in the same manner as he did and you asked me to let you warm yourself in my arms and you did plead so very earnestly that I said you might and then –'

'And then?' said I eagerly.

'Well! I don't quite know how to tell you! However, you got into bed and right on to me and folded me to you so tight – Oh! so tight! and – I don't know what you did exactly – but Oh! – it was so delightful and you were so happy – but I awoke – all of a sudden – and you were not there. I positively cried for – Oh, Captain Devereaux – you know we all love you!'

If this was not straight talk I don't know what it was but the effect on me was magical. In a moment my weakness seemed to leave me and my long dead and useless prick sprang up in all pristine might and stood as it had stood for Lizzie Wilson. The whole atmosphere seemed redolent of fucking; desire as strong as ever assailed me. Fanny's bosom, I could see, was rising and falling rapidly. It seemed to me that she was then and there offering herself to me if

I would but have her. Her hand tightened on mine and I gently drew it forward intending to lay it on my now rigid prick and to show her that I understood and was quite ready if she was so willing. A standing prick, dear reader, has no conscience! All my fine resolutions not to take advantage of Fanny had flown to the four winds of heaven! I could remember nothing but the sweet vision I had had of her dear little cunt, spoiled as its beauty was by the unclean blood of the menses but tempting all the same. Whether she actually felt my prick or not I did not then know for at that moment Mabel came quickly out of the bedroom and said, 'Fanny, mama says you must not stay up any longer and that you are to come to bed.'

Without even saying good-night but with a firm squeeze of her hand on mine Fanny jumped up and ran.

Excited as I was with the tumult of joy and passionate desire in my heart and the stream of luxurious wine, I jumped up too and, taking Mabel round the waist, I kissed her again and again, pressing her two nice young little bubbies as I did so to her vast delight.

'What a regular woman you are growing, Mabel! What a fine bosom you have! What perfect little bubbies! I suppose you have plenty of hair here,' and I slipped my hand down to her motte and pressed my itching finger between the thighs to her little cunt.

'Oh! Captain Devereaux!' she exclaimed in a low tone. 'You bad naughty man!' but she made no defence; I sat down and pulled her to my knee and had my hand under her petticoats like a shot and my finger buried in her little warm and virgin cunt before she knew what I was up to!

'Mabel! Mabel! You are a woman!' I exclaimed, quite beside myself with excitement. 'Don't you think you want a husband?'

'Yes,' she whispered, hotly returning my burning kisses. 'I often feel I should like a man.'

God only knows what I should have done, but I think I might say that Mabel's maidenhead would have been done for there and then had it not been for Fanny's voice ringing angrily out of the room, 'Mabel. Come to bed!'

With a last feel of the sweet little cunt which alas! I had not had time to make spend and with a last kiss, fully returned by the gratified girl who at only twelve was precocious indeed, I let Mabel go, whispering to her 'not to tell' and rejoicing over my fully regained power and 'standing'. I went home to my tent and quickly undressed and viewed with delight that fine stalwart Johnnie who had so often stood to me so well in my encounters with the lovely foe.

I had ravishing dreams. I fucked I don't know how many of my former lady loves but neither Fanny nor Amy came in for their share. In the morning I woke and found not only my dear old prick to my joy and delight standing as full as in days of yore but also unmistakable signs of a most prolific wet dream – a sure sign that my balls had recovered their power of secreting the essence of man.

As I went to fall in with my company I met the regimental postman who handed me a letter which I saw at a glance was from my beloved Louie. I had a conviction that there would be bad news in it. Bad news! Oh! what had I become when I deemed it bad news to hear that she was starting by the next mail to come to join me in India! And further that she had waited until now to announce that we had another baby to expect – the fruits of our too prolific fucking – about March next. She had not been sure and did not like to mention it until she was certain; the usual signs did not show themselves; but now she was certain that a baby was really in existence and had run nearly six months of its natural life! Then – if she did come – and Louie was a woman of her word – I should have before me a time when I should not have that intense pleasure in fucking her which I had when her womb was free from lading.

She said from my letters my spirits seemed increasingly low, that she was getting more and more alarmed and that *conte que conte* she would come and join me; she did not know where but she would find out in Bombay on landing. Next mail here! she must be in the Red Sea now! Or perhaps in the Indian Ocean and she would get to Fackabad almost as soon as we would! Oh! Fanny! Fanny! How could I have you now? Gods! To think that the day had come when I did not want the woman who at one time had persuaded my soul and my senses that I should never care for another; the woman whose darling cunt alone made my prick stand and had taken the shine out of all others! I was, I tell you, dear readers, torn with contending emotions. It was too late to stop Louie. She was as surely on her way as I had felt Mabel's dear little cunt! I should never fuck it now! No! nor Fanny's either. And just as I had at last made up my mind that I could no longer, without dishonour to myself or either of these charming girls, stay the craving which we all three felt.

No wonder Lavie who soon joined me on the dusty road found me glum and cast down.

'Look here, Devereaux!' said he. 'I know well what it is. You are just killing yourself with the foolish fancy that your prick will never stand again! Now listen to me! Be wise and give up such absurd ideas! You will find the old gentleman lift himself up again some day soon if you will leave him alone and let him wear off his sulks; but if your mind dwells on it you may render yourself permanently impotent, for the mind has great power over the senses. I'll just tell you a little story of myself as an illustration. It happened at Woolwich three years ago; I had been on duty at the Herbert Hospital and a brother officer came walking home with me in the evening, a fellow I was very fond of. It was about nine o'clock and on passing the artillery barracks I saw a very nice-looking girl, evidently a poll, standing on the pavement. I wished her good-night and asked her if she was expecting anybody. "Yes dear," she said, "I was expecting you."

' "Oh!" said I, "then come along and I'll go home with you. Where do you live?"

' "In Wood Street," said she.

' "That is not your street, Lavie," said my friend, "and it is mine, so you had better let me see the young lady home and go to your lodging yourself."

' "Not I," I replied laughing. "I want a poke and I am going to fuck this girl – am I not, my dear?"

' "Of course," said she, "you asked me first and I'll come with you but if your friend likes I'll go to him or he can come to me when you are done."

' "Buttered buns!" said my friend laughing. "No, thank you. Tomorrow night, however, if you will meet me at the road to the cemetery at eight I will take you home and we will have it out then."

' "All right," said she.

'Well, we walked on and soon were at Wood Street and, just as the girl turned in at her gate and I was following her, my friend called out to her, "You had far better have come with me for Lavie is good for nothing and you'll get no change out of his balls tonight." The girl laughed and so did I.

'Well, we went upstairs to her bedroom and undressed and she was as fine and nicely made a little poll as you ever saw: good bubbies, nice skin, good arms and legs, and a fine black bush hiding a soft fat little cunt! But by Jove! I could not get a stand! The words of my friend kept ringing in my ears and I kept thinking to myself my God! fancy if it comes true! – and true it did come, simply because I doubted my own power. The poor girl was very much put about. Everything she could think of was tried – but in vain – to make my brute of a prick stand. I wanted to pay her and leave her, for I was miserable, but she like a little darling would not let me go. "You try and sleep," said she, "I won't touch you any more and I dare say your prick will be all right by morning and we can fuck then." I thought I never would sleep but at last I dozed off and, I suppose in an hour's time, woke up and found I had a glorious stand. The girl was fast asleep with her back towards me. Without wakening her I got one of my legs between hers, working myself round and along her until I had the right direction, and when she woke I had my prick buried in her cunt up to my balls. Well, she would not have it that way but insisted on my doing Adam and Eve and I never enjoyed a night's fucking more. I had her seven or eight times and when I went away after she had given me some breakfast she asked me if she had not done right to not let me go? She said she knew it was only nervous depression and the effect of fancy and that she had more than once had experience with it and so was not surprised when she was disappointed. So you see, Devereaux, how I, who had no such cause as you have to be weak, lost my power from simple imagination. Don't you indulge in fears any more.'

I thanked Lavie heartily for his sympathy and then told him how I had quite unexpectedly recovered; how I had had a wet dream and how delighted I had been. He was glad to hear what I had told him as he had begun to get alarmed for me but he evidently was curious to know why I was so very despondent. So I told him it arose from my having received a letter from my wife announcing her speedy arrival in India with a six months' baby in her belly and I said I was alarmed for her safety. Lavie was quite taken in and the rest of our conversation turned on the folly of pregnant women undertaking long and tedious journeys; the terrors of the hot weather; infant mortality in India and so forth, but my mind lamented the lost chance of dear Fanny's cunt just as it seemed so well within my reach.

On arrival at Akhtora I went direct to the Selwyn tent and found Mrs Selwyn and the colonel sitting in the shade of it, for the sun was burning hot although the air was so cool, it being in the middle of the delicious cool weather of northern India. Fanny who was sitting by her mother's side blushed. Oh! she blushed a beet-red blush which fortunately her mother did not see. Mabel standing in the tent door leaning against the door-pole grinned at me and turned red too for a moment and knowing that she had a dark background she gave me a perfect contour of her rising bosom, swelling out her fine little bubbies as much as she could and showing her legs too by occasionally putting her foot up against the opposite door-pole as high as she could reach. She had extremely good legs and very pretty feet and ankles. Jardine and Amy were sitting at the far corner of the tent. The colonel soon went off to see the camp and I then told Mrs Selwyn about Louie's letter.

Both she and Fanny called out in surprise at the sudden determination Louie had taken and looked at one another. Poor Fanny turned as white as death. So white that I thought she was going to faint. Mrs Selwyn saw it but fortunately did not put it down to the real cause.

'Fanny! Fanny! God bless the child! Did you ever see a mortal turn so white in a second?'

Fanny's faintness, however, only lasted a second. With that wonderful determination which I afterwards found to be so strong a feature of her character, she pulled herself together again and said it was nothing.

'Nothing!' exclaimed her mother. 'I'll tell you what it is, you are overdoing yourself. This march and the long rides are wearing you out. You must ride in the *dhoolie* like Amy and me.'

'Oh! Mother!' cried Fanny. 'I assure you it is really nothing! I really am as strong as a horse and quite fit to bear –' but here she paused as if seeking for a word.

'A husband and get children!' cried the impudent Mabel.

'Mabel!' cried Mrs Selwyn, 'how dare you! How dare you say such things and before Captain Devereaux, too! Go into the tent, miss, and don't presume to come out until I let you! I'll give you a whipping, miss! Go in I tell you!'

Mabel looked at me and as she turned to obey, laughing, acted as though she had a baby in her arms which she was giving suck to. Her mother did not see it but I did and was amused as well as a little, a very little, shocked, of course.

'It is all this horrible India!' cried Mrs Selwyn to me. 'Fanny, dear, is not that your papa coming back? Get up and see, that's a dear girl.'

'Yes,' continued Mrs Selwyn, 'it is wonderful how precocious children become in India, both in mind and body. Now look at that naughty Mabel. She is not much more than twelve years old and as you see I still keep her in short frocks to let her remember that she is not grown up yet. But, dear Captain Devereaux, I can tell you that Mabel is grown up and could marry tomorrow and get children as fast as could be. You would be surprised if you were to see her in her bath. Of course, you are a married man so I can speak to you about such things; if you were a bachelor I could not. So I can tell you that Mabel has breasts like a woman, thighs like a woman and hair – hem! ahem! what was I saying? Oh! yes, she is fully developed.'

I could hardly help laughing at the slip she had so nearly made when she mentioned 'hair', but I refrained for the thought of hair around that pretty little cunt, which I had now both seen and felt, entered my mind and I sighed to think that probably my prick would never gain entrance there, nor indeed, to that darling one for which my whole body craved, that between lovely Fanny's thighs.

'Well, Mrs Selwyn,' I said, 'the only thing for it is to do as I say. Try and not notice anything which is not too openly said and done in the way of sexual precociousness and try to lead the youthful mind into another channel. I promise you I will try and do my best to second you.'

'Ah! my dear, Captain Devereaux, how kind you are!' And the good lady let some tears run down her cheeks. Positively I felt an awful beast. For I had not at all intended to lead the girls themselves into any other channel than that which would the most speedily bring my prick slick into their charming cunts.

Oh! Lizzie Wilson! Lizzie Wilson! What a pity it was I ever had you. But for that I should have been overjoyed at my Louie's coming to me; but alas! Lizzie's delightful cunt had brought back all that old burning love of change which had made me a cunt-hunter before I was married.

I must leave my sympathising readers to realise the contending passions which tore me. There were now dancing before me two sweet, sweet cunts – Louie's and Fanny's; Mabel's did not count. I had the most intense desire to taste Fanny's. I felt so sure it would be superb to fuck the girl on account of her passionate temperament. I had the liveliest recollection of my Louie's and the more I recalled it to mind the more I loved the thought of it and the stiffer it made my prick to stand.

I had fully expected on arrival at Fackabad to have found Louie there or a letter announcing her arrival at Bombay, whereas what I did find was a letter written in the greatest despondency saying that upon application to the agents of the P & O she was told that there would be no room for her until the third steamer after the one she had intended coming by. Sure that she was coming, I behaved accordingly and kept as much out of Fanny's way as I could without being downright rude. Even Mrs Selwyn complained of my making myself such a stranger. The colonel did not mind because Mrs Soubratie satisfied his every want regularly, I having taken a bungalow just at the back of the Selwyns so making it very handy for the poor colonel when he felt cunt-hungry, which was very often. But Fanny was awfully offended with me. There was no deceiving her. She knew quite well what it meant and that I was simply sacrificing her happiness to the exigencies of the case. Yet at times, when I was unavoidably thrown into her society more closely than at others, I could not so well preserve the gravity of my demeanour as to prevent her seeing that I admired her and what a real pleasure it was for me to be with her. Once indeed she said to me, 'Captain Devereaux, once upon a time I thought you the wisest man I ever knew.'

'And what do you think me now, Miss Selwyn?'

'A fool!' said she with emphasis. Jumping up, she walked away with her head in the air and in the most disdainful manner.

After that I thought that the sooner Louie came the better. If once a woman despises a man it is a poor chance he has of ever having her.

But it seemed to me that there would never be a chance of poor Louie's coming. By some extraordinary error on somebody's part she missed the steamer and then came a catastrophe which caused a silence of two mails and indeed nearly ended her life. I think what I felt most was Fanny Selwyn's apparent nonchalance when she heard that Louie's life was in great danger. At one time she would have found it difficult to avoid expressing openly her joy at such a catastrophe, for if Louie died she would (she was sure of it) marry me, but now she coldly hoped that poor Mrs Devereaux might recover. The accident which so nearly put an end to poor Louie very nearly put an end to my offspring also. Our little baby girl, playing at the top of the stairs, very nearly tumbled down them. Louie who was watching her sprang to help her and in doing so tripped and not only fell but precipitated herself and the baby down the whole flight. Fortunately the child was not seriously injured but poor Louie, being in the family way, was terribly hurt. The result was a premature confinement and the delivery of a dead boy and a hovering between life and death for some weeks. My anxiety was fearful. Poor Mrs Selwyn did all she could to comfort me. All the family, even Mabel (who had developed into a very naughty girl, forever talking *double entente* since I had tickled her cunnie at Nowshera), showed their sympathy with me, except Fanny, who openly said that I did not deserve a good wife and so God was taking mine from me. I can tell you that there was much more hate than love between us at that time. Fortunately it was, however, only skin deep. Fanny and I were both deceiving ourselves. She imagined that she detested me as much as she had loved me before and I tried to think that after all she was by no means as desirable as I had at first thought and that if I had the chance now I would not fuck her.

So days and days rolled by. There was an assumed truce between us and things might have gone on so until Fanny and I should have been separated in the natural course of events – but all was in the hands of Venus who smiled at our puny efforts to guide our own course. The time for the sacrifice had arrived; the veil of Fanny's maidenhead was doomed to destruction and in the shrine of her virgin cunt was to be set up that prick which had once been the god of her ardent devotion. Yes, Fanny Selwyn with joy opened her thighs to me and I will now tell you how it all came about.

Fackabad is a large station. A European and a native regiment are always quartered there with a battery of artillery and a squadron of native cavalry; there were plenty of civilians too so that we had some very good society in the place. In this way it was very different from Cherat where there were no civilians and only our regiment and the details of others. At Fackabad we had a judge, a deputy commissioner, a civil doctor, a civil engineer and a number of other civilians, besides a Roman Catholic priest, a Church of England padre and a Presbyterian minister. In addition to these male exhorters, who lived pure and simple and blameless lives, we had a number of very charming youthful ladies known as the Zenana Mission, one of the fair female missionaries being so beautifully furnished with charms both of face and person that she raised desire far more carnal than spiritual in the minds of those mundane inhabitants of the cantonment who like myself worshipped the Creator in his creatures.

Lawn tennis, polo and cricket occupied the quiet ones and all were attractive pursuits on the beautiful evenings when the cool shade made exercise delightful and even necessary, for it can be very cool from the end of November to the beginning of March in the northern part of India; we soldiers had plenty of parades, with drills both morning and evening, except on Thursdays and Sundays, days always devoted to rest and ease in that country. If we had been idle at Cherat we made up for it now at Fackabad and there were not a few who welcomed the coming hot weather – hot winds, hot nights, hot days – for the sake of the nominal parades and the minimum amount of work, for man is by nature an idle animal when his pleasures are not concerned.

Hence my patient readers can readily understand that as the houses of the cantonment spread over a very considerable space and our work lay in very different directions, I really saw very little of my once constant companions. We saw one another at mess in the evenings and would say a few words to one another but I was never much addicted to staying longer than to smoke a cigarette after dinner; I was only too glad to go home and to take off my uniform and, clad in loose clothes, to sit in my long armchair and smoke and read at my ease rather than stay late after mess. Besides I was sore at heart. I was in great anxiety about poor Louie after her accident and I could not but recognise that so far as Fanny Selwyn was concerned the course of true love not only did not run at all smooth but that to all appearances the frail bark in which I had sailed down that current had got stranded if not altogether wrecked. I felt defeated and defeated through my own fears and I felt somewhat degraded in her eyes – in the eyes of a girl who had almost invited me to fuck her. I felt that she despised me and my want of that courage which is so valued by the girl full of desire and passion. But instead of trying to regain my lost footing in her esteem I had quite come to the conclusion that I must give up all idea of Fanny, that the enterprise I was once so naturally embarked upon had been providentially nipped in the bud and that to endeavour again to embark upon it would be to tempt providence to pour down the vials of its wrath upon my foolish head; but I was unhappy all the same; I did not like it.

Venus, behind her ambrosial clouds, naked, loving, beautiful, smiled as she read my heart.

I might have kept up my acquaintance more vigorously with the Selwyns but for Mabel. That little girl, ever since I had tickled her cunnie at Nowshera, evidently looked forward to being fucked by me very soon and she was more than daring whenever I visited her family. She plagued me beyond bearing. Her delight was, by word, look or gesture, to make my prick stand, no matter whether her mother was standing beside us, and my embarrassment was simply enormous. Pretending to consider herself a mere child, she would in spite of her mother's too feeble chidings seat herself on my lap and hiding her hand under her feel for and clutch my infernal fool of a prick, which would stand furiously for her though I wished it cut off at such moments. If I happened to be spending an evening at her father's house and to be engaged in a game of chess with one of the two girls, Mabel would find an opportunity to slip unnoticed under the table, crawl to my knees and with her nimble fingers unbutton my trousers and, putting in her little exciting hand, take possession of all she found there. I should have laughed at it only I was terrified lest this very forward play might be discovered. I had to sit tight up against the table and do my best to seem unconcerned whilst Mabel's moving hand was precious nearly making me spend! – a catastrophe I am thankful to say she never quite succeeded in bringing about. I took every chance to beg and implore her to be more careful of herself and me but her reply would be to toss up her short frocks and treat me to a complete exposure of her lovely thighs, downy motte and sweet young cunt, which she would insist on my feeling and which I was too weak to resist doing. It was the torture of Tantalus I was called upon to endure and the consequence was as much absence as I could keep from the colonel's house and the feeling on Fanny's side that my object was to avoid her. I could not tell Fanny the truth for she would have been madder than ever to hear that I had felt Mabel's cunt for the first time immediately after she had told me of the wonderful and delicious dream she had had of my fucking her at Nowshera.

The month of March had arrived; the sun was daily gaining power which before the end of the month would be tremendous. This is the season when fruit is most abundant in northern India and I daily feasted on figs, peaches, grapes and even strawberries. The letters I had lately received had been of a more cheerful character and you know what it is to be relieved of such killing anxieties.

One morning at the beginning of March I came home from parade and whilst I was drinking my tea and eating my *chotah-hazry* of fruit and bread and butter the postman came and handed me a letter addressed to me by the darling Louie herself. It brought a joy not to be expressed in words. Ah! but if every cloud has its silver lining so does every rose have its thorn. For though her doctor assured her that no permanent injury had been done to her he had told her that on no account must she go to a hot climate and on doubly no account was she to sleep with her husband if he came home for, though so sweetly, so gloriously, so entrancingly genial, fucking was the last thing she should do for at least two long years to come! Else he would not be responsible for her complete cure and immunity from danger. He even warned her that fucking might result, if too soon indulged in, in pain and anything but pleasure, and he said that as I was 'providentially' in India it was well to allow me to remain where I was out of the way of doing her any harm.

Poor Louie. She told me that the tears were rolling down her cheeks as she wrote the sentence of the banishment of my prick from her longing – really longing – cunt.

'It is only for a short season, though two years seems a long time to young people like us, my beloved darling husband Charlie! Still just fancy what grief and utter desolation would be ours if our coming together too soon resulted in what the doctor threatens – the complete death of all that lovely love which made our marriage-bed so supremely delightful to both of us! Oh! I love my Charlie and I desire the staff of his manhood – that splendid "prick" as you have taught me to call it – too much, too well, to like to think of endangering all the happiness and delight I can give him and all the rapture and heaven he can give me. No! I will stay at home and be a nun and who can tell but that when the time comes I may not be, as it were, a new bride for my darling husband to enjoy, without that fearful shyness which to some degree marred the joy I experienced when he first entered the virgin territory of which he and he alone is Lord and Master!'

I was joyful. I was so full of the thought of my Louie that the thought never struck me that part of my joy might arise from the fact that she could no longer stand in my path towards a certain delightful little cunt. That cunt was between Fanny Selwyn's thighs. I say I did not think consciously of Fanny but as my story will now tell I had no Louie to raise a warning finger and say, 'Not into that cunt but into mine only must your prick glide, Charlie!'

I saw Lavie come down the verandah towards me.

'Ah! Lavie, good-morning! How are you old chap? Sit down!'

'No, thank you, Devereaux,' said he with a half-sigh.

'Why what is the matter with you, Lavie? You sigh like a calf kicked away by its mother. Has Jumali or any other frail one given you the clap?'

For some minutes he remained as he was, then, slowly raising his head, he looked at me with the queerest expression and said, 'Devereaux, I can trust you. You swear you won't tell a soul if I tell you what it is?'

'Of course,' I replied wondering what on earth it could be.

'Well,' said he speaking extremely slow, 'I love Fanny Selwyn!'

'Good God!' cried I, roaring with laughter, 'is that all? But man alive! if you are in love it should make you frisky and not as gloomy as a sick cat!'

'Ah! but she does not love me,' he groaned.

'How do you know?'

'Oh! I know it only too well!'

'But, my dear fellow, can you tell me why you know it so well? Perhaps I may be able to give you some comfort if you will treat me as your mental physician and tell me the truth and nothing but the truth.'

Lavie groaned, leant his elbows on the table, hid his face in his hands and at last he said, evidently with an effort, 'Last Sunday evening she would not walk with me to church –'

I roared with laughter! It was so superb! A young lady does not walk to church with a gentleman who admires her and thereby proves that she does not love him!

Well I heard the whole of his story, which was that up at Cherat he had been very much struck with Fanny

Selwyn and in secret he had been fanning the spark of love within him which had at last burst into flame. He had indeed never shown Fanny any marked attention but as she never seemed to avoid him and always spoke kindly and politely to him he imagined she accepted his quiet way of showing his admiration and that in due course she would give him to understand that she quite understood and that she was quite ready to marry him. But on that unlucky Sunday evening he was sitting on his verandah without his coat on, expecting he would see Fanny and her sisters pass on their way to church and if he called out they would wait as they had done on previous occasions until he had got his coat on, for it was very hot and he did not wish to put that garment on a moment sooner than was absolutely necessary. But Oh! grief! dismay! horror! Fanny would not wait and not only did she not wait but when he hurried out after her he saw her and her sisters running – yes, actually running – away. It killed this poor heart! His hopes were violently dashed to the ground! There was nothing in life worth living for now it was plain that Fanny did not love him.

I listened with ever-increasing amazement. Hitherto I had looked upon Lavie as a particularly sensible fellow, but the story he told me and his reasoning were absolutely childish and proved him, when in love at all events, to be an egregious ass and fool. I, however, liked him a deal too much not to feel sorry for him and I set to work to comfort him and succeeded in doing so by telling him that, accepting his story as absolutely true, it only proved that Fanny Selwyn amused herself by giving him a chase after her. I admitted that she was a fine enough girl for any man to take some little trouble in trying to run after and I wondered that she had not been snapped up – young as she was, not quite seventeen – a year ago.

But do what I would I could not screw Lavie's courage up to going at once to see her (she lived only just across the road within seventy yards of my bungalow), declare himself and find out what her real feelings were towards him. He flunked it. I told him in vain that faint heart never yet won fair lady. All I could persuade him to do was to go and see Colonel and Mrs Selwyn and see whether they would countenance his suit. To this at last he assented and went off leaving me more than astonished at his pusillanimity. For Lavie was a man of strong passions, an ardent fucker; he had a reputation with Jumali and her companions of being one of the very best pokes in all Fackabad and I should have thought that where his prick led the heart his courage would have followed. For it was evident to me that he was much more cunt-struck with Fanny Selwyn than smitten with what we mean by the honourable term love.

Whilst I was still thinking over this astounding announcement of his and inwardly congratulating myself on my being free of any form of responsibility towards Fanny, he returned, his face wearing the appearance of satisfaction. He had seen the colonel and his wife and they had been very kind. They said they could not urge Fanny to marry him but they had no objection to his doing so himself. That their girls should choose for themselves and if Fanny chose to be his wife they would not say no. But when I asked him had he there and then asked to see Fanny he said he had not – another day would do! Gods alive! I did my best to make him go at once but it was of no use. He was satisfied to a certain degree and would live on what hopes he had extracted from the permission he had been granted. I said to myself that Fanny would not thank her papa and mama! Well! I knew Fanny better than he. None the less I hoped against hope that she would take him.

Why? Why? Ah! a smile comes; the more I looked back on the past, the more did I think it impossible that I could have even a chance in Fanny's heart. She had deliberately called me a fool. She had in a hundred little acid feminine ways shown me that she despised me and I believed that she would be more than delighted to say something sharply cutting if I ever showed that I sought her love once more. When a girl offers herself, take her, for she won't be likely to ask you again, my dear male friends! Moreover, although my faith in Lavie had been rudely shaken by his asinine ideas of conduct, I thought he would make Fanny a good husband. He was essentially a gentleman, he had a good profession at his back and I knew he would fuck her to her heart's content, and when a woman is well fucked she is always contented and happy.

I have known so many instances of girls marrying against their wills, going from the altar to the nuptial couch perfect victims, yet becoming quite happy women simply and solely because their husbands turned out to be first-class fuckers. This is absolute gospel and my gentle readers may believe it.

I was sitting reading Louie's delightful, loving, passionate letter for the fiftieth time, my prick standing deliciously all up my belly under the buttons of my trousers as it thought of the dear cunt it had so often fucked and spent in, when I was suddenly astonished at seeing Mrs Selwyn and Fanny walking into my room unannounced. It was very hot and I was surprised at seeing Mrs Selwyn, who was so delicate, expose herself too much to the sun.

'Oh Mrs Selwyn! What on earth has made you come over here in this blazing sun? If you wanted me why did you not send word for me? Here sit down under the punkah! Here is a chair! There now! Tell me what I can do for you and you know I will do it.'

Mrs Selwyn looked at Fanny and smiled. Fanny looked at me with the queerest expression of half-fun, half-earnestness in her glorious violet eyes. She looked extremely pretty. She had not lost any of the fresh colour she had brought down in her face from Cherat. Clad in a thin muslin dress, her bosom was that of a glorious nymph. Its two little mountains, evidently much grown since I had seen them bare and uncovered some months before, were swelling out in the most voluptuously tempting manner on either side. Her well-rounded and healthfully shaped thighs were equally well shown off by the soft folds of her dress and her lovely little feet and ankles, crossed in front of her, ended a fine pair of well-developed legs which I did not wonder Lavie would like to open and take his pleasure between. Fanny seemed to me altogether more beautiful this day than I had ever seen her before. But I looked upon her as never to be mine and so schooled was I in this thought that, much as I admired her, my prick grew none the stiffer and was standing simply and solely for the sweet cunt between my Louie's thighs, thousands of miles away.

'Now, Mrs Selwyn, please tell me to what I owe this unexpected and pleasant visit?'

Mrs Selwyn looked at Fanny and smiled. Fanny returned the look and did not smile; on the contrary, she looked rather put out.

'Well! Captain Devereaux, I, that is Fanny and I, have a crow to pluck with you. What made you send Dr Lavie on a wooing errand to my house?'

'I never sent him at all, Mrs Selwyn.'

'Then he told me an untruth for he certainly told Colonel Selwyn and me that you had sent him to ask permission to pay his addresses to Fanny.'

'Well,' I said, 'there is just this much truth in that assertion, Mrs Selwyn, and I will tell you just what took place between Lavie and me this morning. I was sitting on the verandah outside here when he came looking the picture of misery and woe. For some time he would not tell me what was the matter with him but he sat and held his head in his hands and sighed and groaned in the most dismal manner. At last he said that he loved Miss Selwyn.'

Both Mrs Selwyn and Fanny here burst out with merry laughter, Fanny's being sweet, silvery and hearty. There was no unkind ring to it but it was evident that she was greatly amused.

'Yes! and then!'

I said that was no reason to be so miserable and he said, 'But she wouldn't walk to church with me last Sunday evening.'

'The fool!' cried Fanny, again going off into another merry peal.

'That is what I thought, too. I had a long talk with him and asked him did Miss Selwyn know of his feelings towards her? He said he expected she did. I asked him had he spoken to her? He said no. Well, I said, if you have not done that yet you had better do so as soon as possible and not go imagining all kinds of things. But he seemed to be frightened at the idea. At last I suggested that at least he might see you, Mrs Selwyn, and the colonel and see if you approved of his proposal. The fact was I did not know what to do with him. He acted on my hint and went and apparently received a satisfactory reply for he seemed much relieved when he came back to me.'

For a moment or two neither of the two ladies spoke. Fanny looked at me half reproachfully; Mrs Selwyn was evidently cogitating something. My prick, no longer interested in Fanny's cunt and the current of its thoughts recalled from Louie's sweet secret charms, had begun to drop a bit and I waited to hear the next thing.

'Well! Neither Colonel Selwyn nor I would object to Dr Lavie. He is a nice fellow, a thorough gentleman, and no one could have been more attentive or kinder than he was to poor Amy when she was ill after the attack of those horrid Afghans at Cherat, but then both Colonel Selwyn and I think it only right and fair to let Fanny choose for herself. We cannot bring ourselves to advise her at all. Anybody may come forward as a suitor so long as he is a gentleman and has sufficient means to keep a wife, so far as we parents are concerned. So Fanny must speak for herself in this matter.'

I looked enquiringly at Fanny who coloured a little and then turned pale whilst the movements of her lovely breasts showed that some thoughts, perhaps not pleasant ones, were agitating her.

'All I can say at present,' said she speaking slowly and deliberately, 'is that I find he is not the man I can marry!' She laid some little stress on the word marry.

'Perhaps,' said I, 'when you consider Dr Lavie you may grow to think him eligible, Miss Fanny.'

'I don't think so,' said she, 'I like Dr Lavie well enough as a friend but I do not feel as though I could ever love him and I could never have a man unless I loved him.'

'Well, give him a chance,' said I. 'Hear what he has to say and perhaps when you examine him from the point of view he desires you may see more in him than you do now.'

'I suppose,' said she a little sharply, 'you would be delighted to see me take him, Captain Devereaux.'

'I would if I were sure you would be happy with him, Miss Selwyn, but not otherwise. Lavie is a great friend of mine and I know him to be a real good fellow. I think he is a little off his head just now but when I look at you I am not surprised. Is not Fanny looking really very pretty, Mrs Selwyn?'

Both mother and daughter looked as pleased as could be at this compliment, but it was not said merely to please for Fanny did really look uncommonly lovely and I had spoken the words quite unaffectedly and spontaneously.

'I have often wondered,' I continued, 'that Fanny has not been snapped up long ago! Such a pretty girl, a girl so nice, so desirable in every way, should by this time have had a great number of adorers and several offers of marriage. I cannot make out where the men's eyes are.'

'Oh, Fanny can tell you, if she likes,' responded the mother, 'that she has had two or three offers. There was one gentleman in particular who was very much in earnest – a Dr Jardine – who on the march down proposed to her.'

'Dr Jardine!' I exclaimed.

'Yes! He asked Fanny but she said no and then he asked the colonel and me to try to persuade her to take him but we told him we objected to such a course and if Fanny said no it meant no as far as we were concerned.'

'I am glad Fanny did not say yes,' I replied.

'Why?'

'Because Dr Jardine might be a clever doctor but he is a bad man and quite unsuitable for Fanny in every way. At least that is my opinion.'

'I think so too,' said Mrs Selwyn decisively. 'Still if Fanny had said yes we should not have declined though we might have been grieved she should wish for such a man as Dr Jardine.'

'What made you marry, Captain Devereaux?' suddenly cried Fanny.

'My dear child! What a question to ask!' exclaimed Mrs Selwyn.

'I married,' said I laughing, 'because I had at last found the girl I fancied; the girl, in fact, who seemed to me to be altogether superior to any I had seen in my life and the one I fell really and truly in love with.'

'And I suppose,' said Fanny, trying to seem cheerful, 'that you have never seen anyone since whom you would have married had you not met your wife first?'

The question was too plain to me and for the life of me I could not resist giving the answer which I knew she wanted but which the tone of her voice told me she did not expect.

'I can easily and truly answer your question, Miss Selwyn. It is true I am not easily pleased but I have seen one lady since I married whom I should have asked to marry me had I not already been married,' and my eyes told Fanny who that lady was.

The colour again mounted in profusion to her lovely face, her eyes glistened and shone with satisfaction; she looked at me from head to foot and her entire appearance told me, 'Had you asked me I would have said yes and the sooner the better!'

Poor Lavie. I saw now only too well that he was right and whomever it was that Fanny loved it was not him. A secret satisfaction filled my soul and a flood of voluptuous desire came over me as I again ran my eyes over Fanny's graceful form and charming appearance and my slumbering prick once more swelled and swelled until I thought it would burst the buttons and spring out to frighten the mother and daughter.

I saw Fanny and her mother halfway home and the way Fanny pressed the moist palm of her hand in mine sent a thrill through both of us and I could see that she had quite made up her mind to have me at the earliest opportunity. By God! How my balls and groins did ache all that day.

4

Forbidden Fruit

It was in the middle of March; the sun was simply blazing through the day; the crows and fowls, all birds in fact, went about in the shade with their beaks wide open and wings lifted from their bodies, so much did they feel the blasting heat at this time. I was seated in my long armchair dressed only in the thinnest of jerseys without sleeves and the lightest of pyjamas – in fact as naked as I could well be, for the clothes I had on hid only the colour of my skin and even that very imperfectly. The punkah slowly swinging from side to side poured down a breeze of cooling air upon me and wafted away the smoke of my cheroot. It was midday and frightfully hot; I could hear the leaves of the trees crackling under the sun's rays; suddenly to my intense astonishment Mrs Selwyn and Fanny rushed rather than walked into my room.

Mrs Selwyn seemed half demented; Fanny looked as if she had been crying and seemed fearfully annoyed. Both looked reproachfully at me. I jumped up, apologised for my state of dishabille (for I had not even slippers on and was in my bare feet) and got them chairs under the punkah. But before she attempted to sit down Mrs Selwyn cried, 'Captain Devereaux you must, you really must, insist on Dr Lavie ceasing to annoy us any more! He is killing me! He is mad! I am certain he is not right in his mind! He is killing Fanny too! Oh!' and down she flopped into her chair.

I looked at Fanny but said nothing. Mrs Selwyn then told me that Lavie had taken to calling at all hours, even at night when everyone had gone to bed, and that he moaned and raved and wept. That Colonel Selwyn had spoken to him kindly, harshly, every way; had ordered him never to come again and so forth; but it had no effect and they were at their wits' ends because they feared if they took any other – that is forcible – means to keep him out of the house it would only create a scandal and that people were dying with laughter over Lavie's miserable courtship as it was.

Whilst she was telling me this and I was wondering what I could do, in came Lavie, his eyes glaring, his face pale, his lips hard set. He went straight up to Mrs Selwyn and asked her to go into another room which I had and which was empty.

I begged him to sit down where he was but he smiled inanely at me and said he would not keep Mrs Selwyn two seconds and she weakly rose and followed him. Fanny drew her chair near mine and begged me to do what I could.

'Oh, dear, dear Captain Devereaux, do rid us of this monster!' was her cry. I took her hand and assured her that I would; that I had a plan and that was to get him sent to some other station. I knew the PMO very well indeed and I would represent the case to him. Poor Fanny was delighted. She gave me one of those looks which meant 'kiss me!' I hesitated a moment but at last I could resist no longer. Jumping up I seized the willing girl round the waist, lifted her to her feet, and pressing her to me, I kissed her red, red mouth over and over again.

'Oh, my darling Fanny!' I exclaimed in a low tone quivering with passion that communicated itself to her. 'How I do blame myself for having countenanced that idiot's making love to you!'

'Oh! Charlie, Charlie,' she cried pressing her swelling bosom to mine, letting me pull her to me until our bodies seemed to form one and not denying me the thigh I took between my own thighs nor the motte, the sweet delicious motte, against which I thrust myself. 'I know now that you love me as I love you! Oh! my darling darling! I forgive you! But oh! if it were not for that I would hate you.'

'And do you really and truly love me, Fanny? Oh my sweetest own girl. You must be all mine! Every bit of you, heart, soul, body, all!'

'Oh! I do I do!' cried the excited girl in an ecstasy of passion. 'Oh! can you not feel that I do?'

'With your heart, my own love?' and I pressed a delicious and firm round hard elastic bubbie in my hand.

'Yes! Yes!'

'On your soul?' and I glided a hand swiftly between her thighs and pressed the equally elastic and soft motte and delicious cunt with my fingers. For a moment Fanny drew her hips back but on my again pressing her motte and throbbing cunt with my hand, she closed her thighs on it, giving me such a kiss as I had never yet had from her. That was her answer. Gods! Gods! I took my hand away. I put my arms round her yielding waist. My prick, furious, mad, raging to get at her, made a perfect tent pole and stood out from my pyjamas. But for the pyjamas it would have risen at a bound to an angle much too acute with my body to have enabled me to do what I did, but the pyjamas held its head somewhat down and I pressed the mighty weapon against Fanny's quivering motte with all my force whilst I kissed her and felt her tumultuous bubbies, which she was pressing against my bosom as though she was trying to flatten them against it. Feeling my urgent thrusting and putting down her hand, she said, 'Oh! what is that pressing against me?'

'It is me, my darling,' I whispered, in a voice hardly audible or articulate from the excess of passionate emotions, 'it is me! There take me in your dear hand and take possession of the treasure which is yours henceforth and yours only.' (Poor Louie! Had she heard those words spoken in a moment of blinding passion . . . !)

'Oh! my darling, my darling!' exclaimed Fanny, absolutely beside herself with ecstasy. 'My darling, my darling!' and her little hand nervously and excitedly kept clasping my burning prick as if she hardly knew what to say or do but in delight inexpressible.

'Yes! Yes! Darling Fanny! This is for you. For it must be admitted to this abode! To the temple of love!' I again had my hand excitedly caressing her now maddened cunt, between thighs more than willingly opened to admit it!

Fanny could not stand this caressing. She let go of my prick and tried, clothed as she was to impale herself on it. It slipped beneath her motte. She felt it do so. She pulled up her dress a little and suddenly opening her thighs she closed them equally suddenly on my prick which felt just as though it had been in her cunt! Gods! Gods! I think I should have burst – only nature came to my relief and I poured forth a torrent of hot burning spend! This recalled me to my senses.

Gently pushing Fanny away, I begged her to seat herself whilst I went and changed into trousers. The intelligent and excited girl saw the necessity as she looked at me in the quite transparent pyjamas flooded with spend and extended in front by my enraged prick, whose colouring and shape were as clear as if seen in crystal water. But instead of sitting down she came and peeped at me from behind the purdah as I took off my pyjamas and fed her eyes on the galaxy I showed her with pleasure indescribable. She saw the mighty prick, its ponderous well-shaped balls and the forest out of which they grew. She knew that they were now all hers and as she gazed she tried to quiet the throbbing of her hot little cunt by putting her hand between her lovely thighs. But before I had finished putting these treasures away from sight some stir made her drop the purdah and flee to a chair and when I came out in shirt, trousers, socks and shoes she was seated in it. She looked for her new possessions and with burning eyes asked me where they had gone. For all answer I took her willing little hand and laid it on my prick which was buttoned back against my belly. Once more did the excited, 'My darling! my darling!' resound, but in whispered tones; then feeling frightened lest our disordered minds might betray themselves to Mrs Selwyn, who was still talking to Lavie but might at any moment come into our room, I got a book of views and opened it so as to look as if Fanny and I had been examining it during their absence.

'You made the wet come in me as well as yourself, my darling! my darling!' whispered Fanny.

'Did I? Well! my sweetest, next time such wet comes it must not be outside of us but inside you! Inside here! Do you understand?'

For an answer Fanny kissed me, whilst she pressed the hand I had slipped between those thighs which if ever opened for a man would first be opened to admit me!

Whilst thus engaged in deliciously feeling one another and talking the language not the less eloquent because it was dumb, Mrs Selwyn came almost staggering into the room. She was evidently overcome with emotion and was far too excited herself to notice any appearance of heat in either Fanny or myself. She managed to reach the chair to drop into it but for a moment or two could not speak a word. Fanny and I, both in alarm, were at her side at once and waited for Mrs Selwyn to speak.

'Oh! Captain Devereaux!' she whispered and then paused for breath for she was panting with agitation. 'Go in! go in to that – that – madman and for goodness' sake, for God's sake, I implore you to calm him and tell him he must not persecute me in this manner. He talks of cutting his throat if I do not give him Fanny!'

'I will settle him, Mrs Selwyn,' said I as quietly as I could. 'I will go in now. Fanny, look after your mother, there's a good creature,' and so saying I made her eyes speak volumes. They said to me, 'Get rid of Lavie and then we will fuck, my Charlie!'

I went into the next room and there I found the miserable lover who had that very morning been talking whilst I had been acting! That very morning! Why it was not yet five minutes since I had had my prick not in Fanny's darling little cunt indeed but between her thighs and had spent a perfect flood and had shown her my prick and balls naked and had had her hand caressing my prick and herself calling me 'darling' and telling me I had made her spend as she had made me! I must say I felt a considerable amount of contempt for Lavie and wondered where all that good sense had gone for which I had once given him so much credit. Poor devil! The fact was he was quite out of his mind and his lunacy had taken the form of a passion for Fanny Selwyn, but no one knew or suspected the facts at that time. No wonder it was no use my speaking to him or advising him to desist from following Fanny for a while at least. He moaned and groaned and wept and behaved in the most extraordinary manner. At last I persuaded him to go home, promising I would see him again the next day, but when he had gone and when I had ascertained that Fanny and Mrs Selwyn had gone too, I put on my helmet and went myself to Dr Bridges our PMO and put the whole case to him and begged him to get Lavie removed to some other station. Bridges hemmed and hawed at first but at last he said that he had noticed that Lavie was not doing his work as well as he used to and he would see him and come to a conclusion in a day or two. I had to be content with that; it was something.

That afternoon I got a little note from Fanny saying that mama had desired her to write and ask me to dine with them unless I had a prior engagement. That was the propriety part but in the corner written very small and hurriedly was, 'Do come, my darling!' I sent reply that I should have much pleasure in accepting the invitation and I went.

As I suspected it was for the sake of a council of war that I was wanted and I told Colonel and Mrs Selwyn that I had seen old Bridges and both thought it was an excellent move. The poor colonel was especially anxious to get rid of Lavie, for that fellow used to come in by whichever door of my bungalow happened to suit him at any time of the day he wanted to see me, and as he used to come some nine or ten times a day the colonel was twice nearly caught in one of my spare rooms fucking Mrs Soubratie and for a week or more he had been entirely without his accustomed greens as he never knew when Lavie might perhaps find him partaking of them between Mrs Soubratie's brown thighs. The colonel also naturally wanted to put an end to the courtship, which was ridiculous and scandalous, so he determined to see Bridges himself and insist on Lavie's being sent away.

After dinner we all walked up and down the fine avenue in the cool evening air, under a sky lit up by a myriad of lovely stars. We talked of nothing but Lavie until Mrs Selwyn, getting tired, took the colonel in, leaving Fanny, Amy, Mabel and me walking together. Amy got rid of Mabel and I would have been as glad as Fanny if we could equally have got rid of Amy too. Our conversation naturally turned on love and matrimony and Amy said, 'Well! I only hope nobody will ever ask me to marry them. I will surely say no!'

'Why?' said I laughing.

'Oh! Fancy going to bed with a man! I should die of shame!'

'Your mother goes to bed every night with your father, Amy, and she does not die of shame.'

'Oh, that's different!'

'I don't see it.'

'Well! anyhow I should die of shame. Would not you, Fanny?'

Fanny hesitated. She had hold of my hand and gently squeezing it she said, 'I think that would depend upon whether I loved the man or not.'

'Exactly,' said I. 'I know my wife was rather ashamed the first night I came to sleep with her but long before morning she laughed at her foolish fears!'

'Oh! Do tell us all about it!' cried Amy, who seemed to have an eagerness to know how such a change could come over my wife in such a short time.

'Well!' I said, 'I will tell you willingly but mind you if I do I shall have to touch on subjects it is not usual to speak of to young virgins.'

'Never mind,' said Amy, 'it is dark and you will not be able to see our blushes.'

I was delighted at the prospect of being able to inflame still more if possible the already highly raised passions of

Fanny, whose little hand trembled in mine, and I commenced, 'Well! I will not tell you all about the marriage ceremony because, I dare say, you are familiar with the open-daylight mysteries of marriage. It is of the secret side of matrimony, of the nuptial couch, of which I speak and I warn you once I begin I can't leave off. So if I say anything which sounds shocking you will have to hear it in silence. Do you care for me to go on?'

'Yes!' cried both girls and glancing at Amy I saw her press her hand for a moment between her thighs, for dark as it was it was not too dark for me to see that much. I was satisfied. It was evident that her little cunnie was tickling and I was determined that it should tickle her a good deal more before I was done. Not that I had any designs on Amy's cunt; I aimed at Fanny's rather.

'Well! my bride and I went to Brighton to spend the first night or so of our honeymoon. All the way in the train we had to appear calm, to speak to one another as naturally as could be, but I could see that Louie was not quite the same as she had been before that day. Had we been going to Brighton unmarried and not as we were, bride and bridegroom, I am sure she would have talked and laughed in a free and open manner whereas now some thought which I could easily guess at was oppressing her. That thought was of course that her whole life was going to change now that I had rights over her body which I had never had before and that surely in a very few hours' time I should be exercising them. She told me afterwards she had often longed for that time but now it had come she felt nervous.'

'No wonder,' said Amy again, pressing her cunnie with a trembling hand. I saw the movement quick as it was and made my prick more comfortable under the buttons of my trousers, an act which Fanny saw and which she responded to by a hard squeeze of my hand.

'Ah! no wonder! as you say Amy. And yet if our courtships were more natural and less conventional than they are, there would be none of this unnatural restraint. Why I loved my Louie as I had never loved a girl before. There was not a part of her I did not ardently desire to kiss, to devour! The very ground she stood on, the chairs she sat in, were all sacred to me! In fact, I loved her! I had fancied I loved others before but I now knew for the first time what love was. Ah! it is not all a matter of the heart alone but of the body also. I wonder if either of you two girls has any notion of what passion is? When all one's being is stirred up by the thought of the presence of the beloved, of the desired one! I suppose in fact I know that girls do experience much physical excitement when the passion comes on but in a man the change from quiescence to storm and fury is enormously marked. Yet in our cold way of making love, which is the conventional way, it would appear to be proper to forget all ideas of knowledge of difference of sex or even the meaning of marriage. A lover may speak of his mistress's beautiful face, her beautiful figure or her beautiful hips or her beautiful legs or thighs but never under any circumstances of that most exquisite and beautiful charm of charms which, made for him and for him alone, lies between those beautiful thighs.'

'Oh! Captain Devereaux! For shame!' cried out Amy.

'Do be quiet!' exclaimed Fanny. 'Captain Devereaux is quite right, Amy, and you know it.'

Amy laughed and seemed uneasy and remained silent.

'Well! I was thinking all the way down to Brighton of all those charming charms which were now mine and which I was literally burning to possess myself of, but ever and anon would come the thought how might I do it? How was I to dare to lay a hand on my Louie which must startle her modesty, however much her thoughts may have run on the consummation of our marriage? Such thoughts in her I considered not at all unlikely, for modest and virtuous as my Louie was I knew from her general demeanour that, although innocent, she could not be ignorant.

'Afterwards Louie told me that similar conflicts had been plaguing her. She longed for my marital embraces on the nuptial couch with great ardour but she dreaded the first steps. Oh! she longed to give herself to me she said but she feared that in so doing I might lose something of that valued respect for her which I had constantly shown. She feared to be immodest. How could she give me her naked charms without doing that which from her babyhood she had learnt to look upon as immodest to a degree? No wonder we felt an unnatural degree of restraint, a kind of fear of one another, for although when passion drives hard two lovers can be absolutely and unashamedly naked to one another, without such passion that nakedness which ought to be so glorious and so divine may be degraded to indecency and nastiness.'

'I cannot imagine it ever being anything else!' exclaimed Amy, vigorously caressing herself between her thighs. 'However –'

'Amy I wish to goodness you would be quiet and let Captain Devereaux tell his story!' cried Fanny petulantly. For some time she had been walking with her own hand constantly on her thrilling little cunt, quite indifferent whether I noticed it or not. I pretended not to do so, however.

'Well!' I resumed, 'at last we arrived at Brighton. Having eaten our dinner we tried to appear calm to one another. Louie ventured to sit on my knees with her arms round my neck but was careful not to press her bosom against mine. Having exhausted every available topic of conversation and, I admit, having behaved like a pair of fools, so terribly afraid were we of one another, I ventured to hint that it was time to go to bed. "Oh!" said Louie (hiding her hot and blushing face in my neck), "not yet, Charlie darling! It is not half-past ten! I never go to bed so early!" Then for the first time did I pluck up a little courage. I kissed her over her lips and I whispered, "This is our wedding night, my darling, darling Louie."

'She darted at me one quick little look, then cast down her eyes, gave me a kiss and whispered, "Well don't come up too soon, there's a good fellow. Oh! Charlie! I wish it was tomorrow!" then she jumped up and ran out of the room.

'Thus having ventured to hint at what was to follow on this our wedding night I felt inspired with some degree of courage and with courage came desire in floods far greater than I had yet experienced with Louie. I literally burned to have her! How long would it be before I might go up? There was a clock on the mantelpiece and it seemed to take an hour to mark one minute. At the end of ten minutes I could stand it no longer. I was in real pain – for you must know if passion means pleasure it means pain too until it is indulged.'

Here Fanny looked at me and pressed my hand. Ye gods! I wished Amy anywhere else but where she was. My voice trembled as I resumed.

'On going upstairs to our bedroom I saw Louie's pretty little boots outside the door. I hailed this as a good omen. I picked them up and kissed them and then, giving a little warning knock but without waiting to be told to come in, I turned the handle and entered. Louie was in her night-dress, just getting into bed. She gave a little cry, "Oh! you have come sooner than I expected!" and she huddled her-self under the clothes showing only the upper part of her face. Oh! once she was in bed I seemed to shake off my most unnatural cowardice. I closed the door and running over to her I turned the clothes off her face and neck and I put one arm round her shoulders and rained the most burning and ardent kisses on her sweet lips; at the same time I slipped my hand into her bosom and for the first time took possession of the two most beautiful globes which adorned it. Louie did not draw back. She in no way tried to prevent my caressing her there. I was more than tempted to let my hand stray much lower and to seek for the temple of love of which the closely barred door is to be found at the foot of the forested hill sacred to the god-dess of love!'

'Gracious!' cried Amy. 'Where and what is that?'

'As if you did not know, Amy!' exclaimed Fanny indig-nantly.

'You will soon hear, Amy,' said I. 'Well! I did not do so. Louie had both her arms around me and held me tight but I should have liked to have undone the front of her night-dress altogether and to have kissed the beautiful breasts I had found there, but poor Louie, who would have liked me to have done that too, was still a prey to the struggles of her dying modesty. At last I slipped my hand under her armpit and tickled her. With a loud shriek she let me go but she did not cover herself up any more. She lay looking at me with really longing eyes whilst I rapidly undressed. I put my watch on the table. I managed to get off my clothes and put on my nightshirt without offending modesty very much and I was just going round to the other side of the bed to get in when Louie told me I had not wound my watch and that she had not wound hers either. "Oh!" I cried, "let them run down, my Louie, never mind now!" "No!" said she, "Charlie darling, don't let us begin our mar-ried life by leaving undone anything which we ought to do." Oh bother! To please her I wound up both watches with a hand trembling with excitement and then jumped into bed.'

'Did you not blow out the candle?' asked Amy.

'Amy! if you interrupt any more,' cried Fanny angrily, 'I will ask Captain Devereaux not to let you know what happened next.'

'No, I did not blow out the candle, Amy, Louie said something about it but I pretended not to hear. I jumped into bed and put my arms around her and I hugged her to me. For just a moment she resisted a little stiffly but the next moment she yielded; she hid her face, which was all on fire, in my neck and whilst I kissed her frantically I put down my hand and gently drew up the veil which interposed itself between me and those glorious charms which could not much longer be kept from me or remain virgin. With as much delicacy as possible I passed my trembling hand over the smooth surface of her exquisite thighs until I reached the "bush with frizzled hair implicit", as Milton says.'

'Captain Devereaux!' shrieked Amy.

'And finding the sweet entrance to the temple I caressed it with an ardour which Louie could feel pouring in burning flames from my fingers. All she did or said was to hug me closer and murmur, "Oh! Charlie! Oh! Charlie." Finding her so quiet I –'

'What?' cried both girls in suffocating tones.

'I begged her to make place for me and let me worship her with my body as I had promised to do in my marriage vows. Gently she turned on her back and putting one knee first and then the other between hers I gently, but in the greatest excitement, lowered myself on to her beautiful body and then awoke every hidden source of pleasure and passion in her as I made the High Priest enter the Holy of Holies. Oh! dear girls, the rapture of that moment! To feel that I was really and truly joined to her and that the same throb which pulsated in and through her equally pulsated in and through me! It was a glimpse of heaven! It was love! Love in its very highest fulfilment. Louie gave herself to me without further restraint – all fear was gone, all ill-placed modesty was banished – and before morning light had come to take the place of that still yielded by the nearly burnt-out candles, my Louie lay perfectly naked – and not red with shame – in my equally perfectly naked embrace. There was not a part of our bodies which we hadn't mutually caressed and gazed upon and eaten up with kisses ardent and plentiful! Our sacrifices were without number! We kept no count! but the entire night was spent in revels which the angels, sexless and passionless, must have envied had they the means of realising, even in imagination, what they were like!'

Neither Fanny nor Amy had done more than breathe during the last part of this recital and their steps had grown so short that we hardly moved over the ground. It was evident to me that what constrained them was the fact that each of them was trying to control the powerful throbbing of her little cunt by squeezing her thighs together tightly. We were near the front of the bungalow and Amy, without a word but with her hand still pressed between her thighs, suddenly darted into the house. Fanny remained with me. I took and put her hand on my burning and terribly stiff prick whilst I at the same time kissed her and caressed her delicious cunt.

'Come! Oh! come! quickly,' said she.

I felt her draw me towards the lawn on one side of the house where some thick shrubs grew. I guessed her intention. Arrived at the edge of the grove I unbuttoned my trousers and taking her hand slipped it in. Fanny eagerly seized the tremendous weapon she felt but alas my shirt was still in the way and so excited was she that all she could do was to exclaim, 'My darling! My darling!' as her little hand nervously clutched and grasped my burning prick in alternate tightening and loosening of her fingers. Not expecting Amy to return since I suspected she had gone in to solace her little cunt with the help of a finger or a plantain or anything which could imitate the 'high priest' I had spoken of, I stood and enjoyed to the fullest Fanny's excitement and the pleasure her hand gave me; yet, whilst so standing, I suddenly and luckily saw Amy coming. I whispered to Fanny, 'Take care! Here is Amy!'

'Ho! ho! There you are!' she cried, 'kissing I do declare.'

'No,' said Fanny in muffled tones, 'I have sprained my ankle!'

'Yes!' said I immediately, glad and delighted to find Fanny so quick witted as to invent a reason on the spur of the moment for my not turning round. I had my prick sticking right out of my trousers, covered still by my shirt indeed (which had interfered with poor Fanny's endeavours to feel it naked in her hand), but it would have been instantly seen by Amy if Fanny had not leant against me, as it were for support, whilst I did my best to put back my most unruly and raging member.

'Yes,' I repeated, 'poor Fanny somehow turned her ankle and I am afraid it is hurting her very much, poor girl!' Then addressing Fanny I said, 'If you will let me apply my grandmother's remedy I am sure I can relieve the pain even if I cannot take it away altogether but the sooner you let me do so the more certain the result.'

Fanny gave a kind of groan as she said, 'Oh! do whatever you like and quickly for it is hurting me so!'

I knelt on one hand keeping myself close to Fanny's petticoat whilst with rapid fingers I managed to fasten a couple of the more important buttons so as to keep my beast of a prick a tight prisoner. Then taking hold of her right ankle with my left hand I pretended to press it with my other hand but the temptation to do more was too strong and Fanny felt with delight my wicked delicious hand rapidly find her well-turned and beautiful leg and press her calf most voluptuously and amorously as it got higher and higher. She bent a little more over me, resting her hands on my shoulders, and gave a little groan from time to time.

'It will be better soon I think,' said I as my hand reached her smooth, warm, polished and plump thigh. Fanny had really beautiful legs and thighs. My prick bounded and throbbed.

'Yes! I think it will!' gasped Fanny, 'if you continue as you are doing now.'

Amy stood by looking on and sympathising but quite unable to see what I was doing.

I rapidly moved my hand up that glorious virgin thigh, pressing it and feeling it delightedly as I mounted, until I arrived at the spot between the delicious columns of ivory. I turned my hand back down and gently seizing the two soft full lips of her plump little cunt I pressed them together by alternate squeezes, so as to tickle and excite the clitoris, until Fanny could hardly stand still. Then slipping my big middle finger in up to the knuckles and using my other finger as a fulcrum against her swelling and bushy motte, I imitated what my prick would have done had it had a fair chance, until, almost expiring with pleasure, Fanny deluged my exciting and lascivious hand with a perfect torrent of hot spend which ran down my wrist and arm. I caressed the sweet responsive cunt with my most voluptuous touches and then, hardly able to keep a steady face, I asked her, 'Well, how does it feel now, Fanny?'

'It is all right! Oh! thanks – that was nice! Now the pain is quite gone.'

'Did what he did really do you any good?' asked Amy wonderingly.

'Of course it did, you silly girl!' cried Fanny, 'or I shouldn't have said so!'

'Well! That is wonderful!' said Amy, 'I'll tell mama!'

'Don't do anything of the sort,' exclaimed Fanny, 'you would only frighten her, I dare say. It was nothing but a sprain. Anyway I'm all right now.'

'Mama told me to tell you to come in,' said Amy.

'Oh bother!' cried Fanny, 'Amy, there's a good girl, go and ask her to let me stay on a little longer.'

Amy was not inclined to do so and much to Fanny's and my dissatisfaction we had to go in. Before we did enter the house, however, Fanny managed to throw both her arms round my neck and give me two most ardent kisses without being seen by Amy. Gods! how my balls and groin did nearly split with aching.

After I got home I had the inevitable visit from poor Lavie. What a terrible plague he was! I did my best as usual to try to reconcile him to his fate and I strongly urged him to do as much fucking as he could.

He said he had been doing this regularly and irregularly every night but could not work off his passion for Fanny and I resolved to do my best to get him removed before going to bed. I wrote to Dr Bridges and I told him that I feared that Miss Selwyn was not safe; that Lavie prowled about all night round her house and that he had a perfect lust for her which might induce him to attempt to rape her. I really believed this, for Lavie was like one mad for Fanny. He had begun a habit of muttering to himself and I had overheard a semi-threat to fuck Fanny whether she liked it or not. Calling Soubratie from his slumbers I told him to take the letter first thing in the morning to Dr Bridges – and the results will be seen in the events of that never-to-be-forgotten day, the seventeenth of March, the very next day, the day on which Fanny Selwyn attained the double dignity of seventeen years of age and woman-hood, the day I at last took her most charming maiden-head, fucking her both to her and my heart's content and relieving her sweet cunt and my balls and groins of the load which had oppressed them since we had declared our mutual passion.

I knew the seventeenth was Fanny's birthday but I had no idea I should be invited to assist at keeping the feast. However, after breakfast I had two very agreeable visits. As usual I was very much undressed, having nothing on me but my short-sleeved jersey and pyjamas, for it was much too hot and there was far too blazing a sun outside for me to expect visitors. The first who came to see me was old Bridges our PMO, who seemed very anxious about Lavie. He said he had lately noticed a considerable alteration in him, a laxity in the way he carried out his duties which he could not account for until he heard of his unfortunate love affair. He now wanted to know about the subject of my last letter because it was of a very serious nature and if I did think there was any danger he would telegraph to Simla for permission to send Lavie to Benares where he understood there was room for another doctor. I easily satisfied Bridges on this head.

During our conversation I had noticed his eyes constantly directed at the still-blue-and-red-looking scars on my left arm caused by the knife of the brutal Afghan who had buggered poor Amy, and after he had finished speaking about Lavie, the good doctor went in for a complete history of the scars. I showed him the rose-looking ones on my chest and Bridges exclaimed that I ought to consider myself the chosen of Providence for I had had the most extraordinary escape he had ever heard of. Of course, I did not tell him about poor Amy's catastrophe but he had heard the rumour that she had been buggered. I lied to him. I told him the rumour was false and I was glad to be able to do so (although I had to tell a lie) because I knew that Bridges would talk and would look upon anyone who persisted in believing in the buggery as a slanderer whom he must at once put down.

Hardly had he gone and I resumed my book and cheroot than in ran Mabel in real hot haste. She sprang into my arms and gave me a number of hearty kisses and then, looking over her shoulder to be sure that no one had come yet, she pulled at the strings of my pyjamas and before I knew what she was up to had my prick in her hands as stiff as a poker. As I have said before I should never at any time object to so great a pleasure as having my prick and balls handled by a very pretty girl, whom I knew to be fuckable, but Mabel was so frightfully daring I guessed she had not come alone and asked her. To my horror she said that her mama with Fanny and Amy were on their way over and she had run ahead to peep at her pet if she could manage it before they came into the house. As she spoke I heard Mrs Selwyn's voice and the footsteps of the three coming along the verandah. Hastily pushing Mabel to one side I ran to my bathroom where I at once splashed myself with water as though I had been bathing my face and neck and then fastening my towel around my waist so that it would hang down in front and hide the evidence of my terribly excited prick, I came into the sitting room and, as if quite surprised, greeted the ladies and begged them to excuse my dishabille.

My open jersey showed the really terrible-looking scars that Mrs Selwyn and Amy had not seen since the bandages had been taken off. With little cries of horror and sympathy, which did me good to hear, all three inspected them and Mrs Selwyn laid her finger on one on my chest and asked was it still tender. I said not. There and then my darling Fanny – pretending to feel one – took as much of my left breast as she could gather in her hand and gave me a tender little squeeze as I would have done to one of her own sweet pretty bubbies had I had the chance. Amy exclaimed at the thick hair between my breasts and I made her blush by saying softly to her and Fanny: 'Ah! Amy you are as beautiful as can be! You've Jacob's beauty in your face and Esau's where it should be! Whereas I am Esau all over!'

'For shame!' said Amy.

Fanny only smiled and reddened and I knew she longed to let me see that she, too, had Esau's beauty covering the mount above her lovely cunt.

Well, the visitors, having talked the whole story of the attack on their house at Cherat over again, now declared the object of their visit, which was to invite me to dinner that evening. They were not going to ask anyone else, but Mrs Selwyn said she had looked upon me so much at one time as quite one of the family, that she hoped I would let myself be prevailed upon to come and see them very much more frequently than I had recently done. Fanny looked at me with imploring eyes, full of passion and desire, and she looked so lovely, so delicious, so voluptuously tempting, that I could not have declined, even had my old virtuous intentions returned again. Ah! no! Those virtuous intentions had altogether died away and my prick stood upon them, stiff and erect and swollen with pride, as a perfect conqueror naturally feels when he has overcome his foe. I therefore accepted, with every manifestation of real and unmistakable pleasure and as I escorted Fanny out of the house, following her mother and sisters, I took the opportunity of letting her judge the sincerity and strength of my passion by the relative force and intense stiffness of my prick. But for the friendly towel I might have made an exhibition of myself, that is sure, and I felt thankful to Mabel after all, though at first I was vexed at the insane liberties she had taken with me under such dangerous circumstances.

Now, dearest reader, I hope you are as interested in Fanny's sweet, thrilling little cunt as I was. As interested in hearing about the fucking of it as I would be. Girls, darlings, who may read these dear but naughty pages, I hope your delectable little cunnies are moistening and tickling with sympathy, and, Oh! ye, my male readers, may those pricks, which I trust are stiffly standing, have sweet cunts in which to cool their ardour not far off!

Fanny, seventeen years old, was this day promoted to the dignity of *décolletage* and when she welcomed me that evening I found her as proud as a peacock, in all the glory not of extended tail but of a very lovely exposed bosom. The two darling little breasts were indeed more hidden than I could approve of, but I could see some small portion of their smooth and polished globes and my delighted eye gazed on the sweet path between them which, followed lower, would end in her exquisite little cunt. Alas! the presence of her father, mother, sisters and little brother Harry, prevented me taking my privileges as her lover and once more feeling those beautiful bubbies, but I gave my eyes such a feasting that I found it necessary to be very careful how I moved for fear of displacing my terrible prick, which had, as usual, become unmanageable. I sat next to Fanny at dinner and whenever occasion offered gently pressed her thigh, a compliment she returned as often as she could.

At length Mrs Selwyn proposed that we should all go in and play a round game of cards but, once it was set going, Fanny and I very quickly managed to lose all our cards. We then pretended to watch the game very eagerly; in reality I had one of her legs on my knee with her foot hanging between my calves, where I pressed it. I whispered to her to come out, but she seemed afraid to attract attention and did not stir. We were near the corner of the table, which was a long rectangular one.

Everybody else was deep in the game going on. I became desperate. We were losing an opportunity which might not recur that evening. I unbuttoned my trousers and getting my prick out, free from my shirt, I took Fanny's hand and put it on it. She gave a perfect jump! Her hand tightened on the subject of her delightful thoughts and wishes and her bosom rose and fell to such a degree that, together with her intense colour, made me fear she would burst! But in a moment or two she got up and said she would go out for a moment, it was so hot.

'Do, darling,' said her mother, 'I dare say Captain Devereaux will go with you.'

Fanny went at once and I, rising quickly and turning my back on the company, walked with rapid strides after her, my prick completely out and pointing like a bow-sprit at the ceiling. Oh! that walk across the room! How I dreaded anyone calling me back. But Venus, dear Venus, protected her servants and I joined Fanny on the verandah safe and unsuspected. Neither of us spoke a word to the other; our feelings were too intense and hers altogether too agitated.

Quietly and swiftly we made for the friendly shrubs, of which I have spoken before. Arrived on the grass between them, I put my cracking prick again into Fanny's trembling hand, whilst I rapidly undid my braces and unbuttoned the rest of my trousers; for though poor Fanny tried her utmost to manage this, she was in such a state of nervous excitement that her strength seemed to fail her. However, all strength did not fail me. I soon had the pleasure of putting my heavy and painfully swollen balls into Fanny's curious and eager hands and she, with the instinct of pleasure and extreme tenderness, felt and touched them as though the slightest rough handling would surely destroy such delicate jewels. All this was delicious to me, but I was all the same in a desperate hurry to get our first fuck over for fear of interruption. I rolled my shirt up, so as to leave as much as possible of my belly naked and then pushing my trousers a little down off my hips, I took the sweet and eagerly longing Fanny round the waist and laid the willing girl on the ground. Not one single attempt at playing false modesty did the dearest girl make. She allowed me to lift the front of her dress well up and lay it carefully back upon her, so as to crease it as little as possible and next to do the same with her petticoats and, last of all, to take up her chemise so as to leave her lovely, sweet, dimpled belly as naked as mine; for Fanny, as I had discovered the evening before, wore no drawers and from her waist to her knees she was quite and sweetly naked. Dim as was the light, there was enough to show me her beautiful thighs, shining white, and the dark triangle of her bush; yea, even the soft line of her delightful little cunt was apparent! I gave it one burning kiss, which made the excited Fanny jump, and then, without further delay, I took my position between her thighs, put my left hand under her head to give it support, to raise it above the rather harsh and rough grass beneath it, pressed my lips to hers and adjusted the point of my eager prick against the soft portals of her equally excited cunt!

Glory! glory! I am in!

As he entered that beautiful temple of heat and passion, my prick doffed his headdress and did not stay his progress till pulled up by the virgin veil of Fanny's maidenhead! Whispering to her to 'Raise your hips a little, my darling, to let me put my hand under you,' I drew back for a strong forward thrust. I had not time to spare her. Fanny did not require to be educated up to that point which makes the rending in twain of the maidenhead a less timorous thing for the sweet victim. She wanted all my prick in and showed it by the firm way she pushed up against me and the frank manner with which she gave me her delicious little cunt. I made the thrust. For one hardly appreciable little space of time the doomed maidenhead resisted. There was a little check, a sudden yielding, accompanied by a slight tremor of Fanny's form and a very, very little cry, and I was in the Holy of Holies. God! but I acted as I always have done. I remembered that, whatever my pleasure might be, my chief object in fucking a girl must be to give her pleasure. So it was when by rapid movements backwards and forwards, by thrilling sweeps of my burning prick, commencing at the very outside of her cunt and only ending with the feeling of resistance to further progress, I finally succeeded in being buried up to my balls and motte in the cunt of the exquisite and passionate girl, who helped me all she could! I felt as if I had never taken a maidenhead before, as if this was my first conquest of a maiden's cunt! – delightful love which can make even old pleasure appear new! Long before I came to the thrilling and maddening short digs,

I had Fanny hardly able to keep from crying out aloud with the hitherto unknown rapture of being fucked! Of an ardent and generous temperament she 'came' frequently and always with a thrilling tremor which shook her from head to foot and she spent abundantly and copiously. As long as possible I kept back my offering, for once in Fanny, I did not care who came. Not that it was so in reality, but my blood was up, my prick was up and nothing now should interfere with the bliss I found I enjoyed. So that I made the first fuck of Fanny last as long as I could. But alas, how short! how much too short is even the longest fuck a man can make! I could not restrain the lava torrents very long and amidst a chorus or rather a duet of sighs, voluptuous groans and little cries and at the rushing end of the maddening short digs, at last came that burst of spend which makes a man drive in his prick as though he would send it through his lovely comrade and press his motte to hers as though to flatten it forever. Certainly Fanny was well anointed with the holy oil that first time. I had only spent once, or rather twice, since I had fucked Lizzie Wilson. The first time was when I had the wet dream at Nowshera and the last time was when I had sham fucked Fanny yesterday in my bungalow and I was boiling over. But all things come to an end and after enjoying for a while the leaps of Fanny's motte and the compressions of her lovely little cunt, I withdrew my still iron-stiff prick and wiped the sweet girl between the thighs with my handkerchief. Fanny lay still on the ground, her eyes turned up to the stars and her thighs open in the most voluptuous attitude, whilst I rapidly restored the disorder of my attire. She seemed like one in an ecstasy. At length I roused her and assisted her to rise to her feet. For a moment she seemed hardly able to stand without support and then she threw her lovely arms around me, and pressing me to her, she gave me a shower of kisses which I returned with interest.

'Oh, my darling!' she cried, 'at last you have loved me as I have so longed, longed to be loved! But oh! I am all wet down my legs!'

Of course. Her overfilled cunt was overflowing and that reminded me that I must take care of Fanny. Kneeling down and telling her to let me do what I liked, I passed my hand up her thighs and introducing two fingers as far as they would go into her hot, soft little cunt I used them like glove stretchers and succeeded in bringing another flow of imprisoned spend down my hand and wrist and so relieved Fanny of what might otherwise have proved a dangerous burden. She asked me why I did that.

'I will tell you another time, darling. But come, let me wipe you once more and then we will take a turn of the avenue and see whether anyone is coming out.'

Fanny submitted to the further wiping with a voluptuous surrender of herself, which was exquisitely delicious to me. Oh what a jewel she was, if I could but wear her properly! What an immense pleasure did I see before me in training this ardently voluptuous girl to enjoy in its fullness the pleasure she could give! She loved me, I knew, and she loved my prick even more; but it should, if possible, be my care to make her adore my prick without loving me the less.

We walked slowly together, arm in arm, for we feared any more lover-like attitude lest eyes might see what none must even suspect. Twice we walked up and down before the house and looked in to see whether any move suggested an exit of anybody, but as far as we could see all were busily engaged. Then Fanny did one of those bold things which made me respect her so much. She went in, spoke to her mother and asked when someone would be coming out and was told to go and enjoy the walk with me as the game was not likely to end very soon. She came to me all radiant and joyful.

'Come, darling Charlie!'

I knew what she meant. We hurried to our temporary nuptial couch between the shrubs. Here Fanny performed my toilet and I performed hers and when we were, both of us, as naked as could possibly be without actually taking off our clothes we joined in another one of those particularly rapturous fucks which neither man nor woman forgets all the days of their lives. Oh! dear readers, my pen fails me when I try to write down the burning reminiscences of those burning moments, but all my soul, my heart and my life seemed to be centred in Fanny and the seat and acme of pleasure to be in her cunt, between her beautiful thighs!

'Oh! Fanny!' I said, as we walked up and down, 'to have you properly we should both be in a comfortable bed and naked as we were born! How can we manage it? Can I come to you, darling? Could I not come in by the far bathroom door, across your room and into your bed?'

'Oh, no! It is impossible,' she replied. 'Amy sleeps in my room and my bed creaks – and – but, leave it to me, darling Charlie, and I will find a way! In the meanwhile let us enjoy one another as much as we can, as we have done. Oh! Charlie! I never, never, never could have enough of you, or as much of you as I should like!'

The remainder of the evening passed quietly and I went home about eleven o'clock. Arrived there I carefully spread my handkerchief to dry, for it had on it the precious bloom, mixed with our offerings, of the sacrifice of Fanny's maidenhead.

Before going to bed I, as usual, sat in my chair and tried to view calmly all the immense happiness I had attained. But I was still in quite a state of excitement. I had indeed fucked Fanny twice, but here were my balls aching. Was it really so impossible to get at her in her house? Should I risk going over presently and having a try? I knew I could make her hear me from the verandah, for I could whisper her name through the lattice of her window. I must fuck her again and very soon! I was rapidly coming to the conclusion that I could not really wait any longer, but must go to look for Fanny, when to my great surprise and intense joy – as well, however, as alarm – in came Fanny herself.

'Oh! Fanny darling, how did you come here?'

'I walked over, of course,' said she. 'Oh! my own love! Oh, my own darling Charlie, I could not sleep after I went to bed. I lay and tossed about. I longed for you, my darling! my darling! and at last I made up my mind that no matter what would happen, I would risk all and come to you – and

233

now, see! I am come to give myself, wholly and entirely to you! Naked as I am by nature, I give myself to you all naked, there!' she exclaimed, as she tossed aside the grey cloak and the nightdress she was clothed in and took her feet out of her slippers, 'there! see! do you like me so, Charlie? Am I pretty enough to please you, my own, own darling?'

Was she pretty enough? There standing before me, lit up by the light of the reading lamp, shining white against the darkness beyond, stood a perfect nymph. A perfect incarnation of youth and freshness and beauty!

Fanny had one of those fresh, clean-looking skins, so desirable in women. Her arms were full, round and beautifully shaped. Her shoulders sloped exquisitely and her bosom, like that of a young nymph, was adorned with a pair of well-separated, boldly self-sustained breasts, so often seen in sculpture and yet really so rare in nature. The little coral nipples showed clear and red, a lovely brilliant red, like that of her lips, and each sweet bubbie looked a little away from the other. Her form was the perfection of elegance, that of a really well-made girl, and her ivory belly, dimpled by a lovely navel, was a couch fit for Jupiter himself. Below that fairest belly was the swelling mount of Venus and with pleasure I saw that her bush was considerably grown, as indeed were her breasts, since I had last looked on them at Cherat. But below that mount, receding between her really beautiful thighs, was that most tempting deep line, which formed a cunt to be desired by the gods themselves! A cunt all mine now! A cunt no man had ever caressed or fucked before. I had done so today! A cunt which longed for me and which was brought over by Fanny for me to fuck, to love now! A cunt which I had indeed tasted, but had not yet fully savoured, but of which the first rapid, incomplete taste had made me eager to devour more and more!

Fanny had, as I have said before, really beautiful thighs. Indeed her arms, legs and feet were among her strongest points and could be models for any artist. They struck me as particularly beautiful in the light in which I now saw them and the sweetness, the glowing sweetness of really healthy youth shone from them, much enhanced near the groins by the dark curls of her fairly grown, dark brown bush. The more I gazed at all these exquisite charms, the stiffer did my prick grow and the more did I realise what a prize I had so fortunately obtained. Fanny, as though conscious of the power her beauty had over me, stood smiling, with lips slightly parted, as though waiting for that burst of praise, admiration and passion to which she felt she was entitled. Had she been conscious of not being well made, of her skin not being really pleasant to look upon, she would never have given herself, all naked, in this manner to me, for women's modesty too often is the quality under which they hide their blemishes. I have never yet fucked a really pretty and well-made woman who, from the first, objected to appearing naked before me. On the contrary the better the forms were the easier did the fair and beautiful owners of them find it to exhibit them to me without disguise.

'Oh! Fanny! you are lovely. My darling girl, you are the very perfection of beauty! Come, let me eat you up!'

Fanny's eyes blazed with pleasure, happiness and passion! She came with a little cry of joy and threw herself on to me as I reclined in my long chair. My prick opposed her belly and she pushed it to one side to enable her to lie on me and press me in her energetic arms, whilst she rained hot, burning, happy kisses in my equally responsive mouth. All the while she was murmuring little passionate love sentences into my ears and she moved her breasts from side to side over my bosom, so that I could feel the hard little coral nipples scoring it, as it were, and the firm elastic bubbies passing like waves across it. I gently pressed her lovely haunches in my two hands and tried to reach her warm little cunt from behind, but she laughingly kept it from me. She lay along my left thigh and side, with her arm round my neck, her left hand moving up and down my excited prick, occasionally grasping and feeling my balls most tenderly, whilst she said in tones of greatest excitement and the deepest feeling, 'Oh, Charlie! Charlie! You don't know how I love and adore you, my own darling. I thought I knew what love was, but I did not. There was a time when I thought I never could give myself to you, unless I was sure that I could call myself your wife and make you marry me. But now! now! I feel that I do not want to marry you. What I should like to be would be your own beloved concubine. Yes! to have you I would willingly be a servant in your house and wait upon your wife if I might, from time to time, sleep with you and have you as I had you this evening on the grass! I wish concubines were allowed now. They had them in the old days – why should not a man have more than one wife now? Why should he

not have concubines, too? Let me speak. When I went to
bed I felt so happy. I had had you – twice! Think of that!
Twice had this darling thing of yours been buried deep in
me. Twice had I felt it pour the splashing essence of my
Charlie into me! Oh! I could feel it so well, so distinctly,
and each time it seemed to kill me with pleasure. The more
I thought of it and remembered all you did, the more did
I long to have it again, the more did I want to feel these'
(she gently handled my balls) 'pressed against me, for they
told me when my Charlie was all inside me! And I remembered what you offered to do, to come to me and have me
in my own bed, how you said you could so easily come to
me, by the far bathroom door and I was almost sorry I had
said no, for after all we might have gone into the next room
and lain on the floor and there would have been no creak-
ing bed to waken Amy. I tried to sleep, I could not – my –
I don't know what you call it, Charlie, but in Hindustani it
is called *choot* –'

'Cunt, darling!'

'Cunt? Is that the English name for it? A nice soft name.
I won't forget it. Cunt! Well, my cunt troubled me terribly
and called for this – what do you call it, Charlie, dearest?'

'Prick, darling!'

'Prick? What a funny name! Prick! well, never mind. My
cunt then called for its darling prick and at last I could not
stay in my bed any longer. I jumped up. I went and looked
at Amy. She was fast asleep. I went and looked into the
nursery. Sugdaya was asleep on the floor. I listened at papa
and mama's room and could hear them both snoring. So I
took my grey cloak and slippers and ran out of the house,

by the bathroom door, and here I am with my own Charlie. Are you glad, darling? Are you glad that Fanny has come and is in your arms now?'

'Oh! my Fanny! My Fanny! How could I be anything but glad, darling, darling girl. Yet I feel a little nervous on your account, Fanny, if you should happen to be missed! What a row there would be if you were found here! Now if I were found in your room, it would not be half so bad, because no one could say that you had invited me there, but it would be different if you were found in my house!'

'Oh! I am not at all afraid of that, Charlie! I feel sure in my heart that no one will miss me or find me out.'

'But, darling, Lavie is such a night bird, he often comes much later than this to see me and – by Jove! I hear him coming now!'

Fanny started up into a sitting posture. She still had my prick in her hand and we both listened for a moment. The footsteps came rapidly towards the door. We could hear them crushing the gravel on the avenue and it was plain that in another moment Lavie could be in the room. I recognised his footsteps and knew it was he. Fanny was about to jump up but I held her tight. The footsteps paused beside the door then paused a little longer then passed on! Lavie appeared to me to hesitate and it was clear to me that he was changing his mind and that, as he so often did, he would go first and walk around the Selwyns' house and then return to bore me. The moment he had commenced his walk again I told Fanny to pick up her chemise, cloak and slippers and run into my bedroom and lie down and cover herself with the cloak; if possible, I would stop Lavie and send him home.

Fanny darted with her goods into the bedroom and I went out on to the verandah. My fright was so real and sincere that my prick had at once lost all its stiffness and hung with very abashed head whilst I again tied the strings of my pyjamas. I got its hood on to its poor shrivelled head again and set off to catch Lavie, but when I got round the corner of the verandah he was nowhere to be seen or heard.

Uneasy, I hurried back to my sitting room, meaning to visit Fanny and see that no light entered my bedroom in case Lavie happened to return that way, for each of my rooms had four doors by which it could be entered on all four sides, as is common in Indian houses where every provision is made for the most thorough circulation of air, and as I entered my sitting room I met Lavie coming out of my bedroom.

I am sure my anxious and generous-minded readers will not accuse me of cowardice when I confess that my hair stood on end with fright when I saw the unhappy doctor coming out of the room where I believed Fanny to be lying naked on my bed! In any case, I trust they will give me credit for not losing my presence of mind under great peril. It was not for myself I feared. Fanny! Had Lavie seen her? Then goodbye to her reputation and future happiness. One glance at his absent-minded, moody face, told me that that misfortune, or rather piece of evil fortune, had not taken place. I steadied my face as much as I could, for I was indeed intensely agitated, and said, 'Why, Lavie! where have you come from? I thought I heard your footsteps outside and went to call you in, but I could not see you. I fancied I was a victim of imagination.'

'I did pass your door. I meant to come in but changed my mind and went on. Then I thought I must come in and tell you what I think. So I came in by the other side of the house.'

'Well, sit down old fellow. What do you want to tell me?'

'No, Devereaux! I will not sit down! I will never sit down in your house again.'

'Goodness! Why not?'

'Look here, Devereaux!' said he in most menacing tones, 'I believed you were my friend. I told you that I loved Fanny Selwyn and you promised to help me to get her. But it is my belief, I am sure of it, that instead of speaking up for me you said and did everything to make the Selwyns and Fanny in particular think me a fool and a bad match! You can't deny it!'

Now in reality, nothing could be more untrue and unjust than this stupid accusation. I had, at first, done all I could to help Lavie with Fanny. Lavie's words offended me. Nevertheless, I am sure I should have forgiven him, if I had not already fucked Fanny. Instead, I seized the opportunity of banishing him from my house forever, and all the more eagerly because I knew that my naked darling was waiting for me on my bed, in the next room.

'Lavie!' I exclaimed in determined tones, 'if this is what you have come to tell me, let me show you the door. Do you see it, sir? Out you go and never come into my house again! I consider you the most ungrateful wretch I ever had to deal with!'

Lavie glared at me, hesitated, then slowly walked to the door, where he once more paused and, turning, said, 'Yes! I will go! I will never call you friend again! You won't succeed in keeping Fanny Selwyn from me for as sure as God is in heaven I will fuck that girl!!'

I thought it prudent not to answer him. He glared again at me for a moment and then slowly walked down the avenue, out to the road, and departed in the darkness.

I stood watching him for a moment or so and was just going to close the door when I saw a light approaching. Cursing in my heart whoever was coming to interrupt my solitude on such an evening, I waited to see who it was. It was Dr Bridges' *chuprassy* with a note:

Dear Captain Devereaux – Make your mind easy about Doctor Lavie. I have permission by telegraph from Simla to send him to Benares and he shall go tomorrow.

Yours very truly,

J. Bridges

'Thank Dr Bridges and give him my regards!' I told the *chuprassy,* who, with a lordly salute, turned and departed. I shut the door and bolted it, took my lamp and swiftly went into my bedroom.

Fanny was lying on my bed covered with the grey cloak. She raised herself on her elbow, holding the cloak ready to cover herself with in case of need, but displaying to my delighted eyes almost all the glories of her lovely nudity. I saw her bosom to perfection and her body, foreshortened, offered itself to my eyes in a position new to me in her. Oh! how I can see even now the delicious bush of her motte making a sharp-pointed triangle towards her thighs, for she had them close shut and was leaning on her left elbow. My prick had been about dead from the alarm it had received, but at this exquisite sight it raised itself again in all its glory; running to Fanny, I clasped her in my arms and told her all was safe so far, Lavie had gone, and I gave her Bridges' note to read. Fanny was delighted. She threw her arms around me and called me all the loving names she could think of. Then casting her cloak completely off her on to the floor, she opened her arms and parted her knees and with eyes darting the most voluptuous desire and in a voice thrilling with passion, she said, 'Oh! Charlie, darling, don't let us lose any more time!'

Although the scenes I had gone through were enough to make me forget everything, yet the delicious pleasure I expected to take between those lovely thighs I kept before me constantly. Foreseeing that I should, now that I had once fucked Fanny, fuck her many times, I had prepared that indispensable *savoir* sponge which should render innocuous those otherwise pleasant but dangerous streams of spend which would naturally gush from me and inundate the shrine of love. I did not expect Fanny in my house indeed, but I had the sponge in a little glass wide-necked bottle, with a weak solution of phenyl and water, ready to be carried in my pocket for use in her house, where I hoped next to have the joy of fucking her. This I now got and placed handy on the floor. Then I stripped. I stood completely naked before her. She gave a cry of joy and admiration and put forth both her hands to grasp my big, swollen and immensely strong prick and the potent balls beneath it; with delicious rapture, I felt her lissome fingers twining round the objects which by touch alone filled her with still more delightfully voluptuous and deliciously lascivious longings.

'Oh! let me kiss it! let me kiss it, Charlie!' she cried and smiling I brought the head of my excited prick to her ruby lips. With unmistakable rapture she pressed her mouth to the rounded tip and her tongue to the little orifice in it. I took my part: bending over her, I parted her willingly opened thighs with my hands and covering her glowing little cunt with my mouth, I shot my tongue as deep into it as I could. Fanny, who had never been so caressed before, uttered a little cry of pleasure. I could feel her hands, both hands, grasp my prick with renewed force and ardour and, as though to repay the compliment she felt I was paying her cunt with my tongue, she took the head of my prick right into her mouth, passing her tongue all over it and making me thrill through and through with the rapturous sensation!

But such caresses serve only to excite to madness almost. Turning to her I caught her arms and pushed her on her back. I took the sponge and squeezing the super-abundant moisture out of it, I pressed it into her little cunt, her tight little cunt, and getting between her thighs, I quickly followed it with my prick and then, mouth to mouth, bosom to bosom, belly to belly, we had our first really luscious, fully voluptuous, deliciously delightful and rapturous fuck.

Fanny, voluptuous by nature, was truly formed for fucking. Not even Lizzie Wilson could have better or more fully evinced the pleasure, the rapture she felt, than did Fanny. Although she had never been taught the refinements of fucking, she seemed, instinctively, to drop into them and nothing could have been more graciously superb than the way in which she gave a firm little buck each time she felt my balls come against her. Had I not known that it was I who had taken her maidenhead that very day, I should have concluded that Fanny had often been fucked before that night, but my heart was easy on that score. With some girls it seems natural, others can be taught, but most require to be trained.

When the hot, quick, rapturous short digs came, Fanny almost lost her senses, so much was all that was sensuous in her touched. Her voice rattled, or rather gurgled in her throat, her eyes opened their widest and seemed more gloriously beautiful than ever. In her agonies of pleasure she nipped my shoulder with her teeth, whilst I thrust my tongue into her ear and she met my torrents of hot spend with foaming floods of her own.

Then came that exquisite period when, as though exhausted, we relaxed our grasp on one another and lay quite still, her bosom heaving under mine, making me feel the full elasticity of her lovely bubbies, her belly rising and sinking, her motte leaping and giving mine little blows, whilst her cunt squeezed my prick with a force which made me fully conscious of how powerfully pleasure had affected her.

Then came all those sweet, sweet little expressions of love, devotion, passion, those kisses over such parts of the body as we could reach, and then finally the withdrawal from one another's arms and the immediate and satisfactory inspection of those charms which had been the chief extremes of our mutual pleasure.

'Oh! Charlie! How grand! How big. Who ever would have thought so small a thing as I have could take in such a lovely monster?'

'Ah! darling Fanny! But your sweetest little cunt is really very tight! But not too tight all the same.'

'Oh no! It can take it, Charlie! But why did you put the sponge in?'

I was glad to explain. I gently drew it out by the thin silken thread I had fastened to it; the outer end of the thread was tied to a little crossbar of silver to prevent the sponge being entirely sucked up into her cunt by the backward and forward strokes of my prick, and I showed her the great quantities of spend which I had poured into her and I explained to her the formation of her womb and how, in order to avoid a possible baby, the mouth of the womb should be prevented from being watered by the prolific produce of my balls and that, still further to deaden the vitality of that spend, I had used phenyl.

She quite understood me as I explained and kissed me again and again, thanking me for the great care I took of her and saying that she had never thought of any danger. I told her I had written to Cawnpore for a powerful enema and sent a receipt to be made up which would be more effective and pleasant than the phenyl, as it would have rose-water as one of its ingredients and would have a more pleasant aroma; and then I proposed that she should get up and let me wash her pretty cunt, so that I might pay it again the homage of my kisses. To this she joyfully assented. I got a basin of water and a towel and bathed her hot little cunt. She enjoyed the freshness of the water and when I had dried her bush and cunt and thighs she insisted on washing my prick in her turn, laughing and happy.

'Now!' said I, 'my darling, lie across the bed and put one leg over each of my shoulders. That's right!'

I hid my face between her thighs, my mouth on her sweet, sweet cunt and my upstretched hands grasping each a polished globe of her bosom. Fanny lay still for half a minute, while I searched the depths of that voluptuous little cunt with my tongue and pressed my nose on to her excited little clitoris, but at last she snatched those charms away from me and said, 'Oh! at least let us lie so that I can do the same to you as you do to me, my Charlie!'

Delighted to find her so ready to play every air on the sonata of voluptuousness, I stretched her on the bed and took my position over her, leaning on my elbows, embracing each of her thighs with an arm and again searching her cunt with my tongue, whilst my chin tickled her clitoris and I gave my prick to her mobile lips and sweeping tongue and my balls to her agitated and excited fingers! And then once more placing the sponge of safety within the rosy portals of the temple, I reversed my position and again thrilled the deliciously lascivious and voluptuous girl with my impassioned fucking.

And so the night wore away. We laid no plans for the future. Here in the happiness of one another we never thought how we were going to manage to meet and fuck without fear of detection. We were just like a bride and bridegroom and this, the first night of our marriage.

Towards four o'clock Fanny, thoroughly exhausted from the strain on her nerves and senses, sank off to sleep in my arms after the last ablution and I must have fallen asleep too. Suddenly I felt a hand on my nose, gently pressing my nostrils, and opening my eyes I saw Sugdaya!

'Hush, sahib!' she said, 'Miss Fanny *baba* must come home now, before the day breaks!'

'How did you know she was here, Sugdaya?'

'Oh!' she said, laughing softly, 'I have known a long time that Miss Fanny *baba* meant to be fucked by master. I kept my eyes open and I saw you in the shrubs last evening. I saw you go twice and I saw everything! Miss Fanny *baba* did not tell me, but I said to myself, when the honey does not come to the bear, the bear goes to the honey. I went to see if Miss Fanny *baba* was in her bed at midnight and I found it empty. I came over here and have been watching your pretty pranks through that door and now you must wake her up, sahib, and let her go with me!'

'Wait a moment Sugdaya,' said I, gently withdrawing my arm from under Fanny's neck and getting out of bed. 'Come into the next room.'

Sugdaya followed me. I unlocked my dispatch-box and took a roll of twenty-five rupees out and laid them on the table. Then taking Sugdaya's right hand I put it on my balls. She smiled and gently grasped them, with a voluptuous folding of her hand and fingers which made me know that she was not at all unwilling to feel them on her own account and knew why I had put them into her hand. Then slipping my right hand under and between the folds of her robe, I found her cunt and covering it with my palm, I dictated to her and she repeated: 'May my cunt wither and burn and shrivel if I betray the girl against whose bottom these balls have pressed. May Vishnu, Ram, Sita and Lakshmi curse me if I break my oath.'

Sugdaya laughed on the completion of this very necessary ceremony and said, 'Oh! sahib! no oath was required to bind me not to betray Missy *baba* or you! I am more than glad Miss Fanny *baba* has had the pleasure of being fucked. No girl needed it more. She will eat and drink and sleep all the better for it and I know that the sahib will not proclaim his conquest in the byways but hold his tongue!'

'You may be sure of that, Sugdaya!' said I, kissing her, 'and when Miss Fanny *baba* goes away from Fackabad, will you let me fuck this nice cunt of yours?'

'Before then if the sahib wishes!' laughed Sugdaya.

I had been caressing her well-formed, elastic, prominent and perfectly smooth motte, for Sugdaya like all Indian women either plucked out or shaved off every vestige of hair from that region. She had, in her turn, been caressing and feeling, with hands evidently not strange to the act, my prick, which was in that vigorous condition women love to find.

'Now, sahib!' said Sugdaya, pressing her swelling breasts against my chest, 'there is time for one more.

Come! wake Miss Fanny *baba* as a lover should rouse his
beloved!'

Nothing loth, I accompanied her to my bedroom, quite
ready to do as Sugdaya had suggested, but Fanny, tired out
with the long and exciting night's arduous and always
ardent combats, was lying on her side, fast asleep, with one
hand between her knees. She looked so lovely as she lay
slightly curled up and her dear little face looked the picture
of sweet innocence.

Sugdaya read my thoughts, for she said, 'Her cunt is
asleep, sahib, but when I waken it up you will see another
expression on her face!'

Looking round for something she evidently wanted,
Sugdaya saw some peacock feathers, and selecting one
which suited she approached Fanny and deftly commenced drawing the soft feather along the line of her
cunt, which, gathered up as she was, I could hardly see
anything at all of. At first there seemed to be no effect,
but Sugdaya, with the utmost patience, continued those
soft caressings with the feather and Fanny presently murmured something in her sleep and turned a little more
over forwards as though she felt too tired for any more
fucking and deprecated the invitation. I glanced at
Sugdaya who smiled and seemed in no way discouraged.
She withdrew the feather and passed it several times over
my prick, up and down, before she recommenced oper-
ating on Fanny. Whether the feather conveyed any subtle
influence with it from my prick or whether, what seemed
more likely, the continued soft rubbings of the down
along her soft cunt lips caused a sweet excitement within,

Fanny murmured again and, slowly turning on her back, opened her lovely thighs a little, so that the rays of the lamp distinctly lit up the whole of those domains of which, in the name of love and Venus, I had taken possession. Sugdaya reversed the feather and with the quill stroked Fanny's bush, occasionally touching the tip of her lovely cunt also. Presently out peeped the little ruby point, glittering with generous moisture, and the slight tremor of her motte, with the almost imperceptible, but still marked, parting of the rounded lips of her cunt, told us that desire had laid his wanton hand on the charm which we wished to arouse from its state of torpor. Still Fanny remained fast asleep. Her bosom rose and fell more rapidly. Her lips moved and her eyelids quivered. A smile wreathed her lovely mouth and she parted her lips as though to speak, but, except for those of her delicious little cunt, all her senses were still locked in the embrace of sleep. The sweet girl's thighs opened wider and wider and her feet separated. She drew up her knees. It was evident, from her quick breathing and the rapid quiverings of her motte, that voluptuousness had fastened itself on her. Sugdaya gave me a nod and I, very gently and with as much quiet as possible, got between my darling's knees. Bending forward I rested on both knees, as I had done with Lizzie Wilson, and Sugdaya, seizing my prick, directed it so as to strike the doors of the temple at that very spot where they opened with the least pressure. I glided in, still keeping my belly from touching that of Fanny, and it was not till my balls touched her that she awoke.

'It is true, then! Not a dream!' she exclaimed. 'Oh, my Charlie! I forgot for a moment that you were my real lover and I thought that I was only dreaming my Nowshera dream again! I was afraid to open my eyes till I felt your dear balls against me!'

I stopped her further speech with my ardent kisses and Sugdaya, who had discreetly moved a little to one side, out of reach of Fanny's eyes, witnessed the voluptuous combat, which judging by the vigorous way she crossed her thighs and the occasional passing of her hand between them must have moved her very much. What a grand, grand poke that was! I enjoyed it more than any I had hitherto had and when I withdrew my proud and delighted prick from the overflowing cunt of my darling, she exclaimed, 'That is the best one we have had yet, Charlie!'

Sugdaya came forward. Fanny seemed no way put out by her presence and I afterwards found out that for months Sugdaya had been inculcating the joys of love in all three girls and that she had urged Fanny in particular to do all she could to seduce me. It accounted for the extraordinarily bold conduct of Mabel who, before Sugdaya entered the Selwyn house, had, like her sisters, been very modest and reserved. It accounted too, to a great degree, for the free conduct, if I may so call it, of Fanny in telling me of her dream when at Nowshera, for when I first knew the Selwyns there were not three purer-minded girls in all India than these three young maidens and I certainly did no more than foster the plant of desire when I saw it was growing.

It was still dark when the two girls left my bungalow; having seen them depart in safety, I returned to my room, put out my lamp and lay down, certain of a grand sleep, for there would be no parade that morning and I need not get up early. I remembered that in our last fuck I had not used the all-important sponge, but it gave me no cause for alarm, it being a well-attested fact that the last few spends of a man who has fucked all night are not at all prolific.

5

Sibling Rivalry

The colonel continued fucking Mrs Soubratie very comfortably in my house, where, in the spare room next to my bedroom, I had a special bedstead for him and his dusky concubine. So papa and daughter got their greens regularly and all went on as tranquilly and as happily as could be. But alas! a terrible crisis overhung this happy family.

I have spoken of Mrs Selwyn's delicate health. About July she began to fade rapidly. The close, hot atmosphere of the rains, with its accompanying relaxing effect, pulled her down, hand over hand. To the terrible grief of her husband and children she breathed her last. That night, by the most extraordinary good fortune, Fanny was not with me. The only night that she had not come over for weeks. Thus did Venus watch over the safety of her tender adorers.

I will pass over that sad time, during which I was for a period deprived of my Fanny's company, but it did not last long and once more we were united.

But the poor colonel, I grieve to say, took to driving away his cares, as so many do, by the aid of the bottle. For some weeks he did not even come over to fuck Mrs Soubratie. The loss of his wife brought to his memory those many years of sweetest happiness he had had with her and he used to speak to me of the grief it gave him to think that he should have committed adultery, and with a native woman too, during Mrs Selwyn's last year of life. This stung his conscience. But I knew that a man with such balls as he had could not long remain a monk and little by little I cheered him up until desire returned and he once more made Mrs Soubratie happy and drew upon that storehouse of happiness between her luscious thighs.

Of Mabel's pranks I have hardly time to speak. She used to implore me to fuck her. She would use every possible inducement, but I was too fond of Fanny to wish to give her a rival, especially as her affectionate passion for me seemed to increase with our intercourse. I had what I loved, a charming girl, all mine, to be my companion by day and by night. Mabel could make my prick stand indeed and I would willingly, gladly, have fucked her but for Fanny. Little by little Fanny was taking Louie's place in my heart and she wisely hid all signs of jealousy of Louie, if indeed she felt any. We both lived in the present hour; it was so happy, so congenial and neither of us looked ahead. If we regretted anything, it was having lost so many months and weeks and days when we might have enjoyed one another as we did now, but if such thoughts entered our minds they simply served to make us all the more determined to lose no more time.

About the time that the colonel recommenced fucking the (to him) delightful cunt of Mrs Soubratie another death at Fackabad caused a change in our world. 'Brigadier'

Colonel Wilson suddenly left this world for the next and
Colonel Selwyn was appointed to the vacant post. This was
a capital stroke of luck for me, for Major Mortimer, the
station staff officer, son-in-law to Colonel Wilson, had to
go home to attend to his late father-in-law's property and
look after his wife's interests and I was, on Colonel Selwyn's
recommendation, appointed acting staff officer. But for my
darling Fanny's sweet cunt I do not think I should have got
this appointment, not that the colonel thought me in the
least unfit for the office, but Fanny turned his thoughts to
me and gently but persistently urged that I was the one
who should get the post, though, by rights, some other
officer who had been longer in India than I should have
had it. But you see, dear reader, that the sweet delights I
gave Fanny, through her charming little cunt, made her
very solicitous about me and *amor vicit omnia* in this
instance. So my soldier readers, if you want to get good
appointments through your colonel, fuck his daughter
well, as I fucked my darling Fanny. Really and truly, all jok-
ing apart, this appointment was very pleasant. I had no
longer to command my company. I had nothing to do with
my regiment as an officer of it in the way of duty. I had
therefore no morning parades, no drills, nothing to lug me
out of bed at ungodly hours in the morning. I only
attended general parades when the colonel did. I had a
good deal of signing my name to letters, etc., prepared by
my clerks, but as everything was in good order the work
was light. The emolument of my office did not matter
much, as I had no need of money, having plenty of my
own; but for all that the extra rupees were not by any

means a nuisance to receive. Darling Fanny profited by my not having to go to parade. Some mornings when we had slept later than usual it had happened that she had had to run home without her daybreak fuck; now she always had one and sometimes two and she was just as ardent and eager for them as ever my sweet Louie had been. Oh! I was really very happy and contented.

But, although no real harm was done, yet a circumstance occurred which might have brought all this happiness to a disastrous end.

Colonel Selwyn's command comprised all the army, not only at Fackabad but also several other stations where there were detachments of troops. Amongst these was Rampur some seventy miles off and to be reached only by dak *gharry*. One evening early in October, that is just a year after I had seen my darling's cunt for the first time and since Amy had been buggered, the colonel electrified Fanny and rather astonished me, who had no notion of his intentions, by saying that he thought he would go in a couple of days' time and commence his inspection of the troops at Rampur and that he would take Fanny with him.

'Oh, papa! but I would much rather not go!' cried poor Fanny, looking at me with an aggrieved and startled face, 'could you not take Amy?'

The colonel, who had not yet drunk enough brandy and soda to be befuddled, looked rather angrily at Fanny. 'No! I said you were to accompany me, Fanny! And I shall not take Amy, I don't like to be dictated to by my daughters!'

'I did not mean to dictate, papa,' urged poor Fanny, who struggled visibly to restrain an outburst of temper, 'but I should really be obliged if you would let me remain here and if you would take Amy or Mabel instead. Come, there's a dear, good, kind papa. Do.'

Now the colonel was a weak man and therefore obstinate. He was offended at Fanny's outburst and he had got into a sudden rage. He looked black as thunder and roared at Fanny, 'Miss Fanny! I have said that you will go with me! Let me hear no more about it!'

He turned his eyes to me and for a moment I wondered had he any suspicions as to the very intimate terms Fanny and I were on? Yet how could he have discovered them so suddenly? I was mistaken, however.

'Miss Selwyn,' said I, seeing Fanny ready to cry with vexation. 'Do you know I rather envy you? I hear that Rampur is a very pretty place and that the road there takes you through some very lovely scenery, though it is all plains. I only wish the colonel would take me too, as his staff officer.'

'Well, Devereaux, so I would, but for that confounded new order which requires special application to be made for permission to take a staff officer with one when on these irregular inspections. I am afraid you must wait a little longer. But I will take Fanny.'

There was living in the compound next to mine the Protestant padre of Fackabad, one Mr Corbett, a married man with a very amiable and young and not too straitlaced wife. These people were great friends of the Selwyns and Mrs Corbett, who knew I was fond of Fanny, often teased me about her. I had even 'confessed' to her that I admired Fanny so much that had there been no Mrs Devereaux, I should have been very much inclined to ask Fanny to become that lady. But long practice had made me a consummate actor and Mrs Corbett, without thinking me a saint, never suspected that the cunt she knew I must fuck (she was a woman of the world), whilst Louie's was not available, lay between Fanny's thighs of snow. No, she fancied that I relieved my necessities between some brown thighs and more than hinted that Sugdaya owned them. I rather encouraged the idea and if ever I had cause to mention Sugdaya, I spoke of her with that apparent consciousness that made Mrs Corbett more certain than ever that I did fuck Sugdaya regularly. So we were both contented.

It was with the Corbetts that Colonel Selwyn arranged to leave his children during his absence with Fanny at Rampur. Their house was large enough to accommodate them easily and no country in the world makes such temporary movements more easy to perform than India. All that was required was that a few bedsteads should be carried over and the thing was done.

The last night had to be a very short one for Fanny and me. Her father intended starting at four in the morning and Fanny had to leave me at half-past two. She was ravenous. In the few hours she still had to enjoy my prick she lost not a moment and the interludes between act and act only lasted just as long as it took the pretty hands to operate the resurrection of my prick, a thing extremely easily performed, I am glad to say. I may tell my fair readers here that as a little boy, when I first began to understand why I had a little prick and girls had little cunts, I had marvelled at the story of Hercules and wondered how taking fifty maidenheads and putting fifty virgins in the family way in one night could be considered a 'labour'. Well, I had had no practical experience then, but later I learnt from women of all classes whom I fucked, that I was more abundantly blessed than any man they had ever met in having an unconquerable prick and a pair of balls which never ran completely dry. I do not mention this to boast, but only to say how thankful I am that such has been my lot. So poor Fanny left me with her sweet cunt throbbing with pleasure and a heart grieved to think that it would be perhaps nearly a fortnight before it would throb again from being well fucked by me.

For my part I was as grieved as Fanny. I loved that girl. She was a second edition of Louie. I never could have enough of her, by day or night. I was certain that her absence would be as grievous to me as my separation from Louie was. It took me a long time to feel desire again after I had left Louie, as the readers of my first chapter will remember, and I felt very nearly the same now that Fanny was gone. There was this difference, however: when I left my Louie I had an idea it might be years before I should again know the glorious pleasure of fucking her and fucking her meant in my mind, then, fucking at all. I really and truly thought that I had done with women, i.e., all other women than my Louie. My readers may remember the soft influence of Mademoiselle de Maupin and the realisation of that beauteous power in the person of the lovely and delicious and really lascivious Lizzie Wilson. Her cunt proved its power and the far distant one, between poor Louie's thighs, no longer tyrannised over my (till then) moral prick and modest balls. Well then, I did look forward this time to some more luscious fucking, at no very remote day, for Fanny's dearest little cunt would surely again be mine within a fortnight to caress, to kiss, to fuck to my heart's content. Still it was a grievous annoyance to lose it, even for that short time.

The day passed wearily, far more so than I anticipated it would. My thoughts were all with Fanny. I knew she went away grieving and all my sympathies were with her. I went to bed early, hoping to get some sleep and so pass away as many hours in an unconscious state as possible.

I don't know how long I had been thus sleeping, when I woke, feeling my nose gently pinched, and there was Sugdaya!

The first idea that came into my mind was that Sugdaya, mindful of my little speech to her on the first night that I fucked Fanny, had taken advantage of my words literally, and that Fanny having left Fackabad, though only temporarily, she had come to be fucked herself. The dear reader will remember that I had proposed to Sugdaya to fuck her whenever Fanny went away (I meant for good) and now I imagined that Sugdaya wanted to take my words literally.

'Well, Sugdaya, what is it?'

'Sahib! Miss Fanny *baba* wants me to ask you to come over to her. She is in bed and wants master!'

'Good God! Has there been an accident, Sugdaya? What made the colonel come back? I hope no one is hurt! How is Miss Fanny *baba*?'

'There has been no accident, sahib!' said Sugdaya laughing, 'no one has been hurt. Miss Fanny *baba* is quite well but her cunt is hungry for this,' and she took possession of my prick. I did not repel her. I never repel a pretty woman when she takes hold of me there.

'I'll come at once, Sugdaya! But tell me, why did the colonel come back?'

'He has only come back for the night, sahib!' said Sugdaya, sitting on the edge of the bed and gently moving her hand, in the most delicious manner, up and down my prick. I lay on my back and let her. It was so pleasant and I wanted to hear particulars. 'They got as far as Dharra, that is the first stage, you know, sahib! – Ah! What a handsome grand prick you have, sahib – no wonder Miss Fanny *baba* loves it! And grand balls too! Some day you know, sahib, you must fuck me, you know you promised!'

'So I will, surely, Sugdaya. But take care. Don't make me spend.'

'No, sahib,' said poor Sugdaya with a sigh, 'Miss Fanny *baba*'s cunt must make it do that! I'll play with your balls only,' and she began those caresses with the fingertips which are so exquisitely delicious.

'All right, Sugdaya. That is very nice. Now tell me, what did they do at Dharra?'

'Oh! sahib! There were no fresh horses ready. The colonel sahib wanted to go on with those which had come with him from Fackabad, but the *gharry* man would not. Then they found it would not be possible for them to leave Dharra that day and the colonel sahib waited and when the horses were rested came back slowly to Fackabad. He and Miss Fanny *baba* will try again tomorrow morning – now! Come, sahib. Poor Miss Fanny *baba* wants you badly.'

I jumped up, fastened my pyjamas, felt Sugdaya's nice little brown cunt and bubbies, kissed her, sham fucked her a little and saw plainly that I had only to say, 'I'll fuck you instead, Sugdaya,' and she would gladly have taken Fanny's place; but although all this sporting was dangerous, I had no idea of being unfaithful to Fanny and, with steps as noiseless and swift as possible, Sugdaya and I went hand in hand over to the colonel's bungalow.

Before Sugdaya let me in by the bathroom door she said, in a low tone, 'Don't speak to Miss Fanny *baba*, sahib. The colonel sahib is not sleeping well and he might hear you. For that reason, too, Miss Fanny *baba* has only a small light in her room. Just go in – get right into bed with her and fuck her quietly and nicely.'

This was the very first time I had ever been in the colonel's bungalow to fuck Fanny in her own bed. I had fucked her in the compound and, on one or two occasions which I have not mentioned, I had fucked her in the drawing room, taking her on my knees, but I had never fucked her in her own bed and the idea seemed delicious to me. Though no longer a virgin herself, her bed was a virgin and it seemed to me it would be like taking her maidenhead a second time. I went into her room then, palpitating with desire and with my prick as vigorous as if the long week or ten days had passed during which I had expected to be a widower.

The room was all but pitch dark. There was a light indeed but so covered that not even its miserable feeble rays could fall on the bed which I dimly saw and on which I could just discern the figure of a girl, who looked naked. I could not distinguish any features, only a general form, but Fanny's bush struck me as looking much darker in this darkness than usual. Sugdaya led me still by the hand and when at the bedside whispered in low tones: 'Don't make any noise, sahib. I will go and lie at the colonel sahib's door.'

And she left me and glided out into the pitch darkness of the other room.

Delighted to be with Fanny again, so much sooner than expected, I gently got into her bed, fearing to make it creak, but it was firm – now at any rate – for it made no sound. A gentle but nervously hurried hand took possession of my prick whilst I drew honey from the warm lips and pressed the lively bubbies I found one after the other. I longed to speak, but the first attempt I made was met with a warning 'hush!' from her, whilst a gentle little pull at my burning prick told me that the darling girl wanted to draw it, in silence, to the equally burning little cunt, of which the soft lips were already moistened in anticipation of the delight it expected. Carefully, making no creak occur from the bed-stead, I gently turned over on to the dear girl, whom I could feel panting with hot desire, and taking my place between her exquisite thighs I drew my quivering prick against that throbbing and excited cunt, enraptured at the idea that I was now at last fucking her in her own bed. Fanny kissed me as though in an ecstasy, my prick glided in, doffing his cap as he did so, and then – to my extreme surprise – was met with a complete denial of further ingress.

At first I imagined that Fanny was practising on me. I had taught her how to imitate a virgin bride – that by straighten-ing her legs stiffly, raising her belly as high as possible and withdrawing her cunt from the invading prick, as well as by taking a slightly crooked position sideways, she could make it difficult for her husband, when she had one, to get into her. But on putting my hand to feel how her thighs were placed, I found her knees well bent. I could not detect any wilful upraising of the belly, nor any refusal of her darling cunt. I tried again. No go. There was a real obstruction. What could it be from? I tried again. There was the same result. I began to feel hot with shame and wondered could my prick possibly be failing me. Oh no! It was as stiff as when I first had Fanny. As stiff as it always had been when between the delicious thighs of a girl! I quietly and suddenly slipped off Fanny and put an enquiring finger up her cunt. I imagined that she might have manufactured a *savoir* sponge – for Sugdaya had not asked me to bring mine and I had forgotten to do so – and that this was causing the obstruction. Fanny let me feel her without making the least objection and I felt – a maidenhead! Oh! There was no doubt about it. In a moment the idea flashed upon me that it was not Fanny, but Mabel. I strained my eyes, but could not make out the face so close to me but yet so hidden in the darkness.

'It is not Fanny!' I said in my lowest tones. 'Is it you – Mabel?'

My question was answered by a peal of loud, merry laughter which, considering that I still believed the colonel to be in the house and just across the drawing room, astonished me for two reasons – first, it was not Fanny's laughter nor Mabel's – but Amy's – and secondly it was so noisy!

Sugdaya came running in. When she saw me with my finger in Amy's cunt, which she easily saw by the lamp she carried, and my look of astonishment and Amy writhing in uncontrollable laughter, she joined in and rolled about in excessive merriment!

'Ah! sahib! sahib! What a lucky man you are that all the Misses *baba* think that there is only one sahib that can fuck and that one Captain Devereaux, sahib. Well, Miss Amy *baba*. Did he fuck you nicely?'

'No,' cried Amy, 'he can't do it.'

'Can't do it,' cried I in anger, for I felt I had been most cruelly deceived. 'Can't do it, Miss Amy. I'll show you that I can do it and well, too.'

And so saying, I again plumped on top of her, inserted my indignant prick and, stretching Amy in such a manner that she could not possibly escape me, I forced my excited weapon as hard as I could against the rash maidenhead which had by the voice of its owner sneered at me.

'Oh–h–h! Captain Dev–er–eaux! O–h–hh! for God's sake! Oh! You are killing me – you – are – killing me! Ah–hh–h! Oh! Oh! Oh! Oh! –'

It was a rough job. Amy's maidenhead was thrice as strong as Fanny's and much more unyielding than the majority of those it has been my excellent good fortune to take. And I did not feel tender-minded towards her. I am afraid I was more rough than I should have been – but oh! had she not deceived me and robbed her sister? So without mercy I went way up, until that really sweet little cunt was filled and stretched to the uttermost and my balls rattled against her bottom, just at the exact spot where the Afghan's had first had that pre-eminent happiness.

But Amy, though she said I hurt her dreadfully forcing my prick in so roughly, was by nature voluptuous like

Fanny. Her, 'Ah! Now that's nice. Ah! Do that again. Oh, my! Oh, Captain Devereaux! How you tickle!' told me that and, my temper having been satisfied by my first burst of anger, I fucked her as sweetly as I could and was rewarded by her spending copiously and ravishingly, at the exact moment that I inundated her cunt with the first boiling torrent which had ever been poured by man into it.

Sugdaya stood by holding the lamp and watching with keen and voluptuous interest the real combat between my prick and Amy's cunt and when she perceived by the cessation of my movements and the way in which Amy was holding her breath, that I was inundating the shrine, she gave vent to the prolonged 'oh–h–h –' as though she envied the girl who was getting such delight.

'Now! Miss Amy *baba*! Now! You have been well fucked,' she cried.

'Yes. I suppose I have,' said Amy, in a kind of dreamy manner, usual with her when her thoughts were much occupied; then waking up as if from a trance, she clasped me tight and gave me kiss after kiss.

'Ah! that is all very well, Amy,' I said, 'but I have a bone to pick with Sugdaya and you. A very nice pair you are. Do you know what you have done?'

'Yes, dear,' said Amy, laughing and closing her legs over me for I had commenced to withdraw my prick from her strongly palpitating cunt. 'I do. I laid a very neat trap and caught a very splendid bird and I have him now in my cage.'

'It's all very well, Amy. You have won this round – but oh!' and I felt my voice quiver with the anguish I really felt, 'you do not know what you have done! Here! Let me go.'

'No, indeed,' said Amy, folding me tighter and tighter and forcing her cunt about my prick, which had been half pulled out of it. 'No! I won't let you go. You are my property now, Captain Devereaux, I have fairly caught you! To think of letting you go yet! Oh dear no! You will have to fuck me now as often as you have fucked Fanny. And as she has had you ever since last March, you will have to pay me a good deal of attention before I shall be even with Fanny.'

'Oh, Amy!' I cried, bitterly, for I assure you, dear reader, much as I love fucking and well worth fucking as Amy was and still is, I felt that I had been betrayed, and though done in perfect innocence, doing what I now had done would come nigh to breaking Fanny's heart. Now I loved Fanny. I was passionately devoted to her and not for all the cunts in the world did I feel inclined to outrage her by fucking her sister before her own sweet cunt could be said to have ceased throbbing from the very recent fucking it had had from my prick. I did not desire Amy. The stand I had, when I got into bed with her, was not for her cunt, nice as it was, but for Fanny's. 'Oh! Amy! I'll tell you what you have done! You have broken poor Fanny's heart.'

'Pooh! Ha ha ha,' laughed Amy. 'What do I care? Broken her heart indeed. Oh! Poor Fanny! Much I pity her! What more right has she to you, I should like to know, than I have, or Mabel. She is not your wife. But to hear her talk and to hear you too, Captain Devereaux, one would think there was no Louie in the world. I tell you I have every bit as much right to you as Fanny has, and mind, if you refuse to fuck me, you will never fuck her again, I can tell you!!!'

This thrust I felt was no empty one. Amy had once said she could not imagine herself going to bed with a man and that for herself to be stark naked in the presence of a stark-naked man would be something too horrible to contemplate. Here she was, however, stark naked in my stark-naked arms and the will to fuck was all on her side, not mine. It was plain all her former ideas had become completely changed; and her whole tone and manner was that of a strong-minded woman who knew what she was about and that she could compel, if she could not gain her ends by any more gentle means. Unfortunately it lay in her power to put an end to the delicious liaison between Fanny and me. I lay quietly in her arms, thinking how I could escape this terrible dilemma.

'How do you know that I fuck Fanny, Amy?'

'How do I know? Now, Captain Devereaux! Do you take me for a complete fool? Do you think that Fanny could leave this room, with me sleeping in it, night after night, without my knowing it sooner or later? Do you think I cannot put two and two together as well as yourself? Why! I have known it these five months at least. I taxed Fanny with it and she could not deny it and she told me herself too, about how you fucked her twice that evening of her birthday, when she and you left us playing cards. Well! I didn't care! I thought her a fool for her pains, but by degrees I began to think it must be nice – as Sugdaya has always told me it was – to be fucked and the moment I heard that Fanny was to go to Rampur with papa, I laid a plan with Sugdaya to catch you! Ah! now, my boy! You wanted me to go to Rampur but here I am. You wanted

Fanny's cunt, did you? Now you are in mine and I think mine must be every bit as nice as Fanny's. I have better and bigger breasts, too, and more hair than she has and I don't think you have any reason to complain of Fanny either.'

I saw it was no use trying to urge a higher tone with Amy. It was no use talking to her of love. Fucking was all she could see in my intimacy with Fanny, nothing nobler.

'So you see, my dear Captain Devereaux, you will now have two wives in India and one at home; perhaps three wives in India, because Mabel, I know, wants to be fucked too, and you will have to do it.'

'I will not!' I cried passionately and angrily.

'Oh! dear, yes, you will. The thing is in a nutshell. Do you really love Fanny? Are you really so fond of her as you say?'

'Oh, Amy! You don't know how fond.'

'Very well! Then I suppose you would be awfully sorry if anything happened to prevent you fucking her again.'

'Don't speak of it!'

'Oh! but I will. I have only some night to pretend to be ill, call papa and let him see Fanny's bed empty and Sugdaya not to be found in the house and I think Fanny will never see your prick again, Captain Devereaux.'

I groaned.

'What an ass a man is!' cried Amy, half angrily, half laughingly. 'I should like to know who has such a grand chance of having three pretty girls all to himself, all ladies of his harem. And the idea shocks him. Now! Captain Devereaux – and do be careful what you say. Is it a bargain? Do you promise to fuck Mabel and me whenever we like? For if you don't you may say goodbye to Fanny.'

Now I had had a good deal of experience with girls and women and have often been helped into a nice little cunt by the owner of another, but I never was treated in this way before. The idea that if I did not fuck Amy and Mabel I should lose Fanny was paradoxical! I felt a child in Amy's arms and that I had learned my lesson wrong. I thought I should lose Fanny if I fucked her sisters, not if I did not do so. It seemed it was all wrong. Yet a little reflection told me that the laws of ordinary life did not obtain in this instance and that to keep possession of Fanny's dearest cunt, I must fuck those of her sisters also!

'I think you very hard-hearted, Amy. I see I have nothing better to do than surrender; when the Devil drives, needs must.'

'Thank you for the compliment,' laughed Amy. 'Well, the devil in this instance flatters herself that she has a very nice cunt and desires her slave to amuse her for the rest of this night!'

All this conversation having taken place in English was unintelligible to Sugdaya, who looked on with surprised and perplexed eyes, but when Amy told her what the result of the conversation had been, that not only had I consented to go on fucking her, but that I would fuck Mabel, too, she was delighted and said: 'Oh! sahib! Now I am very glad indeed. Won't Miss Mabel *baba* be glad to hear it too!'

I begged her to go over to my bungalow and bring my enema and *savoir* sponge and I asked Amy to get up and let me assist her in washing her cunt, which required it badly. Sugdaya left and Amy rose. Of course, the sheet was a sea of blood. Amy was rather frightened when she saw it, but

I comforted her by saying that no girl who has really lost her maidenhood, ever did so without losing a lot of blood. Whether the tone of my voice was more gentle than it had been, or whether my comforting words struck a chord of gratitude in her heart, I don't know, but she put her arms around my waist and lifted her face up and kissed me affectionately.

'Ah, Captain Devereaux, now let us be really good friends; we need not quarrel because we fuck, need we?'

The absurdity of such a question struck me with all its force and I could not help laughing heartily. I looked at Amy. Naked as she was, I could see all her form and person perfectly and she was really a splendid girl. Her hair, both of her head and bush, was darker in colour than Fanny's and very much more abundant. Her arms, thighs and legs were full as white and as well formed, her waist was more slender and her hips were wider than those of her sister; and her bubbies, beautiful, round, full and coral tipped, were fully one-third larger. Her hands and feet were small and well shaped and as her face was very pretty, with a fine oval form and with large, dark, lustrous eyes, she was altogether very desirable and a fine addition to my 'harem'. My angry feelings and the regret I so sincerely felt for having been made to be unfaithful to Fanny began to die away at the sight of all these beauties and Amy received caresses from my hands and kisses from my lips which made her as proud as could be, for she rightly judged that had her beauty not been very real, she would hardly have got off so soon for her cruel treatment of me.

'Come!' said she. 'Come, Captain Devereaux. Help me to wash myself and let Sugdaya find us fucking when she comes back.'

The ablution was quickly performed. Amy had never seen my prick and balls before, nor indeed those of any man, though she had had a very big one up her bottom once! She therefore delayed a little while washing me and thoroughly enjoyed the sight and feel of those treasures.

Sugdaya returned just in time to see me getting home well for the first time and consequently was an excited spectator of the first goodwill fuck I gave Amy. Like the voluptuous-minded creature she was, she greatly added to my pleasure by manipulating my balls, which she took possession of between my thighs from behind. Amy seemed frantic with pleasure. Every stroke I gave her threw her into ecstasies. I think Mrs Selwyn must have had a voluptuous nature and I know that the colonel dearly loved fucking. Certainly Fanny and Amy had inherited their parents' disposition towards sensuousness and it was my extreme good fortune to have been the first to inspire their loving cunts with desire and make them throb and overflow with pleasure.

Once more, good friends, Amy and I passed the rest of that night in the most delicious manner possible. Long before the hour, four o'clock, at which she had to leave to go to the Corbetts' bungalow, whence she had come, we had become very confidential and I had managed to extract a promise from her that she would not insist upon my fucking Mabel yet awhile. I pleaded hard. I said that poor Fanny might forgive me having fucked her, Amy, but that it would be almost too much to expect her to accept that two more cunts were to share my prick with hers. But Amy was determined that nothing should be done outside the strict bargain and she only agreed to this arrangement on the understanding that I was to fuck her every night until Fanny returned. I willingly acquiesced. It was agreed that I should meet her where we then were, every night at ten o'clock, for the Corbetts being early people and going to bed at nine regularly, Amy could easily keep that appointed hour. Sugdaya was sorry for Mabel, but at least I had promised to fuck her in due course; she only hoped I would not delay too long.

We left the Selwyns' bungalow together. I had nothing on but my thin jersey, pyjamas and light slippers. Sugdaya and Amy walked as far as the entrance to my compound with me and we exchanged caresses and kisses, hot and strong on either side; Amy, in happy good-natured con- tempt for the proprieties, even requested me to stroke Sugdaya's nice brown cunt before kissing her for the last time! With my fingers still throbbing from this exquisite contact with two such blooming cunts, I walked rapidly up my avenue, not thinking of anything but what I now considered my extreme good luck, for I had had a really delicious night between Amy's fair thighs and had enjoyed so much undeniable pleasure both from her cunt and from her curiously improper mind that, for the present at all events, my sorrow on Fanny's account was considerably deadened.

All this part of my history is still painful for me to remember. I do not deny the sweetness of Amy's really delicious little cunt. It was of the very finest sort and I had very real pleasure fucking it. It had the advantage of being a new one for me. It had been deflowered by me. It belonged to as pretty a girl as there was in India. It was extremely sensitive to pleasure and a perfect fountain under my vigorous treatment of it, but . . . alas for the buts – Oh! how much more delightful to me it would have been had I not been so entrapped into it. I could now understand what a woman feels like who has been fucked against her will and without her consent. Over and above these latter feelings was the absolute certainty of the pain – the mental and heartfelt agony Fanny would surely experience – when she came to hear that, within twenty-four hours of my being between her thighs, I had passed between those of her sister, and that subsequently, night after night, I had fucked Amy.

Amy certainly gave me no rest. I don't think she realised it was possible to exhaust a man. Feeling herself always ready to be fucked, she regarded the stand of a prick as quite voluntary on the part of the lover. Thanks to the splendid constitution I had been born with and the powers which, from what women have told me, I fancy very few men are endowed with, I was quite 'able' for Amy and never disappointed her a single time. In fact, I believe she would have been the first to say, 'I've had enough', had we continued this night-after-night fucking. She was quite prepared to share me with Fanny and wished, really wished, me to fuck Mabel too.

She knows differently now. She is married now and has discovered that there are men and men. In her last letter to me, received not a week ago, she spoke very penitently of the way she treated me at Fackabad and says she had no idea of what a treasure she had in me. It is very nice to be told this now but I did not enjoy being used by her as a complete tool at Fackabad.

The colonel wrote only once from Rampur and Fanny not at all. I was glad and sorry not to have had a letter from her. She told me, when she came back, that she was burning to write, but feared her father's asking questions and perhaps seeing her letter; she said if once she began to write, she could not have kept her pen from speaking the sort of passionate words she was so accustomed to use when we were in our skins together.

So she thought it best not to write except one short little note.

On the morning of the day we expected them back from Rampur, just as I was putting on my pyjamas and jersey and looking at the naked Amy, who had so cruelly robbed me of my peace of mind and Fanny of her full possession in future of my prick and balls, Amy said, 'Oh! by the by, Captain Devereaux, I've something for you here.'

'What is it, Amy?'

'Oh, a letter from Fanny.'

And she put her hand under her pillow and drew forth a little note she had put there overnight and had 'forgotten' to give me earlier.

'Oh! Amy, why did you not give me this before?'

'I forgot.'

'You know I love Fanny. It is cruel of you, Amy!'

'Pooh! What do I care! Lord what a rage Fanny will be in when she hears the news.'

'It will break her heart.'

'Fiddle-de-dee! She will roar and cry and call me names and you too, Captain Devereaux! Oh! she will tear your eyes out!'

'I will tell her the truth, Amy, and then if she can forgive me I shall be happy – but – will she?'

'Of course, she will. Bless you, I know Fanny better than you do, Captain Devereaux. She will try it on. Yes, she will try it on. She will rave and storm and threaten, but if you treat her coolly and let her know that it is of no use crying over spilt milk, but there is more milk for her if she chooses to take it, she will quiet down fast enough. Fanny is not quite such a fool as not to know that half a loaf is better than no bread. But she is greedy. She never offered to share you with me and now she must. It serves her right. And I am rather glad you don't like fucking me, because it serves you right too!'

'But Amy, I do like fucking you! As far as mere fucking goes you are quite as good as Fanny!'

'Thank you for nothing! Mere fucking! You won't per-suade me you see anything more in Fanny than a nice little cunt! I don't believe it. No! no! Captain Devereaux. You are sore because you have to fuck me whether you like it or not. If it weren't for that you would not be sorry to have both me and Fanny, aye and Mabel too, and Sugdaya and every other woman in Fackabad also!'

It was no use trying to make Amy sensible that although cunts may be equally delicious from a physical point of view and all girls equally young, nice and beautiful, yet love distinguishes one above all others and makes one the most delicious of all. I left her in disgust, mad with myself because I could not master my prick and because I could not help confessing that she was a perfect and exquisite poke.

On going back to my bungalow I read the precious note from Fanny. It was full of love and happiness at the prospect of being once more in my arms. Poor, dear girl! She appeared not to have the least qualm about Amy or anyone else occupying my thoughts during her absence. So far from imagining that I should take advantage of her being at Rampur and endeavour to get into Amy or Mabel, she said that she hoped on her return to hear that I had not forgotten that they were her sisters and to find that I had, for her sake, been kind to them and been to visit them at Mrs Corbett's, where she imagined they must have been very lonely without her and papa.

This note gave me the greatest possible pain. What would Fanny say when she discovered the truth? It would nearly kill her! She trusted me so completely. She did not dream of a rival and she could have no notion that she would find a most formidable rival and oppressor in Amy, her own sister. What a deep and designing game Amy had played! And how patiently had she waited until she could put her scheme into action. Herein I saw Sugdaya's hand. No one but a native, or one governed by a native, could have possessed their souls and senses in such a state of entire patience as Amy had done. For she was everything but cool and composed while I fucked her. She was such flame and fury that it was impossible to suppose that she did not enjoy to the fullest the glorious pleasures my prick and balls procured her. She must consequently have endured the most real pains of unsatisfied desire and, like the Spartan boy, have suffered the agonies of having her living flesh gnawed at whilst she smiled in apparent calmness on all. I dare say it was the recollection of these poignant sufferings which made all her words and actions towards me so cruel and spiteful. However, she had been well fucked and perhaps, when I had smoothed down Fanny and calmed the storm which threatened a catastrophe, we might so manage as at all events to render Amy amiable. For if Fanny, as I fully expected she would, declared she would no longer be fucked by me, I determined I would not fuck Amy any more and as Amy liked being well fucked so much, so very much, she might discover that any ill advised attempt to drive a man might result in a revolt whereby her newly acquired kingdom over my prick might be lost.

Full of these turbulent thoughts, I lay down, but could not sleep. Hour after hour passed away. Full daylight came and brought with it, one by one, the numerous signs of life – the birds, insects, animals and men. But I heeded them little; all my thoughts were concentrated on 'What will Fanny say?' and 'How shall I ever recover my position in her love and admiration?' The devil take Amy and damn Sugdaya for her infamous plotting and scheming!

A good swear relieves a man when the cause for irritation is passed and gone, but alas! no amount of cursing will soften the expected pains of approaching doom – else mine would have obviated the misery I expected, for I swore enough to blow all misery to the winds, had the misery been upon me and not still in the offing.

Fanny and the colonel were not expected to arrive until seven in the evening and Amy and the children were not to leave the Corbetts until a little before that hour. I passed that most wretched day in writing a letter to Fanny trying to explain what had happened in such a way as not to inculpate Amy any more than necessary, but yet to exculpate myself.

Needless to say all my efforts were in vain and each letter I wrote seemed worse than the last and all were destroyed by me. Oh! dear readers, may you never, not one of you, have reason to suffer such torture as I endured. It would not have been so bad had I deliberately with malice aforethought been unfaithful to Fanny. But to have been so trapped and betrayed into doing what I really had not meant to do, was a cause of the greatest mental anguish to me. Suppose I told Fanny the exact truth, was it likely she would believe me? Would she not also say and with a great show of justice, that I need not have gone on fucking Amy?

Ah! she had no prick and balls to drive her as I had. It would be difficult to understand, too, that in order to keep Amy in good humour, I had to go on fucking her; and yet I felt I really had no better card to play. I could not help it if I found fucking Amy truly delicious. I dare say a girl who is raped, rather enjoys the sensation, although in her heart she may feel the deadliest enmity against the man who rapes her, because it is done without her consent. I really could not prevent my prick standing and stiffly raging when it was near Amy's cunt. A prick is like a gun. The enemy can take it and use it against its proper owner. It shoots just as straight and as hard for the one as for the other and has no will in the matter at all. All that my prick saw in Fanny was a delicious and sweet cunt between her thighs; it saw exactly the same thing between the thighs of Amy – and its one desire was to get into that one which was nearest. This is certainly not the case with most cunts. It was in Lizzie Wilson's, but hers was by no means the one to give the rule. Look at Amy. Amy wanted to be fucked. Well, she had plenty of friends who would have been delighted to have fucked her, but she never hinted her desire to one of them. Look at Mabel. If anything she was worse and hotter than Amy. The reader will see in time what she did. My prick was always ready for Mabel's cunt and, but for the most determined opposition, it would have got into it. Oh! let a woman understand this: 'A standing prick has no conscience!'

Everything comes to an end and that horrible day came to an end too, but not until I had at last written a little note to Fanny in which I begged her not to come over to see me for a very particular reason which I could tell her as soon as I could find an opportunity on the morrow. This note I took with me to Amy at the Corbetts' and we went out into the garden together, Amy refusing to let Mabel accompany us.

'Well you do look bad, Captain Devereaux. Are you so awfully afraid of Fanny then? You are as white as a ghost.'

'I am not afraid of Fanny, Amy. Nothing she could say to me could be half so painful as what my conscience tells me. But the fact is I could not sleep a wink when I got home this morning.'

'Ha! ha! ha! ha!' laughed Amy, as merrily and cheerfully as if I had told her something more than ordinarily pleasant and delightful. 'Oh! I do like to hear that! What a fool you are, Captain Devereaux! I wonder you don't put more value on yourself. Now if I were you, I should say to Fanny, if she is at all cross, "Look here Fanny! You can take me or leave me – it is all one to me. I can't fuck any the more because I have two cunts instead of one to fuck. Only Amy will get all the more if you leave me." '

'That would be adding insult to injury, Amy.'

'Well! what of it? Is it not the truth?'

'You don't consider the pain such speaking would give poor Fanny.'

'Pain! And pray did she consider what pain I suffered from her not even asking me would I like to be fucked by you when she was. Sisters should share. I only ask for my share. I don't want to take you altogether away from Fanny, but I must be fucked as well as she.'

'Well, I should not be surprised if it all came to an end now.'

'Why?'

'Because I expect when Fanny hears the news she will go into one of her dreadful states of excitement and do or say something rash before your father; and if he hears of what has happened he will certainly take steps to prevent any more of my fucking of his daughters. He could, for instance, as easily get me sent to another station as I could get Lavie sent to Benares. Nobody need know why, but you and Fanny would have to find another beau, if fucking is all either of you wish for.'

This speech made Amy thoughtful. She had entirely lost sight of the possible effects a too brilliant triumph over Fanny might have.

'That is worth thinking about, Captain Devereaux.'

'It is, Amy, in all solemn earnest. Now will you do me a favour?'

'What is it?'

'Will you give this note to Fanny for me?'

'What have you said in it?'

'All I have said is to ask her not come over to me tonight.'

'Have you told her what has happened?'

'No!'

Amy walked on in silence evidently thinking what she should do. I imagine she had intended to crow vigorously over Fanny, but my warning had made her begin to reconsider this. As we walked we approached the stable and Amy, who had been twisting my note to Fanny between her fingers suddenly looked up.

'Oh! Here we are at the stable,' said she.

'Yes,' said I, reading her thoughts, 'but Amy dear I really could not do it now!'

'What nonsense!' she cried reddening. 'I never asked you either – but now, for saying that, you shall!'

'I really can't, Amy.'

'Bosh! come Captain Devereaux, I wish to be fucked now, this instant. It may be my last chance, if so much depends upon Fanny, as you seem to think. I will not throw away a chance. Come into the stable at once and do what you are bid.'

'I will go into the stable, Amy, but you will see I speak nothing but the truth when I tell you that I am not able to fuck you now.'

I went in.

'Now,' said Amy, 'explain yourself.'

'Here is the best explanation possible,' said I undoing my braces and letting down my trousers. 'Look and see if you can get that into your cunt, Amy.'

Amy raised my shirt and saw me in a state she had never considered possible. My prick hung dead and nerveless, my balls were loose in an elongated and relaxed bag, everything denoted the most marked fatigue.

'You are foxing!' cried Amy angrily, stamping her foot. 'Make it stiff, at once! Do you hear me! Ah! Do Captain Devereaux!' she continued in an imploring tone of voice. 'Don't be so unkind to me.'

I heard her with a mixture of amusement and pain.

I was amused at her thinking I was my prick's master and able to make it stand or not, at my pleasure; and pained that I was really unable to comply with her wishes and fuck her, for I felt if I could gratify her now she would be in better humour and be more inclined to spare Fanny and so soften down the announcement of her triumph.

'Amy dear, I would if I could. But the want of sleep and the painful anxiety about Fanny that I have been under all day have killed me; but try if you can make it stiff yourself! I really am not fooling. I should very much like to fuck you, if I could. Here let us lie down in this grass and while you see what you can do with your hands, I will feel your nice, soft cunt.'

We lay down and Amy cuddled up to me, looking at times into my face with a keen gaze as if to see whether I was deceiving her or not, whilst she handled my prick and my balls in the most voluptuously exciting manner possible. It was of no use whatever. I was in a state of mental and bodily prostration and my prick remained as limp as ever, though my balls gradually drew up into a tighter bunch than they had been in before Amy's gentle fingers titillated them.

After about ten minutes of these mutual caresses I withdrew my hand, wet with her frequent spendings, from between Amy's lovely thighs and said: 'I am afraid we must give up the idea of it, Amy. My prick is too dead. Too tired.'

'Too obstinate and too abominably selfish, you mean,' said Amy in great anger. 'Take that for the sulky beast you are,' and with these words addressed to my prick she suddenly gave it a stinging slap with her hand not only hurting it considerably, but making my poor balls throb with pain.

'Oh, Amy! Oh, my! You have hurt me.'

Now if a woman has a tender place in her heart for anything in this world it is for a man's prick and balls. Let my readers think for a second and nearly all must recollect instances where women of their acquaintances have heard with apparent indifference of men being mutilated in any other particular but have shown the very greatest sympathy and have shuddered when they have been told of the mutilation of prick or balls, or both. Amy was no exception.

'Oh! Captain Devereaux! I really did not mean to hurt it so much. Oh, poor thing, poor thing.' She hung over me, as I had turned on to my face, for I had some extremely sharp pains in my groin and a dull heavy pain at the lower part of my belly. I felt Amy's hand groping along my right groin and at first I resisted a little, but a sharp bit of grass happening to run into my prick, I made a sudden move, which enabled her to get at that which she wished to caress and soothe. Suddenly, to my astonishment, for I had no sensation to tell me the fact, she cried out: 'Oh, Captain Devereaux! It's stiff. It's stiff. It's standing beautifully.'

The pain I had endured had been sharp enough, but it passed like a sudden twinge of toothache. Amy's exclamation seemed to drive it away and I could now feel that I had indeed a glorious stand. I felt so grateful to Amy that I turned and caught her in my arms and kissed her before I pushed her on her back and got between those beautiful rounded, snowy thighs, which she uncovered for me with immense haste as though she feared the stiffness of my prick might go as suddenly as it had come. It was a lovely fuck! A completely glorious fuck! and at the end, whilst I was still lying with my motte hard pressed to hers, which leaped and jumped, and whilst I was still enjoying the throbbing and squeezing and twitching of her deliciously excited and melting little cunt, I could not help saying: 'Oh, Amy, try and win Fanny over and we will have many another like this.'

The episode did me considerable good. It gave me more hope towards Fanny, for I left Amy in a much more amiable mood than that in which I had found her and my limp prick and the idea of what might happen should Colonel Selwyn discover that I had fucked Fanny were things both new to her that I was sure were going to do their work on her mind. Fanny would be angry, grieved and more or less destroyed by hearing the news, but bad as that would be it would be so much worse if accompanied by the stinging and triumphant insults which I felt certain Amy, in true sisterly fashion, had prepared for her.

Since I had become station staff officer, I had been relieved of the necessity of dining at the mess of my regiment, so that I used my freedom in this respect pretty largely and seldom dined there two nights running. The truth is, I dislike mess dinners more than I can express and I do not think anybody can like them as a continuance. This night, however, I was glad to go and sit at dinner with my brother officers, for their chat helped me to pass away some of those purgatorial hours between my last fucking of Amy and the time when I was to meet Fanny.

On my way home I looked in at the colonel's bungalow. I knew I had better take the bull by the horns and I rather expected to find Fanny ill or unable to see me. But no, there the sweet girl was, glad and happy – she was all too evidently still unaware of my terrible infidelity. It was clear, too, that Amy had not given her my note, for poor Fanny took the opportunity of whispering to me that she was quite well and that she had a lot to tell me when she came over. Amy was a perfect study. She acted her part to perfection. She was just exactly the same Amy she had been, to all appearances, before Fanny went to Rampur and before there had been any question of my fucking her. I warn Amy's husband, should he read these pages, that he might as well not attempt to keep her under watch and guard. If Amy ever takes a fancy for some young fellow, she will have her way with him and that right under her husband's nose

and he won't know it. Her manner to me was astounding.
Since the moment she had got me in the trap between her
thighs, she had been so unlike the old Amy, that the sudden
assumption of a driving, domineering, hard-hearted, wilful
woman's manner had stunned me, as much as her extraordinary behaviour. She had had me quite under a spell in
consequence. She had jumped upon and crushed me by the
suddenness of the blow. But tonight she had so completely
resumed her old manner, appearance and tone it was hard
to believe we had fucked something like fifty different times
during the past week. Alas! My prick which had refused to
stand that afternoon for her until she had beaten it, did what
it had never done in the old days before Fanny went to
Rampur (those old days, which though only separated from
these new times by a week, seemed so long, long ago) for it
stood stiffly the moment Amy came near me. In the old days
that irrepressible organ would have remained quiescent until
Fanny's approach would have aroused it to assume its grand
proportions, but tonight it grew stiff the moment it perceived
the nearness of Amy's cunt.

I went home then, knowing that the storm had yet to
burst, for I imagined that when she and Amy retired for
the night, Amy would surely tell Fanny all and the first
effect of her grief and indignation would be to make her
take a vow never to see me again.

But instead of going to bed I sat up. My head buzzed
with fatigue and excitement, but tired as I was, I knew that
if I did go to bed I should not sleep. Whilst I was thus
seated in a half-dreamy and truly painful state of mind, I
got a shock which woke me to life and action in a moment,

for I heard the swift, light steps of Fanny coming down the verandah. Before I could rise she burst into my room, as if life, or all that was worth having, depended upon the swiftness of her movements. On seeing me she stopped dead. A glance at her face told me she was in possession of the news. Poor Fanny! Ah! Gentle reader! Tell me, do you know anything in this world so hideously painful, so agonising to the mind and heart, as the discovery that the person in whom your confidence is placed, in whom all your love and devotion, heart and soul, are invested, is false, a traitor! Fanny had never loved before she loved me. With the wholeheartedness of youth she had given herself to me – heart, soul, body – unreservedly and she trusted in me as in her God.

For a moment she stood looking at me, her lovely eyes expressing all the pain she felt but at the same time a kind of hesitancy to believe what she now knew was real and not a dreadful dream. Her lips were parted as though to speak, but no words came. Her bosom heaved tumultuously and her lovely firm breasts seemed as though the struggle going on within her would make them burst their points through the bodice. I had seen Fanny in a passion many times, but never in such a state as she now appeared in. Her look fascinated me. She seemed to be trying to read my inmost soul through my eyes and I remained dumb.

'Oh! Charlie!' she cried, all of a sudden, 'tell me it is not true! Oh, why did you do it? Oh! I never thought that my Charlie would be so – so – so – cruel to me!' She bent her lovely head and commenced to sob and weep violently without noise.

This was awful. I had never been so tried in all my life before. I jumped up and approaching her sat by her side, not daring to lay a hand upon the girl whom I felt I did not dare to touch with my polluted fingers.

For fully five minutes we stayed thus, until Fanny, raising her face, all wet with tears and once more flushed, turned her streaming eyes upon me and staggering forward fell into my arms. I caught her in them. I kissed that face all lovely still though quivering with the devouring pain she felt and Fanny let me do so, let me press her to my bosom, let me draw her towards my chair and let me take her into my lap, where I held her tenderly lying against me, whilst she still wept and sobbed.

Suddenly she rose into a more upright position and looking at me, said, 'Why don't you speak to me? You are crying too! What are you crying for?'

'Because, Fanny darling, I can't help it! I can't see you, the girl I love, in such dreadful grief and not feel sorry.'

'I am a fool for coming,' she said. 'Let me go! I'll never, never, never, speak to you again!'

'Stay!' I cried, holding her. 'Stay, Fanny! You have heard only one side of the story. It is only fair to me to hear mine. I swear to you that I never had the remotest idea of being unfaithful to you and that it was not until I was actually in Amy's cunt that I knew it was not you whom I was fucking.'

Fanny loved me. That is the only explanation of the patience with which she heard me. In her heart, that heart so dreadfully wounded, she wished to find the palliation of my sin. Had her pride only been wounded, she would never, or could never have forgiven me, but love covers a multitude of sins and Fanny heard my story, not only with patience, but with eagerness.

With passions as strong as mine, with a cunt as susceptible to pleasure as my prick, she could understand me when I said that the first fuck with Amy over, I found it impossible to tear myself away from a cunt so fascinating, so blooming as that between Amy's thighs; and as I proceeded and told my story, in such a way as to make it more than evident that, much as I appreciated her sister's cunt, I did not love Amy, whereas my whole soul was bound up in her, she at last threw her arms round my neck and kissed me and then wept again, but without that violence, which was all the more dreadful because subdued, which marked the first outbreak of her passion.

For hours we sat thus talking. Fanny quite understood her position. She loved me too much to be able to carry out her passionately expressed threat never to speak to me again, yet it was but too evident that she must consent to share me with Amy at once and with Mabel later on. She herself remembered what she had said about concubines and, with a sorrowful smile, she congratulated me on having now three really pretty ladies in my harem. As she grew more cheerful, so did I, and venturing at last on an act, I undid the lace of her bodice and uncovered her lovely breasts, which I once again devoured with my lips, in a manner so full of passion that the poor girl all but fainted from excess of emotion. Snatching the lovely bubbies from my eager lips, she put her mouth to mine and beginning with the top button of my trousers she undid them all, one by one, until, reaching the last, she inserted her little hand and, pulling up my shirt, took possession of my stiff and impudent prick, which looked her boldly and unblushingly in the face.

'Yes,' she cried, 'it is not my Charlie, but you who are the traitor. Oh! you villain!'

Hard words, but Oh! what soft caresses. I am afraid my prick, like Galileo, paid no attention to her speech, but was too hungry for that dear little cunt which he had been the first to open. Happy reconciliation. Fanny in a few moments more stood in her naked beauty before me and in another moment had all but forgotten the agonies of the recent hours in the convulsions of the delirious pleasure I presented.

Sugdaya awoke us. That lovely traitress was delighted to find us naked in bed together. Fanny would have quarrelled with her, but she had listened to me and had swallowed Sugdaya with her other inevitable griefs and our last luscious fuck took place under the eye of that lovely native girl and born procuress, who was to be so useful to me in finding me sweet cunts, besides her own, during the next three or four years.

Now, reader, did you think for any moment that things could have turned out so? Did not our beloved goddess Venus stand on my side? I saw her divine and beneficent hand in every turn of our amatory survey and never had she a more ardent priest than me. For I did my utmost never to lose a chance of making her holy altars between the thighs of my lovely 'concubines' smoke with the incense of my offerings.

Oh! those exquisite nights! Those revels when like a god of olden times I sported with my naked nymphs, passing from between the arms of one to between the thighs of the other, the change from one cunt to the second giving me fresh life and greater strength! There was certainly an increase of voluptuous pleasure and delight, but alas! the purity and depth of love which had existed between Fanny and me suffered. We never again were, or could be, what we had been to one another.

And now it remains but for me to show you how, at last, I filled up the cup of Mabel's joy by fucking her and then I will close the history of my association with those three beautiful and delicious Selwyn cunts.

Neither Fanny nor Amy seemed to be in the least degree anxious that I should fuck Mabel. This was natural enough so far as Fanny was concerned, but Amy, as my dear reader may remember, had made it a *sine qua non* that Mabel was to have her share of my prick and balls. Experience, however, began to teach her that a whole loaf is better than half of one, and a half-loaf is better than a third of one. So I never heard any more from her of the obligations I was under to fuck Mabel. But it was impossible to prevent Mabel's knowing of my nightly visits to her father's bungalow, and what went on there in consequence, and I have little doubt she often witnessed scenes of joy, in which she burned to play her part, from behind the purdah. Besides, I am certain that Sugdaya, who felt no scruples, incited her to claim her share and this is how she got it.

Epilogue

Mabel Has Her Way With Me

One lovely day in December (this is in the delightful cold weather) I was preparing to go out to pay some visits when I saw Mrs Soubratie hurrying up from the servants' house. I guessed that the colonel must have come over for a moment to get a morning fuck and, as I wanted to see him, I thought I would wait until he had taken his pleasure and then I would do so. Although it was an understood thing between us that he was at liberty to fuck Mrs Soubratie whenever he liked in my house, yet as a rule we did not meet on those occasions, so that unless I actually saw him between her thighs, or saw Mrs Soubratie pass my door, I rarely knew the exact moment these pleasant meetings were taking place.

I waited therefore, seated in my chair. I had not been sitting more than a minute when Mabel appeared, bursting with laughter which she was finding it hard to contain. Coming on tiptoe to me she whispered: 'Oh! Captain Devereaux! Come here! Come here.'

I rose. She took my hand and leading me into my

bedroom she took me to the door in which was a window, covered with a thin muslin blind, which looked into the room and on to the bed in which the colonel always fucked Mrs Soubratie. There, of course, I saw, as did Mabel, the colonel about halfway through a nice, fat fuck, and Mabel, delighted beyond description, feasted her eyes on her father's splendid prick passing, in measured cadence, up and down and in and out of the brown cunt of Mrs Soubratie. The sight was too voluptuous, especially as Mabel was there, not to affect me greatly and I unbuttoned my trousers and put my now burning prick into Mabel's palm. At the same time I intruded my hand past her petticoats and caressed the little cunt, now well covered with curly locks, which immediately responded to my caresses with such an overflow that it surprised me. Still affected powerfully by seeing her father's glistening member disappearing and reappearing as he fucked Mrs Soubratie in his stolid fashion, and his balls, those huge balls, bouncing as they swung backwards and forwards, Mabel quietly moved her hand up and down my prick, until a sudden thrill of pleasure round its collar warned me that if she continued so doing I should spend; all the more also, because of sympathy, the colonel being now at the vigorous short digs. I therefore kept her hand quiet until, the colonel having finished and Mrs Soubratie having made her salaam and left the room, the show had come to an end.

'Well, Mabel!' said I, when the colonel had walked off with that jaunty side step he always adopted after a good fuck, 'you came in the very nick of time to see that!'

'Yes!' said she, looking at my prick and gently feeling my balls, which she had foraged for and got out. 'Sugdaya told me I should see something, if I came over here now. I thought she meant this,' she continued looking up at me with a smile, 'but I fancy she must have meant that I should see papa with Mrs Soubratie.'

'She may have meant both, Mabel dear! But take care, child! You will make me spend if you move your hand like that!'

'Oh! What fun that would be! Let me? Do, Captain Devereaux! I should so like to see it.'

'Well!' said I, shivering with pleasure, 'all right, dear, but let me take off my trousers first or they will be spoilt.'

I saw that the time had come. This was Mabel's hour and I shut my bedroom door and bolted it.

'Now, Mabel! Take off your frock and stays and stockings and we will go to bed together.'

'Oh no!!'

'Oh yes!'

'Oh, how delightful! Oh, you good, good, good Captain Devereaux!!' she cried in an ecstasy of joy. 'But let us go regularly to bed and take off all our clothes.'

'Very well!' said I, laughing, and in another couple of minutes we were both as naked as we were born.

Mabel was very pretty. Like Fanny and Amy, she had a very nice, pure, even white skin. Her limbs still required a little more flesh to give them the roundness that is so desirable, but her little bubbies were really charming and the plump motte had quite as much hair on it as Fanny's and her nudity charmed me; my nakedness pleased her immensely; though she had often enough handled my prick and balls, she said this was the first time she had ever really seen them.

Now, it is chilly enough in the cold weather to make one's skin rather want clothing, so I picked up Mabel, laid her on the bed and, getting in myself, pulled the bedclothes well up to our chins and there we lay cuddled together. Mabel had again got hold of my prick, which she was working in such a way that I knew I would spend immediately if she did not leave off.

'Wait! Mabel, you will really make me spend all over you.'

'I shall like that,' she cried. 'I should like to see what a man's spend is like.'

'Very well,' said I, laughing, 'then see.'

I threw down the bedclothes and almost at the same moment let fly a torrent of spend which I could restrain no longer. Mabel shrieked, for the first jet struck her full in the face, the second under the chin, the third splashed against her bubbies and the remaining jets I directed to her belly and finally to her bush, taking care so to hold her hand as to give her the benefit of every drop.

'Oh! That was nice!' cried Mabel. 'What a lot. How creamy it is. Like hollandaise, only thicker; but you must have quite emptied your balls.'

'Oh no. There's lots in them, Mabel, and when, in a minute or so, I fuck you, they will go on making more for you.'

I wiped the lovely streaming body of my bedfellow as I spoke and, expecting to find a rather obstinate maidenhead, I thought it wise to begin with her as soon as possible, so that by the time I next spent, she would have had a good fuck.

Judge of my surprise, on taking my position between her open thighs, to meet with absolutely no resistance! There was not only not the ghost of a maidenhead, but it was evident to me that the cunt I was in had been most thoroughly well opened. If Mabel had already been fucked, who had done it? I made no remark, however, for I was too much amused and delighted with her expressions of delight and pleasure. Like Fanny and Amy, her cunt was a perfect fountain, easily made to play by the movements of my prick within it, and Mabel made me laugh with her continuous, 'There I go again!' But when I came to the short digs and in my turn inundated her lovely little cunt with a sea of spend, Mabel clutched me with all her force to her convulsed and quivering body and exclaimed, 'Oh! how much better a real prick is than a cucumber!'

The cat was out of the bag! A cucumber!

The first fuck over, Mabel told me amidst rapid kisses and never-ending caresses that Sugdaya had taught her how pleasant a sensation could be produced by a three-quarter-ripe banana, with its peel half removed. From a small banana she had progressed to one of larger size, always to the detriment of her maidenhead, until one day, seeing a very nice smooth cucumber, the straightness and size of which struck her as being peculiarly adapted for her experiments, she picked it, went indoors and finished off with a vegetable what, but for that, would have been decided by my prick of flesh!

Mabel was a lascivious little girl, a grand poke. Like Lizzie Wilson her mission in life is to fuck. The dear reader will not be surprised to hear that she has joined that select number of fair women who, nominally 'kept' by wealthy lovers, take delight in relieving the pains of numerous adorers, and enjoy along the winding paths of intrigue the voluptuous pleasures to be gathered, like flowers, along their shaded ways. If Mabel's present ties were legitimate she would be the Duchess of –. To her was the glory of having been the first to give palpable proof of the ecstasies of fucking to no less a personage than one of the royal princes.

Neither Fanny nor Amy showed any ill will towards Mabel on account of our mutual participation in the sacrifice, and up to the last night of their stay in Fackabad these amiable girls were poked by me, sometimes in company, sometimes singly, unless 'illness' prevented.

In March of the following year, just twelve months after I had taken Fanny's maidenhead, the girls went home to England, the colonel having retired from the service.

Our parting was extremely painful. We made exchanges of locks of hair from our respective bushes and so eager were the girls for mementoes of mine that it was months before my prick grew out of a forest as thick, or rather as long, as it was when first I pressed it against that of Lizzie Wilson at Nowshera.